OHIO WRITERS'
ASSOCIATION

Resistance

An Anthology

Presented by
Ohio Writers' Association

Editor:
R. Luce

Readers/Judges:

Jim Hodnett

Christine Irvin

Briana Lagos

Brian Luke

Corrina Malek

George Pallas

Candice Jones Peelman

Mandy Young

Resistance

An Anthology

Published by:
Ohio Writers' Group
DBA Ohio Writers' Association
838 Campbell Avenue
Columbus, OH 43223 USA

Edited by R. Luce
Typesetting & Cover Design: Joe Graves

Special thanks to all of our judges and editor who made this anthology possible.

Print ISBN – 979-8-9870174-9-4
eBook ISBN – 979-8-9955383-0-1

Printed in USA.

Table of Contents

Introduction

The book you are about to read is the result of The Ohio Writers' Association's invitation to writers[1] to produce works on the topic of resistance. Knowing that storytelling has long been used as an act of challenging the world as it is and imagining what could be, we invited writers of fiction, poetry, and creative nonfiction to challenge the forces shaping our time and culture through substantive works that confront injustice, apathy, and despair. The response was tremendous.

The writers chosen for this publication demonstrate an understanding that to be human involves a lifetime of making choices about conformity. From birth, we humans are molded by our parents, the cultures in which we live, and the exposure we have to physical and mental challenges in our lives and the extent to which we are educated about the world beyond our immediate communities. As children, we are trained to conform to the expectations of our parents, particularly in the ways of interacting with other members of the family, the community, and the larger culture as we know it while keeping ourselves and our loved ones safe. As we mature, we gain potential to assess what we have learned and our then to make choices about what we can and cannot accept for ourselves as fully functioning adults. However, throughout our lifetimes, we are challenged by others—and by circumstances—to conform to demands that are not aligned with the values we have chosen for ourselves. Demands may come from those who control our paychecks, governmental entities, shifts in cultural values, the law, or

---

1 Born here, lives or lived here, works/worked here, or attends/attended school or took part in other significant events here.

dominant individuals or groups who hold power over us. Much of the time, we accept conformity regardless of any contrary values we may hold simply because we wish to get along in the world unless it dramatically alters our overall sense of well-being or safety.

When faced with demands for conformity that disrupt the values we have acquired about right and wrong, fair and unfair, just and unjust, we may deal with it by avoiding the change; or we may try to reason with those attempting to impose their values upon us; or we may seek others more powerful than ourselves to speak on our behalf (i.e., union reps, lawyers, or respected public figures); if immediate threat to our selves or others is prevalent, we may attack those who are imposing upon us; or, in some circumstances, we may succumb to the overwhelming power of those imposing upon us and accept the notion that resistance is futile and then conform to the behaviors expected while subduing the anger that comes from doing so.

In short, being exposed to dominant forces who have (or want) control over us is a part of being human. We are constantly faced with making decisions about what we can and cannot accept and then deciding how we wish to proceed with our lives. At this point in our history as Americans, we are faced with consequential challenges to our notions of right and wrong. We face threats to our democracy, the rule of law, the constitution, and core cultural values. Thus, many equate the word "resistance" with a political stance against the current regime in Washington, D.C. We are facing an existential threat from our own government. And that is well worth talking about.

In this anthology, our writers demonstrate a wide and holistic view of resistance as a way of moving humanity forward toward greater understanding of human potential to do better by using resistance as a means for affecting our individual and collective moral values, for helping shape the human need to transcend our day-to-day existence to create a legacy of lives worth living, and to overcome the pettiness of those who believe they must impose their myopic views of the ways life "should be" upon others.

The collection of works here deal with the multitudes of experiences we humans have with making decisions about what we will and will not tolerate in day-to-day living amongst the many demands for conformity we all live with. It is not until the final third of the book that the reader begins to deal directly with the major conflicts we face in the United States in 2026 as we resist the actions and policies of a government led by those who openly defy the rule of law and foundational principles of our constitution, who actively work to undermine freedoms and social and legal equality for people who are non-white, immigrants, women, and who are attempting to impose a white, male-dominated, Christian Nationalist control over all aspects of our lives.

I thank the writers who contributed to this publication for reminding me and you what it means to stand up against hatred of others, unjust behaviors, and attempts to impose self-serving control over others. I thank them for reminding us what it means to be our best selves, communities, and nation.

R. Luce, Editor

Options for the Weary and Uncertain

by Steve Abbott

I could pile sealed boxes of books higher in the attic
with winter quilts and a dresser full of rock 'n' roll
T-shirts I'm confident will be very old someday.

I could plant onions and tomatoes in square-foot plots,
string a web for peas to climb, a silver ladder to the sun.
A painted bicycle wheel could become lawn sculpture.

Or with a few clicks I could pry the world open like a can
of tuna, inhale its brine and stories of shipwrecked refugees
and recurring nights peppered by gas spewed from a wall

of robocops. I might flee into the safety offered by photos
of other times and the innocence of their smiles, or mumble
a mush of useless curses. I could slowly sink into novels
or hum an avalanche of blues songs. Run till I drop. Turn

the volume up to 11. If I'm willing to shatter myself and
do without, I could sidestep the market's leg-hold trap.

I could even just settle down for a nap, or sink into
the catatonic and reassuring scrolling of my phone,
disappear into another hour of amusing myself to death.
I could stay here, frozen and trembling in this rabbit skin

I've embraced as my coat. Or I could stir my appetite,
serve myself a ladle of resolve, its gristle and fibrous strands

enough for me to stand and shove my body into the weeping
sea of the streets. I could leave this damp hole, breathe in
and let go. Become another droplet in a wave about to break.

Breathes There the Man

by John Kachuba

Plenty Horses ran.

Beneath the cold stars thrown against the nighttime sky he ran, his bare feet pounding the hard earth in time with the pounding of his heart. Frosty clouds of air puffed from his open mouth.

He ran up a sloping meadow, the winter grass crunching beneath his feet. A line of trees hunkered in the darkness ahead. He ran straight for the trees, as if he were going to vanish among them as he had tried to do the first time so long ago. Twice more he had tried, despite the beatings he suffered each time he was caught. Only with time did he understand how far away were the lands of the Lakota.

The line of trees grew closer. Above his own ragged breathing he heard an owl call, saw the winged shadow sail through the night and wished with all his heart he could take wing as well. Five winters. So much time had passed.

Just as he reached the tree line, Plenty Horses turned and ran parallel to it, aware of the scurrying of nocturnal creatures alarmed by his passing. His feet ached with the cold, but nothing could be done for that. It was impossible to run in the hard shoes worn by the *wasicun*. His new moccasins, presented to him by his mother as he left his father's lodge, elk hide decorated with red and blue porcupine quills, had been taken from him on the day he arrived at Carlisle. On that day, they entered his name in their book as Plenty Living Bear, using his father's name. But he knew who he was. As he ran, he repeated in his head: *Ota Tasunka. Plenty Horses.*

The cold air burned inside his chest, but still he ran, arms pumping at his sides. It was cold, yes, but nothing like winter nights on the plains. He remembered waking one morning to find one of the scraggly steers the *wasicun* had given his father frozen solid among the cottonwoods along the creek. That would never happen here where the livestock snuggled in cozy barns and were given plenty of feed and water. As he thought of the steer, he glanced down the slope to where the dairy barns lay. In just a little while, lamplight like fireflies would flicker in the darkness as the students assigned to the dairy stumbled sleepily through the cold to milk the cows.

He ran along the edge of trees surrounding the Carlisle School grounds on three sides. A dirt road lay on the fourth side. He glanced up at the tall brick dormitories, the dark windows like eyes closed in sleep, but watched more carefully the house of Captain Pratt. It too was dark, yet Plenty Horses could feel someone moving within, perhaps standing at the dark window unseen, watching his shadow racing through the night. He didn't try to run away, not anymore, but when that yearning for home became overpowering, as it often did, he would sneak out of the dormitory and run. His endless circuits of the grounds made him feel somehow closer to his home so far away. He suspected that, after being caught three times, Captain Pratt knew his nocturnal runs continued but chose to feign ignorance as long as Plenty Horses remained at the school. Plenty Horses would run almost to the point of exhaustion and sometimes could barely creep back into his bed. When daylight came, it was all he could do to stay awake.

He could not count how many times he had crept out of the dormitory. He thought if he counted each of his steps as he ran that, surely, they would be enough to bring him back across the Big Muddy to the lodge of his father. Still, he ran, each step adding to the total. He offered those footsteps to Wakan Tanka, and sometimes to Jesus as well, just to make sure. If his voice could not be heard, perhaps his footsteps thudding on the frozen ground would find their way to them and they would hear him. Then he would be guided home.

He was now at the bottom of the slope, running beside a split-rail fence that bordered the road, the wind at his back. It pushed him forward. His feet throbbed. He knew that once he returned to the dormitory he would find them bloodied, cut by the frozen ground. He thought of his father, Living Bear, and some of the other men, performing a sun dance. He saw again the bone skewers tethered to his father's chest tear away bloody chunks of his flesh as Living Bear finally collapsed from exhaustion, having danced ceaselessly for two days and nights. Plenty Horses' own wounded feet were nothing compared to that sacrifice.

He was tiring. He turned back across the meadow, heading for the dormitory. Giving Captain Pratt's house a wide berth, he trotted up to a rear door of the building. He stopped there, leaning against the cold brick wall as he regained his breath. He looked up. The windows above him were still dark. There was no sound except for the wind sighing beneath the eaves. Plenty Horses took hold of the door latch. School policy required all the doors to be locked at night. This door had been locked like all the others, but over the years, Plenty Horses had been instructed in the use of many of the *wasicun* tools. Despite the injury to his left hand he had suffered as a youth, he had learned how to pick the old lock with an awl he had hidden near the door. He had done it so many times he felt as though he could close his eyes and still be able to open it. The door creaked ajar and then was silent. He crept up the stairs like a ghost, but a ghost who dripped bloody spots on the wood steps. Once he had safely returned to the room he shared with seven other boys, he wiped his feet as best he could with a rag and then slipped on a pair of woolen socks. He cautiously retraced his steps, wiping up the evidence of his escape with the rag. Back in his room, he fell onto his bed and was asleep immediately.

Someone shook him roughly by the shoulder. "Come, wake up now!"

He opened one eye. Coming to his senses, he saw the gray light of dawn creeping through the windows like an enemy and saw the face of Kills Hard--Edward, the *wasicun* named him--standing over him. He was already dressed in his school uniform, his short hair neatly brushed.

"Come on, lazy dog." Kills Hard squeezed Plenty Horse's shoulder. "It is time."

He swung his legs over the side of the bed and sat up. Immediately, he felt sharp pains in his feet. He knew he would have to conceal his suffering throughout the day. They could not know that he had been out of the dormitory during the night.

In the half-light around him the other boys were already up and about, donning their uniforms and making themselves presentable for breakfast. Most of them were Lakota, but there were three Cheyenne and one new boy from a people he had never heard of before in a place called New Mexico Territory. That boy did not speak much to the others, and the Cheyenne and Lakota peoples had long been friends, so the eight boys got along tolerably well. In any case, their differences mattered little to Captain Pratt and the other wasicun. Here, they were all one tribe, Carlisle Indians. Even that tribe would not last as Captain Pratt had vowed to "kill the Indian to spare the man." Plenty Horses did not understand exactly what Captain Pratt meant by that, but he did know that the Lakota and the other peoples at Carlisle were all what the *wasicun* called "Indian." And there were plenty of dead Indians lying beneath stone monuments in the school's cemetery.

The first bell sounded, spurring the boys into last-minute action. He stood gingerly, testing his weight. He hobbled to his footlocker and drew out his uniform. He slipped on the trousers and buttoned up the military-style tunic, even as the other boys, all except Kills Hard, were already heading for the stairs. His maimed left hand made it difficult for him to tie his shoes, but he succeeded on the second try, Kills Hard standing by as a valet with a hairbrush in his hand. Plenty Horses made a quick pass through his short hair with the brush. The two boys made it downstairs to the dining room just as the second bell rang.

A bell regulated everything the students did at Carlisle. A bell rang when it was time for them to stand at their places at the dining tables; another rang, telling them to sit. A bell announced each class time, each gymnastic period, each work detail, each chapel service. There was even a bell to order the musicians to band practice.

Just as the other students had learned, Plenty Horses learned to live by the bell, dividing his day, indeed his life, into segments that seemed unnatural, but segments that could be measured by the *wasicun* clocks and watches. At home there was no need for anything more than the movements of the moon and sun, for the lengthening of shadows across the grass. He thought about that now as he sat across from Kills Hard at a table on the boys' side of the dining hall. Above them an inscription painted on the wall read, THERE IS NO EXCELLENCE WITHOUT GREAT EFFORT. On the other side of the room, the girls in their long dresses and high shoes ate at tables of their own. A clock hung on the wall above them. He watched the big hand, knowing that when it reached eight o'clock, a bell would ring and breakfast would be over. In the meantime, there was oatmeal and glasses of milk, a drink previously unknown to him. Even now, his belly sometimes fought against the milk, causing him to be sick. Such sickness was common among the students.

As if reading his thoughts, Kills Hard lifted his own glass to his lips, rolling his eyes at him in a comical way. Despite himself, Plenty Horses laughed out loud, drawing the attention of one of the male teachers, a portly man with thick eyeglasses who glowered a warning at him.

"Stop," Plenty Horses whispered. Kills Hard grinned.

Before Kills Hard could start any further mischief, the bell rang for the first class of the day and the boys separated, each going to his respective classroom. In English class Plenty Horses sat on a hard wooden seat at a hard wooden desk, a hard wooden floor beneath his aching feet encased in hard leather shoes. It had taken him some time to adjust to the hardness of the *wasicun* way of living. Even now, after five winters at Carlisle, he was physically uncomfortable in his surroundings. It seemed strange that people would deliberately inflict such suffering upon their bodies, but then, perhaps that was what made the *wasicun* so strong. After all, there were more of them than there were stars in the sky. He could ride across the prairie for days without seeing another person, but here, in every direction he turned, there would be people. And they would be wasicun.

At the front of the room, beneath a framed portrait of George Washington, Mrs. Littleton was writing some lines on the chalkboard. The chalk squeaking across the slate board set his teeth on edge. She wrote:

> *Breathes there the man with soul so dead,*
> *Who never to himself hath said,*
> *"This is my own, my native land!"*

"This is the first line in Sir Walter Scott's poem, 'My Native Land.'" Mrs. Littleton turned to face the class. "Let's all recite it together."

Along with the other dozen or so boys and girls in the room, Plenty Horses read the line aloud. At their teacher's request, they read the line one more time.

"Very good," Mrs. Littleton said. "Can someone tell me what the poet is saying here?" The class was silent. Mrs. Littleton stood still as a tree, her eyes scanning the faces of her students, as she waited.

He did not look at her, mostly because he had been taught from a youth that it was impolite to stare directly at other people, but also because he thought that in some way that was magic; if he didn't see her, she would not be able to see him. He was relieved to hear the teacher ask, "Lucy? Can you tell me what it means?"

He cut a glance toward Lucy, a newly arrived Lakota girl whose real name was Spotted Bird Woman. She sat mutely at a desk near his. In that brief look, he saw a panicked expression cross her face, but only momentarily, disappearing again behind a mask that would reveal nothing to Mrs. Littleton.

"What do you think, Lucy?" the teacher prodded.

Keeping her eyes downcast as she had been taught, the girl softly responded, "It is a man who is happy in his homeland."

"Lucy, you must learn to look at me when you speak and to speak up so that we all may hear what you have to say. That is a good answer. We will understand the poem more, as we progress."

He glanced at Lucy one more time and saw the embarrassment in the young girl's face. He knew it was not so much Mrs. Littleton's reprimand that caused a flush to come to her cheeks as much as it was her discomfort at being forced to speak. It was not the Lakota way. He remembered how it was when he first arrived at Carlisle. He remembered his own confusion, his fear, as the *wasicun* told him that everything his mother and father had taught him, everything his people had taught him about being a Lakota was wrong. He had been taught to walk the Good Red Road in a manner befitting a Lakota, the people *Wakan* Tanka had made superior to all others, yet here at Carlisle, the *wasicun* said no; he was wrong.

Plenty Horses knew that Living Bear had not wanted to send him to the *wasicun* school, but the threat of losing government provisions if his father refused was real. Resigned to losing his son for several winters, Living Bear had tried to find something good. Might it not be a good thing, he had asked his son, to learn the ways of the *wasicun* since they are everywhere around us?

Plenty Horses agreed. It would be like stealing the enemy's horses. He would steal the ways of the *wasicun* and bring them back to the Lakota; a warrior must know the ways of his enemy in order to defeat him.

In five winters he had learned much of the *wasicun* way of living. They were different in every way from the Lakota, but he had come to find they were not all bad ways. *Wasicun* books did not seem like bad things. Within them were many worlds that even the Lakota *wicasa wakan* knew nothing about, despite their sacred medicine and communication with the spirits. *Wasicun* towns and villages were more organized and efficient than Lakota camps. There was always food and medicine, so the people never went hungry and were rarely sick. And the machines and tools of the wasicun, such as guns and wagons and pots, all of which the Lakota had already been using for a long time, were marvelous things. No, not all these things seemed to be bad things.

So, he understood Lucy's embarrassment and her fear in this new *wasicun* world, but he also knew that in time, she would learn as he had learned the ways of the wasicun. She would still long for the people of the plains, for the very plains themselves, just as he did, but she would find that longing sometimes soothed like a cooling river by the wonders of the *wasicun* world.

The day gradually wore away, as every day did at Carlisle. A class to learn the ways of *wasicun* counting. Another class held in a barn where Plenty Horses, Kills Hard, and several other boys were taught how to bend and shape red-hot iron over an anvil. Everything was hard about the wasicun; even their ponies wore iron shoes. Still later, all the boys together in the gymnasium where they contorted their bodies in unnatural ways, tossed large heavy balls to each other, waved wooden clubs in their hands and did many other silly things he did not understand. He would much rather wrestle or race with the other boys, as he did at home, but that was forbidden here.

His feet still hurt from his run the night before. He did his best to walk without limping, but each step was painful. That night after the evening Jesus prayer, when the lights were extinguished, and all the students were required to sleep, he lay upon his bed, too sore to run once more. It was quiet in the room except for the muffled whimpering of the new boy. He closed his ears to that sound he remembered only too well.

Through the window near his bed Plenty Horses could see the stars trekking through the sky. He knew them as friends and guides. He wondered if he followed them, if he walked their paths, would they take him back to his father's lodge? Would they take him back to the Lakota? He closed his eyes, but the stars burned even brighter, and his feet were already following the shining paths they blazed for him.

Mam's Testimony

by Mistinguette Smith

Dear Lord, here come this child, Opal, again. Burning candles, waving joss sticks, and wearing her knees out in front of some old-timey photograph she done found, trying to get me to pay her some mind. She thinks I done passed over already. Maybe she is thinking I can get the attention of the Almighty more directly than she can. It appears You have not seen fit to answer her prayers up to now.

I can see and hear her as plain as if she was closed up in this little bed-sit room with me. These young people today don't offer the courtesy of a proper introduction, but I knew right away whose she was. I can see my Baby in her cat eyes and red-brown hair. Except that picture she's calling Grandmam is some creased, sepia-tone thing, and the lady in it don't look nothing like me. But how could Opal know that? She say she was born up in Ohio; she ain't never seen me, or any of the places I come through. And here she is, thinking her Grandmam Sadie can intercede with the Heavenly Father on her behalf. Poor thing. She don't know that You and me ain't been on speaking terms until recently.

Opal looks barely grown, flat and skinny like a schoolgirl. But she says she's already married and trying to mama a foster child who is a handful of trouble. The girl don't talk, won't answer to her own name. She wanders off by herself, and when Opal finds her, she won't tell where she's been. Opal's eyes are all shiny with affliction when she comes here for me: *Grandmam, please ask the Lord to help me tame this girl's wild spirit.* Ha! Opal wouldn't be asking for my help if she knew one thing about me. *Grandmam, ask God to help me to find this girl before her daddy gets home. If she disappears on me for real, I don't know what he might do.*

Now, it don't take the wisdom of Solomon to understand exactly what the problem is here. Opal has a husband, and like most men, he is likely a passel of trouble. But the real trouble is that Opal's little foster girl has a rambling nature. Some folks mend their troubles by following a deep walking rhythm inside them. Nowadays, with the interstate and whatnot, it ain't enough to walk, you got to pick up your feet and run if you want to feel the world pulse a little before you land. Don't I remember it. Opal gets worried when the girl is missing, but that child is running from something that happens in the quiet between each one of her footsteps. If you ask me, I'd wager that Opal has got legs for running, too.

But how am I supposed to be any consolation for this Opal and her family troubles, Lord? She calls out to me, but it's not like I have a way to answer her back. I guess that is for you, "The All-Knowing," to sort out.

But for tonight, will You please look over Opal and her rambling girl? 'Cause they are both in sorry shape if the only one who's studying them is me. Amen.

***

Gracious God, I thank You for bringing me through to another morning, even though this here Detroit snow is soot-gray across my window and I can't hardly see the sun. The wind outside is fierce, blowing people along like bits of trash in the street. My late husband's daughter-in-law has been in here twice to make sure my lap blanket is tucked in good, and she turned up the heat on the gas grate. She's real nice like that, always makes sure my breakfast is soft enough to chew. But she don't have much to say, so I guess it's just You and me again today.

Opal has already been here this morning, same as every day. She doesn't bother with the smoke and candles so much now; she mostly talks about her friends and family, the news and whatnot. When she's praying, though, she keeps asking for piddly little things: *Grandmam, please ask God to make a way to get this girl into a new school. Ask Him to take the war out of my husband, to make me a wife with a steadfast heart.* Well, no wonder You don't bother to answer her. You, for whom they say, "no work is too great, no pardon impossible." All she can think to bring you is some little pissant problems like those.

If You was a Mother God, you would tell her, "Get up off your knees, woman. Life is big. Go fetch that girl child because, foster or not, she's your family now. Then, both of you get to moving toward the thing you need. It don't matter what kind of man you married, or if you know where you're headed. You got to be already on the way for Me to meet up with your prayers."

But you're a Father, God. You are all powerful, so You can afford to be gentle as a lamb. Maybe that's why she is asking for Your help instead of mine. Can't say I blame her. My hard ways do not commend me.

Watching people blow around on the sidewalk outside makes me think back on when I was young. Moving around was a good thing back then, leaving one place and going to another before your memories could catch up to you and call your name out loud. In the olden days, people stayed stuck in one place their whole life long. I didn't know a thing about the world except what came past the cabin where I was born, until the day I walked down to the Gunpowder County railroad depot.

They say You know every secret in the human heart, Heavenly Father, so you know I wasn't aiming to leave that blind shack on the hillside forever. Sometimes I dream myself back there, thrashing around a spoonwood hell, or chasing a cloud of lightening bugs as they flit through the dark. I had set out to search for my common-law husband, Walter, when I walked down the mountain. I was looking to conjure him back home to me.

It was by chance I fell in with Elijah, a soldier come back from France. Elijah said he didn't know my Walter, but he told me not to take the next train heading west. Word was that a mob down in Knoxville broke open the prison and let mayhem unloose itself on the Colored part of that town. Later on, I heard plenty such mobs had let Negro blood run that summer of 1919; streets ran red as far as Missouri and Arkansas. Maybe I cleaved to Elijah because I was taken by his knowing about the world

Elijah had the shell shock, but his hands were steady enough to drive a mule cart from Gunpowder County, Tennessee, all the way up to Kentucky. He told me he needed a strong-willed woman to sober him up and keep his house, so I climbed up on the buckboard next to him. Without the whiskey, I thought me and Elijah might stand a chance. But a woman can sojourn into trouble even when she stays close to home.

I tried to be a faithful-hearted wife, Lord. But twice a week I made the walk to Main Street just to watch the train from Lexington carry people to all those cities up north. The last coach was always full of Colored folks with their hands pressed against the windows, waving goodbye, looking for someplace better. I would search every window, looking for my Walter's face. But he was never on that train, so I made my feet carry me back to Elijah's temper and his fists.

Union Station was as far as I let my mind wander right up until the day some Colored soldier got accused of carrying off a little white girl. Everybody knew what kind of trouble that would mean. The night they sent the U.S. Army into Lexington to keep the white folks' peace, that damn fool Elijah packed his pistol and went out 'protecting' the neighborhood with his friends. Him and a few other men against the whole U.S. Army—like having been in the service meant they wasn't still Colored. I knew those soldiers would come bust down our door, drag us both to the street, and hang us from the lamppost outside. Elijah's fists was one thing. But I was not waiting around for white men with rifles to come for me. I stuffed what I could fit into my second-hand carpetbag and walked directly to the station for that northbound train, all by myself. When I got to the furthest place my one-way ticket would take me, I could smell Canada, bloodless and clean, on the other side of the Detroit River. That very day, I found housekeeping work, and a room-and-board for ladies in Black Bottom. Two years later, I married Evans Freeman at the courthouse and hung up my rambling shoes for good. Never did hear from my Walter or Elijah again. Never looked at another train window to see who might be waving goodbye.

Every time the pastor comes from the Sick and Shut-In Ministry to visit me, he tells me, "the eyes of the Lord are in every place, beholding the evil and the good." If that's so, You must know this story already. But the way the pastor tells it, I have to confess each and every sin to You myself, so that You can cleanse from me all unrighteousness before my dying day. If Pastor is right, God, here I am, doing my best. Never before have I told a soul about what I came through to get here to Detroit. Couldn't tell a soul but You now, even if I wanted to. Since the stroke, my words don't come sorted out right.

If I could answer Opal, I would tell her everything. I would tell her about my rambling days and what hard times do to a woman, even one with a faithful heart. I would tell her that today won't be the last time the newspapers say Army rifles got pointed at Colored men who used to be soldiers themselves, same as all those years ago back in Lexington. Opal needs to know some troubles won't ever be new.

Mostly, I would tell her how I lost my daddy before I could memorize his face, same as she did. That's a sorrow that can make you cling to a man who had already let go of himself, and it will have you believing you're the one who can't hold on tight.

Since my mouth cannot make this confession, Lord, could You answer at least one of her little bitty prayers? Or maybe let her know when she comes to sit a spell there's somebody here listening? I'd be much obliged. I mean, Amen.

***

Grandmam, how do I humble my heart to be content as a wife and mother? Mama says motherhood is a gift, a woman's highest calling. But I don't feel gifted or called. I just feel like my own life got choked off before it ever began …

Nowadays, Opal is talking to me directly, instead of asking me to petition You. I can't answer her prayers, but I've been mighty glad for her company. Talking to me seemed to be helping her a little, too. But, Lord, I can't help her now.

Father in Heaven, I have got nothing to say about how to mother a child. Never have. My last husband, Evans, was a widower. He made sure I could stay home to cook and wash up after him and his three boys. But me and Evans didn't have no babies, and by then, I was glad of that. We kept to ourselves in the nighttime, and that suited me fine. But Lord, you know it wasn't always so simple.

Still and all, every confession has got to begin somewhere. Even the story of Your only begotten son begins with the name of His mother.

A mother. Now, that's a lonesome thing. You hear grown children call out for their mama like it's the name of Jesus—somebody who can save you from the ropes and guns on the way to hell. But that kind of love ain't particular. "Mama" is a general kind of name. Like when I took in laundry, the white ladies would call me "Annie," the same name as they called every Colored gal. When I had my babies, I raised them to respect me. Taught them to call me Mam. Not like Mammy, but serious, the way you answer to the white folks: Yes, Mam.

Nothing but a round-rumped girl myself when that first baby come along. No point in me telling how she got here. You know that sorry old story better than me. I called her Sis 'cause I wanted me some kin who would grin at me instead of yelling for me to earn my keep: "Sadie, carry the slop bucket out to feed the pigs" or "Gal, come fetch the linens for bluing." Turned out I was somebody to serve her hungering, piss-soaked needs, same as I was for every-damned-body else. But she was a blessing, my little Sis. She leaned into me and learned how to hold on tight. I bound her up against me with some old strip cloth to keep her from falling into the laundry pot or the fire, so nobody ever touched her. For a lot of years me and Sis growed each other up good.

Now, from the moment that second one slid out between my thighs, her countenance was a trial. The granny handed her to me, worm pale and slick, just as my Walter came in the door. He took one look at her and walked right back out. When he came back, he said it weren't my fault. Doing day work in people's houses, he knew all manner of things could happen to a woman. Walter was my long-time good man, but even he could not stand to look every day at that lily-white face pushed up in the crook of my molasses-sweet arm. I could not say I was surprised the day there was a Mason jar half-full of silver pieces on the table, and his two good shirts gone.

Oh, how I tried to turn my face to the wall after that. But the body can't help what it has to do when it hears a baby cry. My mouth, though, it had nothing to say. When the nurse came to fill out the government record, she had to make up a birthday for the baby herself: six of June 1917. When she asked me what to fill in under "father's name," my eyes fixed on the floor, wishing I could crawl up under the boards like a bug. Vexed, the nurse turned to ask Sis what she should write for her Christian name.

"We just call her Baby," said Sis. "Or sometimes Mam calls her Lily ..."

I found my cracked voice. *Call her May. She may live. She may not. What I want don't seem to matter, either way.*

So, then it was me and Sis and Lillie-Mae-called-Baby, shut up all alone in that no-window cabin on the side of the hill. After a time, I got up and tied Baby on my back so I could use both hands to pick hornworms off the potato shoots and stems of Burley leaf. All the while I was thinking, *Sadie, you need that tobacco money for more than you and Sis now, you got to be somebody's mother.* Putting apples down in the storage cellar, I would ponder shucking off my apron and just walking away. Then I would see Sis tie up a straw dolly and give it to Baby to stop her crying, and I wondered what kind of mother could even think a thing like that.

They were good girls, Baby and Sis, thankful to get fed most every day. I taught them how to wash themselves on Sundays with red soap and a rag, how to twig-broom sweep the dirt yard, to come quick whenever they were called. But I never did grow that tender feeling inside that makes a woman want to rock a baby instead of a man.

One summer came around, and all three of us sat in the dusty yard out by the well, watching carts piled up with household goods roll past. Two-year-old Baby opened and curled her fat fingers in a wave, and Sis called out an offer of a cool dip of water whenever she saw a Colored soldier in uniform walking alongside a wagon. Their womenfolk sucked their teeth when they saw me, saying, "We are leaving behind these barefoot Negroes. We are going to the city." Their scorn didn't bother me none: mountain folk know trouble will one day fall on everybody, same as rain. My mind was busy figuring how many places my Walter, or even one of these traveling mules, might have seen out there in the world.

One morning, when Sis took a pail up to the tramway to pick up fallen chunks of coal for the stove, a strong idea came into my mind: if

I tied up the girls' blankets and clothes inside the quilt, I could put half of what was left of Walter's silver money inside to pay for their keep. I let Baby suck one last time, then tied her swaddling cloth around my own chest, tight. When Sis came back, I sent her running up the road to call for the granny. I buttoned my dress and tied on my apron and shawl. Baby started to wail when the front door pulled shut, as if she could tell what I was doing before I knew it myself. My own tears didn't come in until I got halfway down the mountain, breath caught on that jubilee sun going down. Nobody was there to wave goodbye.

Now, You cannot shame me by saying Mam didn't care for her two girls. The granny would foster them until they could make their own way, same as she did for me. Even if she didn't have a softness for them, she would make sure they were raised up right. Although things turned out a certain way, it was never my intention to forget my girls for good. Sis' face looks back at me from every looking glass. I still keep that piece of Baby's swaddling cloth, wrapped up real careful in newspaper, in the trunk here beside my bed.

Yet, I never told a soul about that blind house up on the mountain, Lord, and them two little girls waiting there for the granny to come take them in. Until this Opal with her fancy problems started showing up calling me her Grandmam, I figured those girls stayed in the hills of Gunpowder County for the rest of their days. During the hard Depression times, my mind wondered if my girls ever found their way back to my daddy's farm. People can always scrape up penny money for tobacco, and you could eat a long, sweet time from the apple and plum trees daddy planted back before they hanged him. I never considered they maybe rambled on to somewhere cold but good, a place like I found in Detroit.

Never told nobody. Dear Father in Heaven, I would not tell it to this Opal child, even if I could. Who could forgive a mother like that? Maybe that's why You took words away from my lips. Some stories are so full of road dust and tears they need to stay in the mud where they are buried. Or maybe it was You who sent Baby's daughter to chastise me for the pride of thinking I was the one who should decide how much I can bear.

The Sick and Shut-In pastor didn't come out in the storm today, but I know how he would guide me: "We all might be in the Last Days, Sister Sadie. You should spend every hour confessing and glorifying his Holy Name." So, if You are truly up there, I confess to You, Almighty God, the affliction of my soul. What I visited on those children fifty years ago is the only sin I know for sure is mine. Pardon for me is too small a thing to ask, so I pray you to unburden my generations instead: Sis and Baby, Opal, the foster girl. Let Opal keep believing in the mercy of that stranger in the photograph her mama gave her, somebody more true and better than me. Let that be enough to carry her, Lord. Let that be enough. Amen.

Unbecoming a Christian

by Jim Hodnett

When Tommy first heard about the age of accountability, it was 1964, and he was a skinny, tow-headed, nine-year-old sitting in Sunday School class at the Victorious Life Baptist Church of Fort Smith, Arkansas. The concept of accountability seemed to pull everyone up short, even the bullies sitting in the row behind him, from whom Tommy worked hard to stay invisible. One of them, Stan, a freckle-faced kid who already strutted a fullback's physique, popped a question at the teacher. "You mean Jesus would throw little kids into hell?"

The Sunday school teacher, Brother Andrews, a thirtyish man with plastic, black-rimmed glasses and thin lips, set his jaw. "If they don't accept the word of God, and they're old enough to know better, He will."

"Dang!" said Stan as he and his cohorts stared with round eyes.

"Jesus loves us, but he also has a temper. That's why the Bible talks about the 'wrath of God.'"

"Dang!" said Stan again.

For Tommy, this new knowledge felt like a cold, dark-gloved hand reaching up from inside his stomach and placing a squeeze hold on his heart. The feeling stayed with him the rest of that day and never completely went away in the months that followed. It took root both in his solar plexus and the base of his brain. The doctrine was a looming threat, undeniable confirmation that he was destined for an evangelical Christian adulthood of discomfort and constraint. He dared not ask his mother about it when he got home. Although she and Daddy rarely attended church—claiming tiredness or busyness— she seemed determined that Tommy and his brothers be present every Sunday, and she did not countenance questioning or doubts about Southern Baptist doctrine.

Tommy was left to grapple with the scary inevitability of the age of accountability on his own. Perhaps, he mused, it would be better to die young, while still an unwitting child, and thus *ex post facto* be assured one of those mansions in heaven—that bright, gold-paved city full of joy and praise—than to live a long, agonized life full of "witnessing" and enduring marathon sermons from the likes of Reverend Jebediah Barton.

Reverend Barton, a pale-faced man with dark, slicked-back hair who preached at his congregants with gritted-teeth ferocity, said he witnessed all the time. His sermons were often punctuated with anecdotes about him sitting next to someone on a park bench or in an airplane and promptly sharing his personal testimony. He would bear down on his unsuspecting seatmates to impress upon them the "plan of salvation."

Tommy couldn't imagine talking to strangers for any purpose unless they spoke to him first. It terrified him to think that it would be his Christian duty to perform that task daily. And even at his young age, he was discerning enough to know that not everyone took the gospel as seriously as Southern Baptists. And they likely would not cotton to being told that they were vile sinners headed for an eternity of excruciating torture unless they took a dip in holy water and started believing in virgin births and dead people walking. Yet he saw no other option for his future—save that dying-young escape clause.

God, it seemed, had laid a trap for him.

He did take some comfort in hearing his Sunday school teacher say that the age of accountability could vary from one individual to another. He kept hoping his was far in the future. But one night, after he had completed his prayers—a tedious, rote list of pleas for the safety and well-being of each of his family members, both immediate and remote—he lay in bed with his eyes on the darkened ceiling of his bedroom. It was summer, and the attic fan was pulling a strong but hot breeze through the windows, billowing the thin, crepe curtains and taunting the skin on his bare legs. Yet the air was close and heavy, and it led him to think of the horrors of hell, as had been laid out in a recent sermon by Reverend Barton: lakes of fire, lashings, forced labor, parched throats, and other continual tortures. It was at that moment that it dawned on him: if he understood the horrible implications of the age of accountability, with its awful burdens, it almost certainly had already arrived. He curled on his side in a ball and lay awake for hours, steeling himself for the bleak and plodding future before him.

The day of reckoning was coming, as he knew it would. Still, he was surprised that Sunday during his tenth year when everyone in his age group was taken into the sanctuary for a special Sunday school service. Tommy could sense something was up. His heart fluttered like a bird imprisoned in his ribcage. He and his classmates were instructed to sit down in the first two rows of the stiff-backed pews. They listened as Reverend Barton told them they had reached the point where they could no longer avoid an eternity of torture and misery in hell if they didn't accept the lordship of Jesus and agree to be baptized. The reverend was not standing above them behind the pulpit on the altar, but right there in front of them, pew-level. That made it seem all the more urgent and personal.

After Reverend Barton finished speaking, deacons and Sunday school teachers paired off with the children and began asking them if they understood what the preacher had said. Tommy was assigned to a fifty-something deacon named Burly Johnson. Brother Johnson was a red-faced mattress salesman with an enormous potbelly on which rested a wide, silk, burgundy tie with an ostrich feather embroidered on it. "Are you ready to accept Jesus into your heart, Tommy?" he asked.

"Yes, sir."

"Are you ready to gird your loins and become a warrior for Christ? A Christian soldier?"

"Uh-huh."

Tommy had learned long ago that it was best to answer "yes" to most questions adults asked him in church. But the stratagem wasn't foolproof. Several months earlier, his Sunday school teacher had asked him if it was true that sons were responsible for the sins of their fathers. Tommy had thought of his own gun-toting, nose-picking daddy and how different and distant he felt from him. It made absolutely no sense that he would be responsible for Daddy's sins. Nonetheless, he answered his teacher's question in the affirmative, thinking it to be the safest response. Logic and Southern Baptist theology, he had found, did not often cross paths. But as it turned out, this had been one of the rare occasions they did. The teacher sighed, as though his student should have known the answer was an obvious "no." Tommy blushed, feeling stupid—church-stupid—yet again.

When the special Sunday school session was over, Brother Johnson patted Tommy on the back and said, "Bless you, son. You ready to be baptized?"

"Yes, sir."

"All right, then. We'll be talking to your parents. Are your parents Christians?"

"I don't know."

"I bet they are," reassured Brother Johnson. "Do they belong here, at Victorious Life? Are they members?"

"Yes, sir."

"Well then, I'm sure they are. Run along to the service now."

"Yes, sir."

The service didn't last unbearably long that Sunday. Reverend Barton's sermon, which was the same sermon he delivered every week—with the addition of some digressive rants against communism, Martin Luther King, and mini-skirts—focused on how salvation was a gift that could not be earned by good works, no matter how good, and how refusing that gift was such an offense to God that no wonder non-believers were cast into lakes of fire.

During the sermon, Tommy slumped at the end of a back-row pew near a stained-glass window depiction of Jesus seated by a fountain. A white dove perched on his outstretched hand, showing no fear of the Son of God. But then, doves didn't have to worry about going to hell. As Tommy listened to the reverend, he tried yet again to reconcile in his mind how the onerous obligations of salvation might somehow also be a gift. Whatever carefree moments his existence had afforded him thus far seemed remote as far as the future was concerned, out of reach.

Throughout the sermon, reliable old Brother Walter "Ernie" Earnest sat in the second row of pews and punctuated the reverend's fiery declamations with shouted *amens*. Brother Ernie, always impeccably dressed in a suit that might have fit dapperly when purchased in the 1940s but now drooped from his shoulders and limbs in folds of excess fabric, sat with gnarled hands resting on a cane in front of him. He bobbed his head in rhythm with the sermon's cadences. He couldn't hear very well, but he was able to discern when Reverend Barton had paused after an emphatic statement that called for an *amen*, which he would then provide with godly certitude.

The combination of Reverend Barton's brimstone rhetoric and Brother Ernie's hearty cheerleading did the trick this Sunday. Three people responded to the altar call, two already-saved souls to rededicate their lives to Jesus, and another person—a middle-aged man whose face displayed the worn and lined look of misspent youth—to accept Him as his personal savior. This head count satisfied the reverend, and he felt no need to resume his position behind the pulpit to deliver his sermon a second time, as he often did after a too-paltry harvest of souls. He knew how to wear down a congregation. That was certain.

Tommy rode home in the back seat of the family car, a blue-and-white, big-finned 1957 Chevy Bel Air. His two older brothers were in the front. While Bobby drove, Phil fiddled with the radio, trying to find some rock-and-roll on the dial. It was almost as though he was looking for an antidote to the previous three hours. Over the strains of Peter and Gordon singing "A World Without Love," Tommy posed a question to his brothers. "Did you guys ever learn about the age of accountability in Sunday school?"

"Yeah, sure," answered Bobby. Phil nodded.

"Well, doesn't it scare you?"

Bobby chuckled. "Maybe. I mean, I guess so. At first, anyway."

"But not anymore?"

Phil smirked, "Don't be a dope, Tommy. They're *trying* to scare you. They don't want you to have any fun. Don't worry about it. Just play along."

But how could he *not* worry about it? Maybe Bobby and Phil could. They were handsome, popular, and athletic. Maybe Jesus would give them a pass, but likely not him—not skinny, sissy Tommy Crow. He would have to *earn* his way out of hell and work hard at it, too.

"Then why do you keep going to church?" asked Tommy, his forehead furrowed, making him look like a miniature, younger version of Brother Ernie, intent on one of Revered Barton's blistering sermons.

"I dunno," shrugged Bobby. "Everybody else does."

Phil smirked again and lifted his furry, teenage eyebrows. "Yeah, especially the cute girls."

Bobby blushed but also laughed. He and Phil then began to speak in reverential tones about the beauty of a certain Melanie Crookson.

Tommy slouched into his seat and listened to Peter and Gordon sing about hiding away in their loneliness.

The brothers arrived home a few minutes later to find that Mother, as always, had spent the morning preparing an abundant Sunday dinner. She was in the final stages, rushing, fussing, and fretting as she brushed back locks of hair from her sweaty forehead. But she did not ask for help nor appear to expect it.

Years later, it occurred to Tommy that perhaps Mother's Sunday dinners were a form of worship, her offering, a way of making Sunday special and holy. In a similar vein was her faithful rousting of her three sons from bed each Sunday morning, cajoling and guilting them through hurried breakfasts, shoe polishings, and necktie cinchings until they were ushered into the family car, which Bobby, the oldest, drove to the church parking lot. When they were younger, Daddy would drop them off at the church door, then pick them up later, though he was not as adamant about his sons' church attendance as Mother was. He tended to regard churches as money-making schemes to finance Cadillacs for preachers. Nonetheless, he made sure his sons arrived on time. Looking back on this Sunday routine as an adult, Tommy realized his parents were attending church by proxy, that they saw it as sufficient that their children sat in the pews as their representatives. But as a child, the phenomenon left him confused as to the status of his parents' salvation. Didn't real Christians show up? Sit in the pews? The men dressed in suits and the women in hosiery and bouffant hairdos?

Mother had the meal on the table by one p.m.: fried chicken, mashed potatoes with milk gravy, biscuits, black-eyed peas simmered in bacon, and iceberg lettuce salad with store-bought Thousand Island dressing. Dessert was pecan pie, made from nuts harvested from the ground beneath neighborhood trees a few days before and then shelled on the back porch by Tommy and Phil.

The family devoured the entire meal with gusto, swapping stories and jabs at each other. But Tommy ate in silence. He didn't tell anyone about his morning in the sanctuary. He was hoping it might have been some dead-end side street he'd been driven down, a detour that went nowhere, resulting in a U-turn back to the main road, toward routine and normality.

For a while, it seemed the U-turn was real. After dinner, Mother, sighing heavily, cleared the table and cleaned up the kitchen. Meanwhile, Daddy went to the living room to watch television. Bobby and Phil made their escapes to friends' houses, but Tommy went to his room. He changed into his play clothes, plopped down on his bed, and began reading a Hardy Boys mystery, *The Secret of Wildcat Swamp*.

When the phone rang around two-thirty that afternoon, it seemed to Tommy like the tolling of a bell tower at a funeral. His heart stopped. The inevitable age of accountability was upon him, he surmised. Mother answered the phone, had a brief conversation, and a few minutes later came to find him. Her approaching footsteps sounded to Tommy like a prison guard doing rounds.

"Tommy, that was a Brother Johnson on the phone," Mother said, as she stood at the foot of her son's bed. "He says you're being baptized at the evening service, and he wants to come by and talk about details with us."

"Oh."

"Tommy, why didn't you tell us?" Mother's voice was aggrieved. "I had no idea what he was talking about at first." She peered down at him with hands on her hips. She was clothed in her plain blouse and skirt, her hair unpermed, which made her appear less sophisticated and holy than the elaborately coiffed and attired women Tommy saw sitting in the church pews every Sunday.

"I don't know," he answered in a shamed voice.

She sighed. "Well, I guess it *is* about time for you to be baptized, but I wish you would've warned us."

"I'm sorry."

"Well, put on some nicer clothes. Brother Johnson will be here in just a few minutes."

When Brother Johnson arrived, Mother seated him, Daddy, herself, and Tommy in the living room. Daddy had turned the volume knob on the Zenith TV all the way down when the doorbell rang but had left the picture on. Tommy was glad. The blurry gray images made him feel he had a friend in the room. Mother and Daddy sat on a pink couch adorned with a squiggly modern design, while Brother Johnson sat in a matching side chair. Tommy slouched in a stiff-backed wooden chair that Mother had carried in from the dining room. He stared at the thick, maroon-and-gray wool rug below him, wishing he could disappear into its intricate, leaf-and-petal design.

Brother Johnson suggested they pray. They all bowed their heads. "Lord," began the deacon, "we are grateful for this good family and for their fine son, Thomas, who is choosing to follow in Your path. We ask for Your blessing as he prepares to be washed in Your blood tonight, to have his sins taken away, and to become a soldier in the army of Your Son, Jesus Christ. It is in His name that we pray. Amen."

"Amen," repeated Mother and Daddy. Tommy said nothing. *Washed in your blood?* When he opened his eyes, he could not stop them from widening and blinking. He didn't even like needles, to say nothing of a trickle of red oozing from a finger cut. Blood horrified him and turned his stomach.

"Now," said Brother Johnson. "I had a nice chat with Tommy this morning, and I believe he's ready and understands what he's doing. He said he didn't know whether his parents were Christians, but I can tell just by being in your nice home that you are." He glanced at the Bible Mother had taken from the bookshelves and placed on the coffee table a few minutes before he arrived.

"Oh, well, yes," said Mother, taking a sidelong glance at Tommy. "We were both baptized when we were children." Daddy nodded. Tommy studied his hands, which he held wrenched in his lap.

"That's wonderful," said Brother Johnson. "I'm sure you're filled with joy to know your son will be joining you someday in the hereafter. Now you're all going to need to arrive about six-thirty tonight, and Tommy's going to need an extra pair of underwear and some dark pants to wear during the ceremony. And Tommy, we'll tell you what to do after you get there, but basically, you're just going to walk down into the baptismal, up there behind the choir loft, and Reverend Barton will take it from there."

"Yes, sir."

"Are you excited?"

"Yes, sir."

After Brother Johnson left and Daddy went back to watching television, Mother came looking for Tommy in his room. "Tommy," she said in a reproving voice, hands on her hips again, "that was embarrassing! Didn't even know we're Christians? My heavens! I just don't know what to say."

"I'm sorry."

"What made you say such a thing?" she demanded.

"I don't know." But then he felt some resentment well up behind his eyes, like the wrath of God itself, and before he knew it, he blurted out a condemnation: "But you hardly ever go to church, and we never pray. Other people's families say grace before they eat, but we don't. And Daddy smokes and cusses."

Mother looked shocked for a moment at Tommy's uncharacteristic impudence but recovered in short order. She had a husband and three sons, after all, and knew her way around the block. "Well, what Daddy does isn't any of your business," she admonished. "And we do go to church sometimes when we can. Your daddy and I are busy trying to keep a roof over you boys' heads and food on the table. But we make sure you and your brothers go, don't we?"

"Yes, ma'am."

"And we say grace at holidays."

"Okay."

"Not Christians? The very idea!"

Tommy's face burned with shame. He had begun his life as a Christian soldier by napalming his own mother.

That evening, Brother Johnson and two other deacons led Tommy, carrying his extra pair of underwear and navy-blue gym shorts in a plastic bag, into the men's dressing room for the choir. Dozens of beige robes with burgundy trim hung on racks around the perimeter of the room, making it look lifeless and mournful. Tommy, six other boys, and Ronald, the middle-aged man who had responded to the altar call that morning, were told to take off everything but their underwear and put on their dark-colored pants. Then they were handed starched, white, collared smocks that came down to their ankles. Once clothed in their angelic garb, Brother Johnson instructed them on the procedure for the ceremony. "Now, do you understand?" he asked when he was finished. "Are there any questions?"

Ronald tugged at the collar of his smock and shifted his weight. "Uh, yeah. I'm a little bigger than these boys here. You don't think the reverend will drop me, do you?"

Brother Johnson smiled. "We get asked that all the time. No, of course not. The water will hold you up, so Reverend Barton doesn't have to do much more than keep you steady. You'll bounce right back up after you go under."

Ronald, who was recovering-addict thin, looked doubtful but nodded. A few minutes later, they were led to the portal to the baptismal, where Reverend Barton was already waist-deep in the water. On the wall above the portal a portrait of a blond, blue-eyed, trim-bearded Jesus stared down at them. His head was haloed and cocked sympathetically, but Tommy took little comfort from the image.

As they neared the baptismal, the smell of chlorine pinched at Tommy's nose and eyes. The voice of a shaky, reedy soprano, accompanied by piano, wavered from the sanctuary.

Blessed Assurance, Jesus is mine!
Oh, what a foretaste of glory divine!
Heir of salvation, purchase of God,
Born of His Spirit, washed in His blood.

A shudder went down Tommy's spine. There was that blood-washing reference again. Once the singer had made it through all the verses, Brother Ernie shouted "Amen!" from the second row, and Reverend Barton lifted his hands above his shoulders to proclaim that this was indeed a joyous occasion as more souls had been won to Christ. While the reverend talked, Brother Johnson lined them up in front of the four steps leading down into the baptismal. There Reverend Barton could see them, although the congregation could not. Behind the minister was a stained-glass portrayal of a dead Jesus on the cross, his bearded chin resting on his chest.

Ronald was first in line, then Tommy second. On the other side of the baptismal, seven girls from Tommy's age group were lined up in white robes, too. But Reverend Barton started with Ronald and the boys. He signaled for Ronald to come forward. "Our first new soul for salvation," he announced.

Ronald pressed his hands together in front of his chest in a prayerful position as he began descending the stairs. No one had told him to do that. It was a piety overreach, to be sure, and an ill-advised one at that. What in the world did he think the stair rail on the wall was for? Of course he slipped, fell backward into the water and hit the right side of his head on the rail. While Tommy watched in horror, Reverend Barton slow-motion rushed through the water to help the new convert. "Are you okay, Mr. Sheridan?"

He was, unless you counted embarrassed, addled, and prematurely soaked as criteria. "Yes, Reverend," he replied.

"Well, come on forward, then," said Reverend Barton, taking Ronald by the arm. As they positioned themselves in the middle of the baptismal, Tommy noticed a spot of red behind Ronald's right ear and a thin trickle of blood coming from it. He also saw that there was a patch of pink in the water above the steps into the baptismal. His mouth dropped, and he felt the scalp beneath his blond crew cut tingle.

"Now, Brother Ronald was just a little over-eager, I guess," said Reverend Barton, to which the congregation laughed with relief. "But we'll do it right this time." He whispered a question into Ronald's ear, which Ronald answered. Barton placed his left hand behind Ronald's back and held his right hand above his own head, palm outward. "Ronald James Sheridan, do you profess your faith in the Lord Jesus Christ and accept Him as your Personal Savior?"

"Yes, sir. I sure do."

"Then in obedience to the command of the Holy Scriptures, I baptize thee, my brother, Ronald, in the name of the Father, the Son, and the Holy Ghost." Ronald leaned back cautiously with Reverend Barton's arm at his back, and just as Brother Johnson had promised, the water made him buoyant enough to bounce right back up. "God bless you," said Reverend Barton as Ronnie wiped his face with his hands and grinned with a celestial glow. The congregation applauded.

"A-*men!*" shouted Brother Ernie.

But Tommy stared in horror at the baptismal. There was a larger, darker circle of blood in the water from whence Ronald's head had emerged. After the new convert made his way ever so carefully back up the steps, Reverend Barton motioned with his hand for Tommy to come forward. Tommy obeyed but held onto the stair rail with both hands and did not take his eyes off the solid circle of red in the baptismal water, which, in defiance of the laws of physics, appeared to grow larger and darker with each dizzying second.

Reverend Barton leaned into Tommy's ear. Even above the odor of chlorine, Tommy could smell the Old Spice aftershave on the reverend's cheeks. A bottle of it sat on the bathroom vanity at home where his daddy stood every morning to shave. "What's your full name, son?" the reverend whispered.

"Thomas John Crow the Third," Tommy replied in a trembling voice.

The reverend, who seemed unaware of the crimson stain in the water, placed his right hand behind Tommy's back and again raised his left hand above his head. "Thomas John Crow the Third, do you profess your faith in the Lord Jesus Christ and accept Him as your Personal Savior?"

It was more a plea, a quavering wail than a protest, but the sound emitting from Tommy's throat was clear and piercing. "*No-o-o-o-o-o!*" he cried, "*no, no!*"

The congregation froze. Reverend Barton stared at Tommy with his mouth agape. For a few seconds, the sanctuary was as quiet as two a.m. in a graveyard. Until, Brother Ernie shouted, "A-*men!*"

***

Tom Crow walked the gentle incline with plodding steps, feeling more winded than he had expected. He was ten years older than he was the last time he had trod this path of finely ground black gravel and many more years beyond his refusal of baptism. He did not return to Fort Smith often. Only Bobby remained here, and they seldom talked. Bobby, previously indifferent to religion, had, shortly after college, married a devout and alluring young woman who skillfully led him to a new understanding of himself as a sinner in need of salvation. Accordingly, Bobby did not approve of Tom's "lifestyle," nor would he approve of Tom's reason for returning to Fort Smith: to deliver a short series of lectures to students and faculty in the Comparative Religions Department at the local university. The lectures were entitled, "Jesus: Man vs. Myth." Bobby was a successful attorney and a deacon at their childhood church, Victorious Life Baptist. To him, Jesus was neither man nor myth. He was God.

When Tom reached his destination, he stood for a few moments with his hands clasped below his chin and read the engravings: *Thomas John Crow, Jr., November 14, 1920 - July 12, 1988,* and *Sarah Louise Crow, May 21, 1921 - January 5,1995.* To the right of his mother's plot was another gravestone, *Phillip Silas Crow, June 29, 1949 - August 9, 1970.* Below Phil's name was a five-pointed star with the word, *VIETNAM,* inside it. Tom stroked the top of each gravestone, then closed his eyes and drew in an extended breath. That was all.

As he turned and walked down the pathway to his rental car, Tom felt comforted by the fact the cemetery was well-maintained, the grounds weeded and mowed, and the ancient, low-branched trees laden with abundant leaves. About halfway down the path, to his right, another gravestone caught his eye. It was decorated with an engraving of two gnarled hands resting on the crook of a cane. *Walter Isaiah "Ernie" Earnest, March 6, 1894 - August 23, 1969,* it read. And below, in quotes, was the word, *Amen!*

Tom emitted a quick, breathy laugh, but then began to cry, crying tears that he had not shed at his parents and brother's graves. "Amen, indeed," he said, remembering that day so long ago when, standing in blood-stained chlorinated water, he took his first step toward living his own life. "Amen indeed."

Counterpoint

by M. R. Vian

Milo 2.0

There's no precise English word for it, but Milo's mother might have called her son's current state of mind *toska*. It's Russian for that feeling of wretchedness or angst with no identifiable cause. But as his days in the closet go on, Milo does identify the cause. Precisely. And he tucks it away. There's too much to do now. So much to be gained. And with very few distractions, he can get the work done. Plus, it's a good living. Finally.

The NSA work for Project Raven had been good for Milo's ego, and good for Miloslav Isloynov's résumé. Of course, none of that work experience would ever be written down. His sort of curriculum vitae is only ever passed along in a whisper—and likely encrypted. But that gig, prestigious as it was in some tight-lipped circles, didn't pay for shit. When Milo's new employer found him, he was living in a barely-two-room apartment, eating packaged meat on week-old bread, the stale ghost of the smoker who lived there before, unevictable. The best thing about that place was the family of exquisite cockroaches he shared the flat with—something he knew a little about from the time before—Milo 1.0.

Milo's new boss is no worse than most. Smart man. Determined. But also crass, overbearing. *Vlastnyy*, his father would've said. And perversely wealthy. So, to be fair, or at least more accurate, the "closet" is really a butler's pantry in his employer's palatial home. And it's outfitted with everything Milo needs to do his work. The sliding pocket door closes, so if the old man ever does get visitors—very rare in Milo's time there—he can seal Milo off.

Milo's work *needs* to be sealed off from the rest of his employer's business. What Milo is doing moves that other enterprise only by induction. While his boss's real business is news and news-like entertainment—meant to inform and influence and, on a good day, provoke public debate—the business *Milo* conducts for him is different. And it's all about the data. What people are searching for. What they buy, like, and loathe. What they read or ignore. Knowing what they drink to, dance to, masturbate to feeds the hungry algorithms. These algorithms that Milo birthed and coached and then set loose. Algorithms that ingest all those patterns and proclivities, make sense of them, somehow (he can't quite explain), and spit out the tactics Milo will claim as his own. A thousand tiny morsels of media, fabricated and aimed perfectly to create trickles of doubt that find their way to streams of discontent which, in turn, flow into raging rivers of conspiracy—drowning any notion of *pesky rational discourse.* His employer's words.

Oh, how the 24-hour news cycle craves chaos.

If he had lived to see this modern world, Papa might've marveled at its intelligent machines. But he surely would have sent its ill-imagined social media contraption back to the drawing board. Mama would've called it an affliction. An *anti*-social infection. A viral variant of the old propaganda organ but even more insidious. The thing is, Milo needs the work. And so he takes all that wisdom and courage and conscience, and he folds it up—and he buries it. Deep.

Out there—outside his little box and the bigger box it sits within—thunder rumbles.

Vadim

As winter surrendered to the spring of 1942, Vadim Isloynov's fortunes began a turn. In stature, Vadim was on the short side, though by most accounts, handsome and very funny. But it was his intellect and self-assurance that earned him the rank of sergeant—the youngest in the 3rd Tank Army. He was stationed in the town of Voronezh where he and his men and the rest of their weary contingent of Soviet forces had taken up a defensive position against the Nazis and their Hungarian and Italian lackeys. It was there, amidst the budding chestnuts and gunpowder and gauze, he met Milo's grandmother, Ilsa.

When he landed in the city's battered hospital after a skirmish, Vadim was first scolded by Dr. Pavlichenko for refusing her field dressing of his "minor" gunshot wound. Then he was snubbed by her when he asked if *un*-dressing was an option. When Ilsa's wintry blue eyes made it quite clear who was in charge, he was smitten with her. With that settled and the war pressing, they quickly married, undressed and, together, made Ilsa pregnant. Later that year when Axis forces invaded and overtook the half of the city east of the Voronezh River, Ilsa fled to the countryside with their newborn son.

By winter, after months of fierce fighting, the city was decimated, with only a smattering of buildings left to suggest a grid of streets. But, not for the first time, the dogged Russian spirit shook off the beating it had taken. The troops gathered their strength and their wits, and readied to launch a killing blow.

In the early morning hours of January 15th, 1943, Vadim led his men across the river, setting in motion their part of Operation Saturn. The assault hammered on for ten days, chipping away, and the ragged Red Army was finally on the verge of ousting the occupying Hungarian and Italian troops from Voronezh. To his men, Vadim vowed certain victory, but with the sun setting, he knew the next morning's gambit could go either way. So in the dwindling twilight, he went to find the kid—a brave, mad, almost certainly doomed young boy with a bike who insisted on staying in the city to move messages and cigarettes between the Soviet captains and sergeants. He never asked for a kopek—maybe only doing his part after a brother or father fell in battle. The scribbled note Vadim gave the boy was not the meditative letter he'd wanted to write. It wasn't beautiful or funny—only desperately short—but it was all he could muster. And off the boy went on his bike. Out of the city. Maybe he'd stay there, Vadim thought, if he had any sense.

The Russian sun rose on the final day of the offensive. And in what would be the decisive push ending the occupation and ultimately turning the tide of the war against Hitler, Vadim Isloynov became a momentary hero.

The battle was over and the enemy swept out. Having taken refuge with their newborn son at a friend's outside of town, Ilsa needed to return to the heart of Voronezh, her own heart broken. She'd tucked the note from Vadim under the child's blanket and now drove back alone to the ruined city to collect her husband. Or at least his remains—a medal or commendation maybe—something to mark there had been a man there. A lover. Briefly, a husband. And even more briefly, a father.

She drove through the rubble, and she wept at all that was lost around her. At the missing places. At the shadows of souls. At the stains of life and death there. And the twisted frame of a bicycle poking from the ruins. She stopped the car on a once familiar street in front of the one building still left teetering. It was the burnt-out shell of the city courthouse where she'd married Vadim, and she imagined the bells in the square ringing on that day not so long ago—sweet and impossibly sad now. Rolling down the dusty car window, she heard the rumble of distant mortar fire. The far-off explosion moved the ground just a little. Just a tremor. Then it was quiet again until the courthouse building shuddered and toppled almost lazily into the street on top of the car, crushing it. And so, Ilsa and Vadim's infant son—Milo's father—was left to grow up an orphan in the dawn of the Cold War.

Mikhail

"Tishe yedesh, dal'sho budesh," the directors of the children's home said to him. Over and over. "The more quietly you go, the farther you go." They'd recognized that he would be the exception—the one-in-a-hundred to dodge the fate of the abandoned child—and that, keeping his head down and following the rules, he might even thrive.

Having been passed around between friends of his mother with families of their own, Mikhail was finally surrendered to the home at five or six. They left him there with a small bundle of artifacts, a handful of stories, and head full of questions. As a schoolboy he was clever, curious, and determined. He would forage for morsels of lore from any who'd known the doctor and military man lost in the haze of the war—a haze that left a lot to the imagination.

Lying about his age, a 16-year-old Mikhail Isloynov got work after school lending his natural problem-solving talent—and in the eyes of some comrades, his irritatingly eager work ethic—to help rebuild his mother's city. He seemed to know the shape of what needed making and how things would fit together to make it. Mikhail's math and physics marks in school, his hands-on civic labors, and his parentage caught the eye of city apparatchiks and then local Soviet military leaders who considered him prospective officer material. Though a sad story, having parents who served and died in the war or its aftermath wasn't an uncommon one. Far from disqualifying him, his sort of orphanhood had a ring of loyalty to it. And so with his aptitudes and his presumed inherited attitudes, they redirected him to the Suvorov Military School in Moscow.

Miki "Mechtatel," as his schoolmates called him, was on a fast track at the elite boarding school. But before long, when Mikhail's big ideas were squelched, he began to question—and even poke at—the bureaucratic ineptitude and highly political system of controls. *Mechtatel* means *dreamer* in Russian, and it wasn't an affectionate nickname. His idealism and his habit of questioning The Party won him no friends.

"You see how things work, Mikhail Isloynov, and how they *do not* work," one sympathetic instructor offered him. "Many prefer the latter not to be seen." So despite his acknowledged talent, he was warned, then marked a troublemaker, and then, less than two years in, he was discharged from the school.

With this formal education stunted, Mikhail made his way back to Voronezh to be closer to the mythic shadows of his lost parents—the doctor and the war hero. *Long shadows*, he thought, so he worked hard. To make ends meet, there were many jobs, including one at the library in the evenings. That one had perks, and it stuck. His beloved Voronezh was trying hard to establish an aviation industry for itself. So lingering in the stacks in his off hours, the orphan and military school reject taught himself about mechanical engineering and, more specifically, about aerodynamics. And vowing never again to eat the tasteless gruel of his orphanhood in the *dyetskii dom*—the children's home where flavor must have been deemed an extravagance—he learned a thing or two about provincial cooking.

Then in his *off* off hours, Mikhail found jazz. Not playing, but listening many nights at the Peshchera club, not far from Library Number One. And in that small, dark, and dodgy tavern, he met Maya. Her voice and the saxophone's alternately spooned and sparred, like lovers. Both of them low and reedy and full of breath. Improvised melodies and rhythms shoving off one another, syncopated and straying out beyond recognition, then back again. Always, eventually, back again. And the spaces between Maya's notes said as much as the notes themselves.

The poster outside said they'd be there all week, and it was only Monday. So Mikhail mustered the nerve to introduce himself, and she didn't dismiss him entirely. By Wednesday, they were chatting between sets, poking lightly at each other's boundaries, tastes, sympathies. At closing time on Friday, by then early Saturday morning, he offered to walk her home, and they talked the whole way, taking each other in—on her stoop, in her cramped kitchen, in the shower. Then, under the sheets, they stopped using words for a while.

It was summertime, and outside her open second-floor window the bush-crickets had long since quieted. Sharing her one pillow, they got back around to music and to politics, which for Maya were not-so-subtly laced. She explained how she came to be singing there at the Peshchera club with this quartet whose very musical existence trod a fine line with the government. How, in the thaw after Stalin's death, the ban on jazz dissolved into a complicated relationship with the art form—at its heart, counter to convention.

"They don't know what to do with us," she said and slid off the bed, wrapping herself in the sheet and shuffling to the window. She drew out and lit a cigarette from the pack on the sill as Mikhail joined her there. "In public, Khrushchev says we are merely a bourgeois American indulgence." She spoke in only barely hushed tones as they watched their first sunrise together. "But in private, they are like the falcon eyeing the vole. Unnerved at how quickly we slip underground. And at the language we speak. A language that moves people. A language they don't understand." And she took a long drag, then named what she meant: "A much needed counterpoint."

Mikhail watched her watching the sky slowly unveiled. The drama of orange and coral and crimson blooming over the distant curve of the earth was beautiful but warned of a storm brewing. He felt a thrill being drawn dangerously into her circle. "Well, I don't know if it's true," he said, feeling the need to say *something*, "but I hear the Americans are sending jazz *ambassadors* here." He borrowed her cigarette, inhaled, and coughed. "Maybe trying to prove they're not racists," he added, hoping to prove he wasn't clueless about this world of hers.

"True enough," Maya said, eyeing him in the dawn light. "Yes, propaganda is a chameleon. It will always look almost like what it pretends to be. Almost. The Americans are mostly pretending to fight for freedom of thought. Ginsberg, Kerouac, Burroughs all look the part. They write their raw, honest, provocative words. But maybe there's not enough there, in America, for a fight. Not like here."

When Mikhail had no response (how could he?), she asked what else he cared about—aside from her jazz and politics—and he explained his obsession with aerodynamics as best he could. She listened, and then she shushed him, and then she taught him a bit more about how to improvise with his *lift* and *drag* and *thrust* and the weightlessness they made possible.

She would teach him many things in the days and months and years that came next about The Sixtiers, as some in their generation were dubbed. About how this new intelligentsia with whom she identified had two faces, not unlike Maya and Mikhail themselves—lyricists and physicists. More about their American counterparts, the Beats, who might have *real* repression to fight one day. And Mikhail would learn the unfamiliar restraint he would need to practice—in order to protect Maya from the falcons she increasingly baited. It wasn't jazz itself that made her and her sort threatening, but rather their new way of thinking about structure and anti-structure, and individuality. She didn't *tell* him these things, she *showed* him. And along the way, she taught him to smoke and to drink as best she could.

They married, and while Maya indulged every subversion and zigzagged perilously, avoiding the eye of the Party, Mikhail landed a solid job at the Voronezh Aviation Plant where he'd spend the rest of his life, if not all of his energy. Some of that energy he reserved—first for sheltering Maya and the *jobs* for the Party that this sheltering demanded, then for his son, who they would call Miloslav.

Miloslav II, Milo 1.0

Miloslav was named for Maya's father. Miloslav (the elder) had helped stoke his own Czech counter-culture before disappearing, literally in the night, in the wake of some insult to Party conformity. This drove his wife, cowed and heart-broken, to move herself and their daughter from Prague to someplace less conspicuous in her native Russia. And it spurred that teenaged Maya, uncowed, to carry on stoking into her adulthood, albeit more cautiously—at least for a while.

When Milo (the younger) was a boy, his papa shared photographs and stories of the world's first supersonic commercial airliner and how he'd had a hand in birthing her. Pictures of the Tupolev Tu-144 transfixed Milo. Even twenty years after its introduction, the needle nose and delta wings looked to him more like a spaceship than any modern airplane, and it fed the boy's fertile imagination. An imagination cultivated by his mama's improvisational till.

"You make the world what you want," she'd say, tapping his head—like an egg. "Change is what life *is*." Then she would sing him to sleep with her whispery, increasingly raspy rendition of *Imagination* by the Americans, Johnny Burke and Jimmy Van Heusen.

When he was nine, Milo tried more than once to fall in with some boys his age who played Cossacks and Robbers in the city park most Saturdays. No luck. Their cold shoulders and cruel jabs of "ne nash" one particular day sent him home dejected.

"Why do they say I'm not one of them?" he asked, more confused than sad or angry.

"Boys can be such—" Maya started, then bit her tongue.

"Listen to me, Milo Isloynov," Mikhail stepped in, "You are very clever. This is something not everyone will love. But just be who you are, and I promise, you will find your people." And they sent him back out into the sunny Saturday afternoon.

Milo found himself back at the park swirling with this question of just who he was. Wandering off the paved path, he stumbled upon a patch of what looked like scorched earth ten times as wide as he was tall. With a closer look at the uncannily circular spot, a thought sparked, and sparked again, and the sparks grew in his imagination into a vivid story about the spacecraft that had morphed from a glowing sphere into a spinning saucer and landed there. Taking up a position there beside the mysterious "landing site" Milo recounted the extraordinary phenomenon for passers-by. The shape of the craft, its luminous glow, the creatures who emerged—towering, but with tiny heads. The details were intricate and believable enough that a few gathered around, looking down and then up to the sky and then down again. Some who stopped said how they might have seen something too. The excitement was contagious, even drawing in the boys who'd spurned Milo only an hour earlier, and before long a local police officer wandered up, joining the crowd to embellish the account into a full-on alien encounter.

At home, Milo shared the story and his excitement to tentative nods from both his mama and papa, and they indulged him to a point. But remarkably, the story spread and within the week it was covered by TASS, the national Soviet news agency. It even made the evening national news broadcast on Vremya. Milo watched his parents as "his" flying saucer story played out on their tiny television in their tiny kitchen. Papa listened as he chopped walnuts, the savor of his kharcho soup with its simmering cherry plum, coriander, and beef filling the space. And he was nodding, maybe appreciating the technical details Milo had woven together. When Mama shot him a look, his father stopped chopping, knifed the walnuts into the pot, and shrugged.

"What?" he said. "Good ingredients!"

But the look on Mama's face was more complicated. Proud, maybe, of the boy's imaginative work, and also profoundly troubled by the untruth of it. That look—the image of her face in that moment— would take its place in the slide carousel of Milo's adult memory. A touchstone. Her conflict in sharp relief: the virtue of crafting something from nothing, *and* the obligation to keep it true. Milo would grapple with this problematic coupling of fiction and truth. Much later.

But this particular fiction was out of their hands now, and it inspired a stream of UFO sightings that never really stopped. More intriguing for Milo were the conspiracy theories it sparked, even years later. He watched his little story spawn more stories, and he followed each of its offspring, fascinated by the schemes and plots and dark cabals people imagined they saw, like elephants in the clouds.

Maybe only a year after the spacemen in the park, his mother took him after school to the apartment of a man—Yuri something. It was the only time Milo could remember his father angry at his mother. But to Milo, that apartment was miraculous. A windowless bedroom hid behind a bookcase. Inside the secret space, there were shelves and tables stacked with reams of paper, cans of ink, silkscreens stretched on wooden frames, and a small, hand-operated printing press. Milo wandered amongst the boxes claiming to be cleaning supplies, but one, still open, was instead filled with printed pamphlets and posters bundled in twine, another with many copies of one book. Their blood red covers with identical titles all read *Counterpoint* in bold black letters. On a desk in the corner, a reel-to-reel tape machine caught Milo's eye, and the man, Yuri, saw it.

"Push the button with the triangle," he said to Milo, who looked at his mother. She raised her eyebrows, and Milo pushed the button. First, a few bars of guitar filled the little room, and then the verse of a song.

> *Untruth roams from field to field,*
> *sharing notes with neighboring Untruths,*
> *But that which is sung softly, booms,*
> *What's read in whispers, thunders.*

"Just an old song," his mother said.

"It is Aleksandr Galich," Yuri said. "Do you like it?"

Again, Milo looked to his mother. Again, she raised her eyebrows in reply, and he just nodded for Yuri.

"Good," Yuri said. "Good! Put it in your head, then, where it is safe from the fairy godmothers." And he showed Milo how to rewind the tape, inviting him to play it again as much as he liked.

On their way home, Milo sang the song, almost under his breath.

"Your voice is good," his mother observed, and she mussed his hair. Then she fixed it.

He ignored the compliment and instead asked her what Yuri had meant, and she revealed, in far too much detail for a 10-year-old, the fact of censorship in their republic.

It wasn't so much that Milo saw all of that at such a young age that upset his father. It was just the starkest evidence yet that, as the years went on, Maya's judgment was decaying. It had always been a race to see if her dissidence or her self-neglect would catch up first. Mikhail's efforts to hide her seditious maneuvers soon became deals with the police to look the other way. And as she and her *samizdat* network distributing banned publications in the shadows became a bigger threat, the "taxes" he paid grew too. As an engineer, Mikhail Isloynov had opportunities to learn things about the Americans' aeronautical technology, their thinking, and their plans. And this became his *other* work. But Mikhail's *extracurricular* jobs could only protect Maya from the apparatchiks, not from the wreckage of her lungs—from two packs of Prima's a day—or from her ruined liver.

Milo was too young to hear what his mama had to tell him—like this, at her bedside—but there was no *later* for Maya Isloynov. So though her voice faltered, her mind was *still* clear, and she gave him what truth she had left.

"Know this, my dear beautiful boy—you have lived up close to us, and so maybe you've seen flashes of light. Might still see them. An occasional spark, a shared laugh, a lullaby. But you also see our seams. More every day. The strain of earning this living. The raw and vulgar edges. Coarse threads worn almost clear through. Mine, most of all. So you have us here at hand, where nothing is hidden. Nothing left to be imagined.

"But for your father, without the burden of his parents' lived lives playing out before his eyes, he could believe anything at all about the healer and war hero who left him. What they left him with was a sketch—nothing more than a few brilliant strokes of the pencil on an endless stretch of parchment—that he could finish in any way he might imagine.

"So for you, Milo Isloynov, I wish away the box we've put you in. Too many ugly marks—in ink." She swallowed, and Milo could see it hurt her to go on. "But the parchment still stretches out for you. It can take you anywhere. Away from here."

Papa mourned. For years, it seemed. Though he'd stopped smoking—too late as it happened—he drank too much and barely dragged himself from bed to work to bed to work. But one day, at the very end of all those pitiful days, he came home to find their too-small kitchen in a baffling state. Drained vodka and wine bottles filled the bin. The week's worth of crusted dishes usually piled in the sink were clean and neatly slotted on edge in the drying rack. An earthy tang of sautéing garlic and dill filled the air. He felt a wave of surprise and then shame. And then something reverent filled Mikhail's watery blue eyes as he watched the boy singing quietly and working his wooden spoon. Only he was no longer a boy. And for Mikhail, it was an unfamiliar place to be. To be the one watched out for.

"I have questions about my trigonometry," Milo said. "After dinner, okay?"

His father only nodded and took his seat at the table Milo had set for them. And they ate. It was that sudden. Like a fever breaking, the veil of self-pity—of lost purpose—dissolved and the terrible dream gave way to something else. *Hope*, Mikhail thought. And with that thought, he took a more mindless job at the factory. Then he turned his energies to his Milo, *their* Milo, and readying him for launch.

Nadezhda is Russian for "hope" and was also the name of the first cockroach to be impregnated in space. After years as a student and then a research assistant at the university, Milo got his first truly practical job helping the mission team to track and record the whole off-world conception on video. Insect porn, he joked. No one laughed. Though his degree was in computer science, Milo learned he wasn't a real scientist when he found himself amidst the astrophysicists, the biologists, the entomologists working with the Russian space agency, Roscosmos. The entomologists were the cruelest. Called him "the technician" with unmistakable derision.

He'd thought it might be different once he left the insular world of academia—a place where people spoke in high-minded platitudes, then acted like adolescents behind closed office doors. Trading favors of every sort. Smart people, kicked from the nest, mindlessly falling into parts they'd be playing in the tragedy of a failed ideology. This cynicism, which Milo came by honestly, fed his growing sense of not belonging. Of being an outsider. Of seeing the establishment for what it was: power protecting power, at any cost.

The last straw came eight years later. On the little television in the corner of the hospital room, a sober news reporter detailed the space program's devastating (and embarrassing) failure and the conclusions of its investigations. They watched and Milo just shook his head. In order to save face, Roscosmos, and then the factory pinned blame for a series of faulty Proton rockets on an order of materials placed by Milo's father who had, by then, fallen ill. While his heart still kept time, the rest of Mikhail Isloynov's organs were falling out of rhythm, out of tune, some refusing to play at all.

"They figure I'll be dead soon anyway, so why not have me take one for the team," Papa said from his hospice bed, a thin tube draped across his upper lip feeding oxygen through his nostrils to faltering lungs. "Just like the old days." And he pulled the book lying next to his pillow a little closer. Its dog-eared cover was still vivid, looking like it had drawn all the blood from his face. And its title's bold black letters invoked Maya's tenor. While she hadn't written it, her voice had unquestionably inspired its plan for their much-needed revolution of heart and mind.

His mother was the second bravest soul Milo had known. He caught childhood glimpses and later heard tales of how his father's bargains kept her free to serve a greater good, and to be here, in the world, with her family. At least for a while. And now this brave man— who had raised himself, who had invented and then reinvented himself, who had brought some of the future into existence, then set it aside for his family—was left holding the bag. For Milo Isloynov, it broke the scales. To keep from crying, he looked away, taking in the grim and grimy hospital room as a cockroach skittered across the floor.

"I came back here with a mind to rebuild this city," Mikhail said, his voice thin and gargled, but with that *mind* and its promise somehow still supplying at least a little lift. "It was a purpose I could pour myself into. But it turns out *the place* isn't the thing." And he pulled a scrap of paper from the book beside him, hands trembling—maybe from the disease or the drugs, or maybe from the weight of the words written on it. "It is what my father left for me." And handing it to his son, he added, "For better or worse, the scraps of love are what we're left with."

Milo 2.1

Visitors have just arrived, so the heavy pocket door to the butler's pantry slides closed, leaving the tiny space almost quiet. Apart from the indistinct murmur of voices through the walls, there's only an unwavering gray noise from the fan cooling the machine spinning on algorithms without him. Then, in the worn and yellowed note he reads once each day, Milo can hear Vadim's ghostly whisper, "Mind yourself. Mind your family. Mind your people." He folds it, slips it into the book where it lives, and buries the book back in his pack, for safekeeping. Milo is working on himself. But there's no longer any family. And lately his angst has him more earnestly wondering who, exactly, *his people* are.

Again, as he does in these meditative pauses punctuating the days, he makes another copy of all his work. *Their* work. It's the telling traces of enemies of enemies, enemies of friends, all strangers to him. It's the little stories he and the machine conspire to create, bred to move each manner of stranger this way or that. With all of that tucked away too for safekeeping of a different sort, he goes back to work. And to quiet the *tosca*, Milo sings softly to himself while outside, thunder booms.

perform.

by p.j. melton

take your time. don't slouch! glide up the aisle with dignity and pomp, as befits an eight-year-old wearing a new pink frock festooned by her mother's own hands with sheer, ballooning ruffles and sleeves. let taut threads fastened high above tug your head and shoulders plumb. don't fidget! your arms should dangle neat and straight as you approach the bench. once there, affix your gaze as though staring through the wallpaper, through the wall, through all the walls and beyond the setting sun. perhaps what you see is divine. perhaps its godliness compels this room's respectful hush as you smooth your puffy skirt against your backside and sit. you may now glance down. permit invisible strings to lift your wrists as you silently, correctly place the right hand and the left hand on the keys. do not let one know what the other is doing! bifurcate, dissociate, compartmentalize. play. your fingers know each triplet, turn, and trill. allow your weary will to leave this stuffy place, the straight-backed gawkers in their awkward, velvety chairs. sense their cool, remote interest in the pianist's perfect braids, in the nimble, compliant fingers. and if, as the two-part invention proceeds, you imagine that one day your feral incisors will snap the hidden fishing lines that position you in proper form, recall your piano teacher's upward-facing pencil point, sharp as a tack; its insuperable silver marks on your pale, slumping wrists; her toneless enunciation as she tells you to try again, and again, until you no longer needed her biting reminders. your hands may now float gently up like heavy drapes lifted by the quiet final chord, which rises, resounding, up to the ceiling, into the attic, through the roof, and into the deified sky. fold your hands in your lap. take your time! take your bow.

People Like Us

by Alan S. Falkingham

The rooftop bar at the Chevalier Hotel is called *The Treehouse* because of its décor of fake bonsais that frame the rich and famous in their Armani suits and backless dresses as they look out over the spectacular sprawl of Los Angeles. My date for the evening talks about himself incessantly while I tilt the stem of my dirty martini glass gently, watching the murky liquid stay perfectly horizontal.

"I did my undergrad at Penn State, then Med school at Johns Hopkins. I'm very driven," he says. "My work makes a real difference. You know? We perform these pig liver transplants that are lifesaving. Literally. We've perfected the technique. Our outcomes are simply phenomenal. Statistically." His name is Nicholas and he pauses his monologue to take a sip at the head of his beer which is frothy in its narrow, trendy glass. "Ultra-low calorie," he tells me. "Because I plan to work out at the gym tomorrow at five am before heading into the hospital to save lives."

I smile, mostly out of politeness. It all sounds exhausting, both literally and statistically. But he is certainly beautiful, there is no doubt about that. Fine cheek bones, square jaw, leaden-blue eyes. My family would certainly approve. And he is American. However, he is also unrelentingly *boring*.

The Australian barman has seen bad dates like this. Every now and again he comes over and checks to see if we are doing OK, as if he is waiting on a safe word. He has a tattoo on his arm that is a scene from Dante's Inferno. He is less beautiful than my date. Muscular and rugged, much more my type. But he is not what I am looking for either.

I pick up the skewered olive from my napkin and eat it.

***

When I get back to the apartment, my roommate Steph is still up. Steph is dressed in her Victoria's Secret designer pajamas and inhabits the sofa like a koala bear on a comfortable tree branch, a bottle of pinot grigio where a eucalyptus frond should be.

"How did the date go?" she enquires, not looking away from her TV show.

"He was perfect," I tell her facetiously. "He suggested we meet up again when he gets back from some conference he's presenting at in San Antonio."

"Think he'll ghost you?"

"Unfortunately, I think he won't," I say. "He just isn't my type. Fucking pig livers! Apparently, he grows pig livers and then implants them. He never even bothered to ask me anything about what I did."

"Implants them into what?" asks Steph.

"Sick people, I guess. Although, who knows? Maybe he's testing the procedure on orphans in Compton for all I know" I go and find a wine glass and pry the bottle out of Steph's mock-defensive grasp.

"You know my point of view" says Steph.

"What's that?" I ask her, although I do know her point of view because she has told me a dozen times before.

"Stop surfing for an American husband. Shit, Ale, your art is on display at the Hauser and Wirth. You're going to be the next big thing, girlfriend. Let them come to you."

But Steph also knows my dirty little secret: that I came to America from Romania five years ago as part of an exchange program at Calstone College, finding a life I loved amongst the California creatives. But then I overstayed my student visa, finding a job in one of the gem workshops in the LA Jewelry District between Hill and Broadway.

"You know there was an ICE raid last week. Right here in this apartment block," I tell her. "The doorman told me they arrested half the cleaning crew."

"This thing isn't about people like *you*," says Steph with a sigh. "You look as American as I do for one thing! You're young, beautiful, well dressed, have at least *some* money. They don't want to deport people like you."

It is easy for her to say. And I hope that she is right. Still, this recent uptick in deportations has scared me half to death.

Steph watches me closely. She knows me well enough to recognize the signs, can sense the stress of it all. "Why don't you come to the vineyard with Brandon and me this weekend. Despite what he promised me, he'll end up working half the time, so we can hang out together. My parents would love to meet you, and you can show off your artwork."

Steph's parents own a vineyard a couple of hours south of here and she is heading there in the morning with her boyfriend, Brandon; a certified jackass who owns a tanzanite blue Maserati and trades futures.

I look skeptical, worried I could end up being a third wheel. But Steph is not about to give up that easily. "Come on, Ale. It'll do you good to get out of the city for a few days. You need a break from all this ICE bullshit."

Suddenly my phone flashes. "See u when I get back from San Ant?"

"Join us, won't you? I insist!" Steph finally corners me, like a prize fighter cutting off the ring.

I delete Nicholas' message. "Sure," I say. "Why the hell not."

***

Steph's idea, it turns out, was not actually so bad after all, I think to myself, as I stand on the porch of the gigantic white estate house, staring out into the shimmering heat haze. Rows and rows of green-topped vines planted in long diagonal cuts run down the hillside towards the river, that slithers by like a muddy brown snake marking the southern boundary of the property. Over on the other side of the river, a red-brown plane stretches away to a ribbon of bumpy foothills on the horizon line. There is a calming stillness to the place, just the hum of insects and a hot-sweet smell to the air. It is everything that Los Angeles is not.

"I'll show you the barrel house," says Steph, pointing to another building set away from the main house. "It's where we age all our wine. I love that place. It reminds me of my childhood. I used to spend hours playing inside there as a kid. And I can introduce you to Jorge. He's a darling."

The barrel house is impressive, a high-ceilinged timber beamed building, cool and airy, smelling of oak, mixed with hints of spiciness: vanilla, cinnamon, caramel. And racked from floor to ceiling, laid on their sides, are row upon row of metal-banded wine caskets.

"This is Jorge. Our head winemaker," says Steph throwing her arms around a huge grizzly bear of a man dressed in blue overalls who we come across seated at a desk that is way too small for him. He is making copious notes in a battered old notebook. Jorge, it seems, is old-school when it comes to winemaking.

He pushes up the peak of his ballcap and his leathery face lights up. "I heard you might be coming home this weekend, *Amorcito*! How is the big city?" His Hispanic accent is thick, but his English is good.

"LA is…well, LA," offers Steph.

"I would hate it," says Jorge with a shrug. "So much traffic. Not enough birds."

"This is my roommate, Ale," Steph says by way of introduction. "She is an amazing jewelry artist. Very successful. She's just landed a showing at one of the top LA galleries."

Jorge extends a paw. His fingers are stained crimson from touching grapes. "Honored to meet you, Miss Ale. Please pardon my hands," he says solemnly. There is a gentleness about Jorge despite his physical size, an old-fashioned chivalry. "What type of art do you make?" he asks me.

This is a question I get asked a lot these days, and it has become my habit to show rather than tell. So, I take the pendant that is hanging from my necklace and hold it up so he can see it. Even in the subdued lighting of the barrelhouse, the amber still shimmers.

"I take individual human hairs and encase them. Maybe one of my own hairs, or sometimes a loved one I want to remember. Perhaps even an eyelash. One day I even want to use a tiny human bone." It is hard to explain.

"Brandon thinks it's weird," says Steph as if to demonstrate the point. "He says it's macabre."

Macabre is a big word for Brandon I think to myself.

"No, it's beautiful," says Jorge, still studying the pendant and the wisp of hair encapsulated in it. "It is the way, maybe, we all feel trapped sometimes, even if our cage is so beautiful. No?"

I am surprised by his take. Because it is *exactly* how I came up with the original idea: the gilded cage.

"Thank you, Jorge," I tell him. "You understand perfectly."

"I cannot possibly compete," says Jorge. Then he gestures to the walls of wine barrels all around us. "But hopefully you will get to sample some of *my* art over dinner."

***

"ICE raided my parents' place," says Elliot, picking up his wine glass and holding it up to the light. "Made a whole bunch of arrests. Mostly fruit pickers. You know how that goes."

Elliot is, apparently, my dinner date, a friend of the family who lives further on up the valley and fancies himself to be a sommelier. He has told us all about it in painful detail, including how he has been accepted to attend the Napa Valley Wine Academy in the Fall. His presence is Steph's doing, her latest attempt at matchmaking, and I quietly hate her for it. It's not that there is exactly anything wrong with Elliot. In fact, he is young, good-looking, rich and single. And American. But there is something about him that makes me want to grind my teeth with his talk about some new electric truck he plans to buy and the Clippers' problems at point guard.

"There'll be more of them. There are always more of them……" says Brandon reaching for the wine bottle and helping himself to another glass.

I shift in my seat, unsettled by the conversation. I steal a look at the faces of the others seated around the huge mahogany table, fading light cascading through the high windows. I try and gauge their reaction to see whether Brandon's assertion bothers them or not. Beyond the vines and the river, the sun has just set behind the ridgeline, and an orange-pink halo streaks the sky.

"Do you also have problems with illegals, Mr. Zoltman?" Eliott directs his question to Steph's father who sits at the head of table.

"Everyone has problems with illegals." Brandon answers for him, before Mr. Zoltman has chance to reply. "*America* has problems with illegals. That's why what we're doing to secure the border is so important."

We are, already, a fat pre-dinner cocktail and several bottles of wine into the evening, and I can tell Brandon is drunk. Steph shoots him a look, which he ignores.

"Best not to ask too many questions if you want the cheap labor though," says Elliot.

I force myself to bite my tongue, irritated by his flippancy. Dullness, it turns out, is one of Elliot's better character traits.

"Yeah," acknowledges Brandon. "But keep your doors locked, and don't leave anything valuable lying around, if you ask me."

I am about done with this, unable to stay quiet much longer, but Steph catches my eye, asking me to give her a chance to close this down.

"Well, nobody did ask you, B." She does her best to disarm him without creating too much awkwardness in front of Elliot.

"Actually, in my experience, most Mexican fruit pickers are good people. They just want a better life for themselves and their families. They are not just…how did you describe them…cheap labor? In fact, without them there would be no vineyard." It is Jorge who speaks up. He says it quietly, but firmly.

"Well, you would say that wouldn't you?" Brandon suddenly bristles with indignation.

"B, please. That's enough." Steph tries again, this time more forcefully. "Jorge has worked here for nearly forty years. He's family."

But I can tell that Brandon is too far into this thing to back down. And the alcohol is urging him on.

"Still, I imagine at some point, someone swam the river. Am I right, Jorge?"

Jorge stays silent while Brandon waits for an answer. When he does not get one, he just nods his head: point proven in his mind.

"They are not after people like Jorge," says Elliot, seemingly eager to ease the tension.

People like Jorge. People like me? I cannot stand the phrase. We are not the exceptions that justify the rule. I place my folded napkin on the table.

But evidently, Brandon is not quite done. "I'll tell you this. If I lived here, you'd find me in a pickup down by the river every night. I'd make sure no wetbacks made it across."

Finally, I have had enough.

"Jesus, Brandon," I put down my silverware a little too forcefully and it chimes on the plate as I stand up. "Why don't you just shut up, you racist, privileged, trust-fund fucktard…"

***

The light has faded to nothing, and I am standing out on the porch. Elliot has left and Steph is inside watching a movie with her parents, the awkwardness of dinner hopefully behind us. I listen to the sounds of the night. The insect chorus is almost one continuous gently modulating hiss of white noise.

"Well, I don't imagine Elliot's likely to ask for a second date after that outburst," says Brandon as he steps out through the screen door. Framed there, I can see he is nursing a bourbon, and he wanders over and leans against the railing to face me, circling his drink around in the glass. "Pretty rude if you ask me when you are a guest in someone's home."

The irony is not lost on me. "I'm not sure I was the only one to make a bad impression," I tell him. "What you said to Jorge was dreadful."

"Who cares about fucking Jorge?" Brandon takes a swig, devoid of contrition. "There are a thousand other Jorge's all getting ready for their night swim somewhere out there." He makes a vague motion out into the blackness.

"I care about Jorge. A life's a life, Brandon, regardless of what you might think. That's what's so wrong about what's happening in this country."

Brandon smirks. "I see I hit a nerve. I had forgotten you and Jorge are soulmates. Steph told me about your little visa problem."

Steph's pillow talk, it seems, might have been my undoing, and I am annoyed at myself for ever having told her of my predicament.

"I tell you what," he moves closer, and I can smell the liquor on him. "Maybe we can make a deal, you and me. You need an American husband so you can avoid deportation, even perhaps find a path to get yourself a green card…"

I don't know where he is going with this, but I know it can't be anywhere good. I try and move away but, he stretches out an arm to block my path.

"Despite tonight's little outburst, perhaps I'm still prepared to be that guy. You know? Temporarily, if you see what I mean?"

He carefully takes hold of my necklace, holding the pendant gently between his fingers. He twists it slightly to tighten it, but not quite enough to snap the chain.

"This is a cool piece," he says. "You're very talented, Ale. You have a lot to lose." He is standing too close to me, and I can smell his cologne.

"Your girlfriend is inside, Brandon," I tell him. "Let me pass please."

But he continues to hold on to my necklace.

"Even marriages of convenience need to be consummated," he says. "In the spirit of authenticity just in case someone was to call ICE with a tip-off. You know?"

Brandon's words are flat and measured, but his eyes are primal.

From somewhere in the shadows, there is a voice. "Miss Ale told you that she is not interested in your offer." Jorge steps forward into the pool of light cast from the house onto the porch.

Brandon turns to look at him. "Go fuck yourself, beaner," he says. Then, he lunges forward and forces his mouth over mine.

I push him away, and as he stumbles backwards, Jorge's punch lands squarely on Brandon's temple. He goes down silently, almost gracefully appearing to crumple in stages: at the waist, then knees, then ankles, but when his head hits the newel post at the top of the stairs leading onto the porch, there is a different sound. A heavy thud, like a bag of sand hitting the ground, and a crack that sounds like a pistol shot. And, standing there together in the darkness, Jorge and I watch as blood immediately begins to pool, seeping out from beneath Brandon's motionless body.

***

When the sun finally breaks over the horizon line, Jorge and I are already deep into Mexico in Brandon's stolen Maserati. We are speeding along the Pacific coastline, the sea crashing ashore below us. Our plan is to try and make it as far as the Yucatán Peninsula, hopefully catch a boat from there to Cuba, out of reach of any extradition treaty.

From the time we got into Brandon's car and took off, I kept checking behind us, half-expecting to see flashing lights closing fast. But as we had eaten up the miles south, I had finally started to relax, eventually falling asleep, curled up in the passenger seat with Jorge driving hard, hands on the wheel, grim-faced.

When we stop for gas, I go buy coffee. It is strong and black and tastes like tar. When Jorge takes a sip, I notice his eyes are moist.

"The coffee's hot," he tells me, as if to explain things. But I can tell from his face that he is filled with doubts and guilt in equal measure; the way he rubs his forehead, the tension in his jaw.

It had not been easy to convince him to run. Initially he insisted that we should call the police instead and explain exactly what had happened. But, in this America, I had explained to him, there is no sympathy when people like Jorge kill people like Brandon. And, if I am truthful, I know I would fare no better, whatever Steph might argue. I am still an interloper, an illegal, someone who has no right to be considered *American*. It will never be a place I can call home. So, while I am deeply sorry about how all this has turned out: sorry for Jorge, for Steph, even in a strange way for Brandon, I know that we had no choice but to run.

When we get back in the car, I take the driver's seat and, on impulse, I take off my necklace and loop it around the rearview mirror, so that the amber catches the light of the morning sun.

"It is beautiful," says Jorge softly, tilting his head as if strangely mesmerized by it.

"Sometimes we don't know we are trapped. Because our cage is so beautiful," I remind him.

"Yes," he says simply.

"So, when we get to Isla Mujeres, we are going to throw it off a cliff," I tell him. "Watch it fracture on the rocks below." And with that I gun the engine and accelerate hard back out onto the highway.

A Secret Unfolds

by Blanche Kabengele

"Do the Smith's live here?"

>Quivering hint of a man asked barely filling in thirteen-year-
>>old girl
>shadowing her deep into the ink well dark hallway, where
>>jelly jar
>like lanterns entombed brittle insect acolytes loitering within.

>Where slumlords rarely replaced lights for *Shakespearian*
>>tragedies to unfold.
>Where colored folk became *Black* folk, in former glory such
>>might have rivaled *Pink Ladies*. Where colored folks now
>>lived, others long deserted.

>As she but ingenue of a girl, word well beyond her grasp,
>never
>>wondered who he, hint of man was,

>to her, just another pimpled face Black boy passing through
>>like most other *Black* boys in the neighborhood rarely
>>hurt anybody,

>in a neighborhood where hardly anything ever happened,
>>long as somebody's woman, man, or money, wasn't on the
>>table, would be trouble brewing like grits cooked fast
>>exploding out a pan seeking vengeance on anybody
>>passing.

*"I don't know, but you can check, some people did just move in last
week"*

>>said barely filling in thirteen-year-old girl, as hint of man
>>like a matador to a bull in a lethal courtship grabbed her,

smothering her thoughts, like only humidity can choke
life out of wind said,

"Don't Scream"

so close, his breath lineup ready, wrestled ingenue like
child-still girl,

"Knife in your back, don't scream"

he said once again—catch just about caught.

One year past twelve, anywhere else she be still but a child,
she screamed, and screamed once more, so young, she
knew nothing about his intent,

pimple faced *Black* boy drops blade and runs through bunker
front door as she took as many steps could be fed legs,
mastered the second, to the third-floor home, to mother,

when mother, her mother knuckle-tired scrubbing somebody
else's floor, voice like a steamboat horn blaringly, hauled
way off, pitcher to player back, and slapped her, said

"Didn't I tell you to stop playing in the hall well!"

Momma now gone for quite some time, did girl now woman
tell a story almost forever went untold.

Big Judy

by Stephen C. Kraynak

Resist: To withstand, strive against, or oppose.
—Dictionary.com

Resist: To keep from giving in to, engaging in, or enjoying
—The Free Dictionary.com

Resist is like when you're standing in front of a big wind and
you try not to fall over. The wind wants to push you, but you
use your feet and legs to stay in place. It's like saying "no" to
the wind.
**—"How to explain to a child
@ en.explaintoachild.com/resist**

"Stay away from Big Judy. Don't talk to her," my mother cautioned
when I sat down at our oaken kitchen table for an after-school snack, a
homemade chocolate chip cookie and a glass of cold milk. She offered
no reason, but the slow and steady way she spoke caught my attention,
so I waited to take a bite. Her tone of voice said, "I am the mother in
this house. Just do what I tell you because it's for your own good." A
plump woman in her mid-forties, she usually asked, "What happened
at school? What did you learn today?" But not today. Her stern brown
eyes spoke their resolve about this matter of Big Judy, a neighbor of
ours. I was to stay away from her. But that proscription planted a seed
in me. Now, I was curious. Why stay away? Why not talk to her? I
realized that now I wanted to find out why I wasn't supposed to have
any such contact with Big Judy. I took a drink of milk.

Ours was a blue collar, pro-Democrat neighborhood north of
Lorain Avenue on Cleveland's west side with a mix of older single
and two-family homes. Some were sided with faded brown asbestos
shingles, others in need of a handyman and fresh paint. My mother
told me that she and my father, newly married, were lucky to get
any house in 1947 because of the housing shortage after the War.
"We were third in line for this house," she remembered. "When the

Streeters didn't get approved for a mortgage, we bought it. And it had an upstairs apartment, so the rent helped us to pay the mortgage."

The neighborhood fathers worked during the day. Steven and Rexie's dad worked at U.S. Steel in the flats. Bob Andrews was a plumber and his union chief steward. Mr. Kirby was gone a lot with his railroad job. My father had a desk job at Shippers Dispatch where he took my sister and me on some Saturdays when he had overtime. The mothers, except Stella Mancini who was a secretary in the Terminal Tower, were housewives and cared for us numerous baby boomers.

Many families on the block did laundry on Mondays, drying clothes outside when it was sunny. My mother often chatted with one or two neighbors over backyard fences, but occasionally I saw a klatch near our garage. When I asked my mother, "What do you all talk about?" she responded, "Shopping, recipes, gardening, and…" as she gently touched her index finger to the tip of my nose, continued, "our children, like you, sweetie." She then cupped her hand under my chin and lifted my face upward toward hers as she smiled and added, "It all comes out in the wash, honey. It all comes out in the wash."

Most homes had front porches where the residents sat after supper on the long summer evenings. Neighbors strolled on the sandstone sidewalks or crossed West 123rd to chat. My father often sat on our top step, his pulpit, with his back against the wrought iron railing smoking his Camels, greeting passersby with his cheerful "How-do!" He talked politics and baseball with anyone who stopped. Although a Democrat, he liked Ike. He reveled in Bob Feller and the Indians in the 1948 World Series.

The children played tag or hide-and-seek among the parked cars, using the street, and almost everyone's front and backyards as their playground until their mothers yelled their names into the darkness, calling them home for a bath before bed.

Many days I rode my bike eight houses down the block to where my friend, Jackie Finlan, lived. "Oh Jack-eee!" I called from his front yard waiting for him to come out and play. "Oh Jack-eee!" During a summer in the 1950s we sat on his front porch watching men build a new home on the corner lot across the street. They dug the basement, hauled the dirt away and laid the foundation. We were excited to finally see the outlines of a house and garage in two-by-fours.

Jackie later told me that some people moved into the newly built Cape Cod house which faced directly across busy Triskett Road toward the Yellow Transit trucking terminal, part of the commerce and industry park between our neighborhood and the railroad tracks. Semis came and went there day and night.

Although I don't remember how we learned the new girl's name who now lived in the corner house, the young neighborhood kids dubbed her "Big Judy" to distinguish her from Judy Schartman, our third-grade classmate and friend who lived on 127th, and because Big Judy was a teenager and taller than the rest of us. My mother accepted our moniker and began referring to Big Judy's parents as "Big Judy's father" and "Big Judy's mother," or "Mr. Big Judy" and "Mrs. Big Judy." No one mentioned the family's surname. I don't think we ever knew it because the family did not socialize with the other neighbors.

Most of the Catholic kids in the neighborhood went to St. Vincent de Paul School. Although it wasn't free like McKinley, the public elementary school just a block down the street, parish families got a discount on the annual textbook bill, and all children were taught and supervised by the Sisters of St. Joseph of Cleveland and diocesan priests.

Decorum was expected. Patent leather shoes on girls were not allowed because their high gloss could reflect their panties and distract the boys. We boys were forbidden to put our hands in our pockets while waiting in line because we might play "pocket pool" by fingering our genitals through our pants pockets. Regimentation was strict. We spent much time lining up and waiting silently in line.

Unlike most boys at St. Vincent's, I was like the "elegant and gay Absolon," the vain parish clerk in *The Canterbury Tales*, "somewhat squeamish about farting and fastidious" in my speech and appearance, behaviors which the Sisters reinforced. My elementary education centered on rote learning and memorizing facts, at which I excelled for eight years. I thrived on knowing the right answer and often raised my hand just to be noticed. On one day in first grade, I left my seat so often to approach Sister Augustine at her desk for clarification on our classwork that, in frustration, she said, "Kraynak, you're a real pill." I was embarrassed and scurried back to my seat.

At my second-grade birthday party after school in my home, while my friends, including Susan Szenky, my favorite girlfriend, waited for me at our dining room table ogling the devil's food layer cake my mother had made to resemble a merry-go-round by using peppermint stick candy and a red construction paper canopy, I sat at the kitchen table copying my spelling words five times each. I paid attention, followed the rules and was disappointed when I didn't get all A's, because my parents rewarded each A with a dime. I loved school. It was my haven, my citadel inside which I felt safe, an environment in which I flourished.

Big Judy was an eighth grader who attended class on the second floor of St. Vincent's. The rest of my neighborhood friends were in the lower grades on the first floor or in the basement. So, during the school day, we never saw Big Judy. However, four times daily, we walked the eight tenths of a mile along Belden Avenue to and from school. Since St. Vincent's had no cafeteria, we all went home for lunch. The kids from our block usually walked together.

Gradually, Big Judy came into focus in our young lives. On our daily walks some of us repeated what we overheard our mothers say on the telephone, that Big Judy was already causing trouble at the otherwise well-disciplined school. She was argumentative and disrespectful toward the Sisters. She was disobedient, resistant to authority. Sister Augustine had taught us that such behavior toward parents or teachers was a venial sin and must be confessed.

Cheryl, Barbara, Billy and Beth Bassett; the twins, Linda and Louise Baronak; Ellen Slanker; my sister, Carolyn and I, all in lower grades, lived on the same block and often walked as a group in various combinations. A few times we encountered Big Judy by chance. While passing us she yelled out questions: "Were you all good little boys and girls in school today? Who is God? What's seven times nine? What's the capital of Indiana?" Her voice was a siren, shrill and sharp. It demanded our attention, slicing into us like a box cutter through strapping tape. She had the breath support of a classically trained contralto, her volume triple forte, which projected not only to us, her young audience, but through us and beyond.

She didn't wait for our answers but just laughed and kept walking. Always alone, she strutted her "don't give a damn" walk as she slapped and dragged her prohibited patent leather shoes on the sidewalk. Although she wore the conservative maroon skirt and white blouse required of all St. Vincent's girls, away from school she opened its top buttons to reveal the cleavage of her breasts. Her strong body odor seemed of no concern to her.

On our way home one afternoon Big Judy pointed out a vacant house on 133rd St. "It's haunted," she averred. "It has ghosts. No one lives there and no one ever will. The neighbors are afraid to go near it." In her presence we feigned disbelief, but as she sauntered away Billy Bassett and I went to take a look while the girls waited on the sidewalk. We peeked through all five of the house's bare basement windows. "I don't see any ghosts," Billy yelled to me from one window. "Nothing here. Basement's empty," I shouted back from another. We reported our findings to the group. Beth Bassett was disappointed and sighed, "Maybe they only come out after dark." Yet, we still wondered if Big Judy was telling the truth. She was an enigma.

On another occasion she stopped Billy Bassett and me and told us that if we put an ant on the soft skin inside our elbows, it would crawl through and live in our arm. She watched our facial expressions as Billy and I looked at each other, our eyes wide. "You want to try one right now?" she dared, pointing to a black ant on the sidewalk. "Try it. You'll have your own personal ant," she mocked as she walked away.

Billy and I discussed her claim. "Nope! I don't believe it," Billy asserted. "I … 'm not so sure," I hesitated, but we both refused to try. What if Big Judy were telling the truth? Would we ever get the ants back out? How long would they survive inside? And where?

I was fascinated by Big Judy. She was unlike anyone else I knew. She spoke with conviction and knew interesting things other than memorizing answers from the Baltimore Catechism, or multiplication tables and state capitals. I never saw her carry a textbook. I was allured, attracted by how free she seemed to me, unhindered by rules or restrictions, by how comfortable she was with herself. To me she seemed happy. As a young boy, in my own way I sensed that I wanted that same freedom and happiness. Although my mother had told me to stay away from Big Judy, and I knew disobedience was a sin, I looked forward to being in her presence.

Later that same school year as the nine of us walked home and talked about the school events of the day, I whispered, "Hey, slow down. She's coming!" because I had seen that Big Judy was approaching us. Immediately we were abuzz and slackened our pace to let her catch up.

We stopped as Big Judy casually swaggered up. Now she had her own class of obedient Catholic school children standing silently at full attention. Big Judy immediately began her lesson. Holding all of us in her self-assured gaze she gushed, "Do you know why your *shit* is tapered at the end?" The satisfied smile on her face was a sign that she welcomed our reaction, a collective visceral gasp, "Whaaaawhh!" Eyes darted around. None of us had expected this kind of language, especially from a girl.

I had heard my father and uncles curse when playing poker and telling jokes in our basement, or after they downed shots of whiskey and P.O.C. chasers, Uncle Mack griping about his "bastard foreman" at Cleveland Punch & Shear and my father calling his "big boss" at Shippers Dispatch "dumber than shit." My mother said "some shit" when she talked on the phone to my Aunt Julie. But I knew that children were not to say "bad" words. Nor should they be said publicly.

How was I to know why my shit was tapered at the end? I wasn't supposed to think about things like shit. I was a good Catholic boy. I had looked at my shit in the toilet bowl from time to time, out of curiosity, but I had never looked to see if it was tapered at the end. It was just my shit—which, at the time I referred to as "poop."

Big Judy watched our faces, waiting for anyone to reply. Not one of us spoke. We all knew we should not be listening to her, but none of us moved. Our feet were cemented to the sidewalk. Big Judy, breathing heavily, outwaited us. Our anxiety level rose; the twins giggled in discomfort. We were spellbound, captivated by her choice of topic and vocabulary. We looked around at each other wondering who would answer.

With a perverse smirk, Big Judy skillfully brought her lesson on scatology to a close. "Your *shit* is tapered at the end, so your *asshole* won't slam shut!" she bellowed. We, her students, convulsed with another collective gasp, "Whaaaaaaawhh!" Her instruction ended, she abandoned us and casually ambled away, her shoes slapping the sidewalk. We, her young students, speechlessly turned toward home.

I wondered what my mother would say if she learned about this encounter, since I was the one who urged the group to slow down and wait for Big Judy. This was my fault. I had put the whole group into a near occasion of sin.

I imagined what Sister Cletus, St. Vincent's imperious principal, whom we referred to as "Cle-Bomb," might do if she heard about my indiscretion. Although an elderly woman, generously sized, she clomped and tromped the school's terrazzo corridors like a lumbering man of authority, her voice within the range of a baritone. Might she come looking for me in my classroom? Her full stern face framed in a wimple, I imagined her stealthily approaching my desk, arms folded across her ample bosom, staring at me, my eyes downcast in shame, and ordering, "Mr. Kraynak! Go to my office! Now!" Everyone knew that Cle-Bomb's office was "the dungeon of no return."

I envisioned going to confession and telling Fr. McCarthy that I had been thinking about shit and assholes, and that I had disobeyed my mother. After what proved to be my last encounter with Big Judy—the teenage pariah—I was walking home guilty because I was intrigued by her and because I resisted being told to "stay away."

I decided to tell my mother about our experience, thinking that my punishment might be more lenient if I admitted what I had done, rather than having my sister tell her or getting a phone call from Betty Baronak or Rosemary Bassett. Although my mother purported to dislike Big Judy's kind of humor and told me never to repeat the joke, I noticed her faint smile. Once more she warned me, "Stay away from Big Judy. Don't talk to her."

Occasionally I rode my bike past Big Judy's house and looked through the chain link fence into her yard, but I never saw her again, just her father cutting the grass or tinkering with his reel push mower in his open garage, alone.

We refocused our childhood conversations on the way to and from St. Vincent's on fire drills, report cards and Fr. Conkle, the new parish priest whom we liked. I never heard my mother mention Big Judy again, and Sister Cletus never came to get me.

As I moved through high school, college and into a teaching career, my memory of Big Judy faded. But she had been a spark which lit a small flame within me as a child, like the pilot light of the old gas water heater in the basement of my family's home, burning steadily in the background, on standby, generally forgotten, waiting for the right time to ignite a larger fire.

***

Thirty or more years later I visited my mother, staying with her on a midsummer weekend. She was now a widow in her late seventies living in the same home I had grown up in, a home she loved—her immaculate sanctuary. On that sultry Saturday evening, after doing the supper dishes, we sat silently side-by-side on her front porch and slowly rocked in a pair of worn green wicker chairs.

No neighbors walked down the sidewalk or came by to talk. Many now had humming window air conditioners and stayed indoors. My mother refused when I offered to buy her one saying, "No. I don't want one of those things. I love the fresh air." I noticed that the once well-kept neighborhood had declined. Next door, trash was strewn in what was once Mrs. Randall's tidy front yard, now choked with weeds. Across 123rd the front porch of the former Mancini house displayed an overflowing black vinyl garbage can on top of a mutilated interior armchair, its stuffing hanging out. My mother never mentioned these changes on my visits, but we now looked directly at them.

As she rocked, my mother began to reflect on her forty-four years in the neighborhood. She acknowledged the missing flowering hanging pots of begonias and impatiens, her pride as a life-long gardener, with which she had long adorned her front porch. "I came out one morning to water them and they were all gone. They stole them all. Bastards," she bitterly complained, almost crying.

Frankie Keller, my former friend from four doors down, and his catty young wife, now lived in the green shingled farmhouse next door. Frankie, who always was short-tempered, came yelling in a rage toward my mother about some misunderstanding she had had with his wife. He returned later and shot a handgun at her house. "I'm not afraid of him," she asserted. In the morning I scanned the front of the house and saw the bullet hole, a dark shadow still evident in the white aluminum siding just below the second-floor windowsill.

Old Mrs. Kirby, who had lived on the corner of Belden Avenue, was robbed by some grifters while she weeded her rose garden. "She had left her back door unlocked. We never used to lock our doors when we went outside in the garden," my mother sighed.

Pointing across West 123rd my mother related, "Those old owners evicted some people for back rent. They set the house on fire when they left. The whole damn neighborhood smelled like smoke. I kept all my windows closed for a week. What the hell is wrong with people today?" she lamented.

She then focused on the former Mancini house. "Those new people weren't friendly. Never spoke to any of us." My mother then recalled the day when Cleveland police cruisers blocked the street and officers surrounded the house in what was, she later learned, a drug raid. "When I went to look, some policewoman told me, 'Mam, this is dangerous. Please get back inside your house so you don't get shot by accident.' All because of marijuana or some shit. Damn drugs," she cursed.

Then she turned her attention to the corner house on Triskett Rd. where Big Judy and her parents had lived. My mother sighed deeply, paused, and began, "Big Judy was a problem at St. Vincent's. She raised hell. The nuns had their hands full." Big Judy refused to obey her teachers. She was obstreperous and defiant. In high school she was pregnant and unmarried, unthinkable in the 1950s for a Catholic girl. "Probably some truck driver from that place right there on Triskett," she offered. "Knocked her up and left her. I don't know what happened to her. Maybe some girls' home run by nuns. Baby got adopted. Mrs. Slanker and I talked. She lived right across. Never saw them. No one knows."

My mother concluded by relating that one day after work, Big Judy's father came home and found his wife dead, hanging by her neck, in their unfinished attic. Apparently she had hung herself. She "died from shame," my mother allowed. "Shame and a broken heart."

***

"Who's that?" I asked my Aunt Mary when I was still a boy. "That's me when I was a young woman on my wedding day. That's your Aunt Ann and that's your Aunt Vivian," she said. She then named each person posed in the gold metal framed bridal party photo which I had noticed on top of the RCA television in her living room. Aunt Mary wore a white gown with a veil, and all the other women had matching floor length dresses. "That's your Uncle Steve, my groom," she continued and explained that all the men wore tuxedos, a new word for me. "We were married right here at Immaculate Conception in Kenmore," she concluded with her wide toothy smile. Looking down over the top of her amber glasses at me, she licked the palm of her left hand and unsuccessfully tried to tamp down my unruly cowlick. "Oy yoi yoi," my mother laughed. "That cowlick! Yoi!"

I was intrigued to find similar wedding photos in the homes of my mother's other three sisters in Cleveland, on bedroom dressers or, at Aunt Julie's, on a lamp table with a doily under it. When I asked my mother, "Where's your bride's picture?" she admitted that her sisters had married while they were young and had Catholic church weddings followed by wedding receptions. She then explained, "Your father and I did not have a church wedding. And we have no pictures." As a child I was satisfied with that explanation.

In one of our conversations as adults, I learned more of my mother's story as we sat at her kitchen table. "I was the black sheep in my family," she offered. "I was the one who was different, who was always left out. Your father and I were married by a Justice of the Peace in Solon. We could not have a church wedding because your father had married before. He divorced his first wife. Andy Demko told him that she had been with other men after he was drafted by the Army. The Catholic Church refused to marry us because of his divorce."

"Your father and I," she continued, "met at a social club, The Ramblers, in Bay Village. Your Aunt Irene and Millie Carpenter, my girlfriends, invited me to join them at a party." She noted that my father was a banjo and ukulele playing guy, a self-proclaimed Irish tenor. "He loved to have a good time and a few drinks. We both did. When he drank, he wouldn't stop singing." They fell in love.

Overhearing our conversation, my father joined us. Leaning back against the stove he added, "I went to see Monsignor Dubosh at St. Cyril's in Lakewood, my boyhood parish. Dubosh married me and my first wife. That marriage was never annulled. I asked him for a dispensation. Your mother and I wanted a church wedding, like her sisters. Dubosh wouldn't hear of it. He yelled, 'You're living in sin!' and he shoved me out of the rectory door."

I later related this story to Fr. Karg at my father's burial at Holy Cross Cemetery. "Oh, Dubosh!" he allowed, "Yeah, yeah. He was known as the Hitler of the Catholic Church."

Because of the divorce the Catholic Church punished and shamed my parents by forbidding them from receiving communion. My father then shunned church, but my mother, a devout Catholic, was deeply humiliated. As children, while my sister and I went to Mass with all St. Vincent's students in the main sanctuary, my mother faithfully went to Mass in the church basement, sitting in the rear corner, her head bowed saying her rosary when it was time for communion. "I don't want anyone to see me," she whispered to me when I once attended with her. The shame imposed on her was resurrected every Sunday morning.

After thirty-three years of marriage, the patriarchy relented and permitted my mother to begin receiving communion once again. In the presence of her two adult children, three of her sisters and the one surviving brother-in-law, extended family, friends and neighbors, my mother approached the communion rail during my father's funeral Mass. "Until death do us part:" the invalid marriage was now ended, and my mother was no longer a sinner.

My mother loved to sing as she dusted furniture or cooked dinner. One of her favorites was "Pistol Packin' Mama." I learned to sing along with her, "Lay that pistol down, babe, lay that pistol down. Pistol Packin' Mama, lay that pistol down." We danced and sang that verse and laughed as I pretended to shoot the bad guys with my fore finger and thumb. The song seemed to fit well with her love of Marjorie Main as Ma Kettle and other roughhewn, independent minded and cantankerous women whom she knew from the movies.

That sense of independence lasted throughout my mother's lifetime. In her eighties she developed maturity onset diabetes, resulting in debilitating dry gangrene in her right ankle. The surgeon she consulted recommended amputation, "To save your life, Ma'am" he warned her. "This will not get better." When she and I discussed this, she told me, "No! I will not be like Martha Bunjak. First they cut off one leg. Then the other. That damn diabetes! Doesn't stop. That's no life. I don't want that. No, no, no! I will die and be in my coffin with both my arms and legs. Nope!" As the gangrene progressed, she spent some of her final days in bed curled in a fetal position.

My mother, Helen, daughter of a Slovak immigrant coal miner, from Walhonding, rural Guernsey County, Ohio, with an eighth-grade education, made her own way. Not following the pattern set by her sisters, she married a divorced man, withstood the shame imposed on her by the Catholic Church, and had her children in her mid-thirties. She made and lived by her own decisions. My mother died as she had decided, intact. She resisted to the end.

***

We have our secrets and our needs to confess. We may remember how, in childhood, adults were able at first to look right through us, and into us, and what an accomplishment it was when we, in fear and trembling, could tell our first lie, and make, for ourselves, the discovery that we are irredeemably alone in certain respects, and know that within the territory of ourselves, there can be only our footprints. --R.D. Laing, *The Divided Self* as quoted by Mary Karr in *The Liars' Club*

***

She was gone, but the memories linger ... the water gurgling as it went down the drain after my evening bath, and I hung over the tub's side with both arms to watch it swirl away. "All gone," I said. I then marveled at the trapped steam as it wafted over my head, slowly drifting out the bathroom window which was ajar. "All gone," I laughed. "Stephen, come here to me," my mother said softly. My mother enclosed both of my hands within hers and gently guided me toward her, seated on the yellow floral tufted toilet lid cover. She dried me with a worn terry cloth towel, combed and parted my fine hair, and helped me pull on my pajama top. I looked down at my wiggling toes. "Look at me, please." I looked into my mother's brown eyes. "You smell like Ivory Soap," she said as she kissed and sniffed my forehead. "Clean as a whistle."

As was her habit, she leaned in toward my right ear and whispered, "I love you. I love you. I love you. I love you. I love you." Then she whispered the same into my left ear and I grinned broadly. As I stood between her legs, she said, "I have a question for you," and then briefly paused. "Would you rather have been born a boy or a girl?"

"A boy!" I blurted out. I wanted my mother to love me. To continue to whisper, 'I love you,' to me. I knew she found joy in having a son. I wanted to be that son, that joy. So, even though I wasn't sure what I preferred, being a boy or a girl, I answered her question with the response I thought she wanted to hear. 'A boy,' I had said. I lied.

Yet as a young boy I knew that I was unlike many other boys in our neighborhood. I purposefully avoided their rough play and loud voices at the McKinley School ball diamond, opting for the swings and teetertotters with girls. When I walked to Angie's Deli on Lorain Avenue for penny pretzels or popsicles, I went along the West 125th side, a block away from them, so they wouldn't taunt me. I furtively glanced at them through the wrought iron fence as I passed by, most of them with their shirts off in the sun. I didn't want to take my shirt off outside because my father never did.

When I returned home on spring break as an undergraduate at The Ohio State University, an elderly neighbor, Mrs. Mae Lane, hobbled over with her cane to greet me as I unloaded my red Fiat in the back driveway. After exchanging hugs she looked up at me, her crooked smile betraying stained and missing teeth and, pointing her finger toward my face, asserted, "I will never forget the day your parents brought you home from St. John's. When they got out of that old blue Plymouth, your mother carried you, and your father…" She paused. "He was smoking and carried a potted plant. A goddammed plant." She laughed, patted my wrist, and continued, "After all your mother went through with that pregnancy, he could have at least carried *you* into the house."

As a child I don't remember my father carrying me. I don't remember my father holding me. I don't remember my father singing to me or showing me affection. I don't remember my father telling me, "I love you." As a child I thought it was my responsibility to get my father to love me, but I didn't know how. I wanted a father who wanted me as his son.

I envied our four neighbor boys; Skipper, Michael, Anthony and Jimmy DiLeonardo; as I watched them through my parents' bedroom window. Their father, Frank, who usually had his shirt off exposing his muscular hairy chest and arms, would playfight and wrestle with his older boys in their backyard. They had water balloon fights in the summer, and he grabbed his younger two sons and swung them around in circles as they screamed in delight. I wondered what it would be like to have a father like that, and if he would love me.

As a child, cooking interested me. While doing my addition and subtraction worksheets at our kitchen table, I was distracted by my mother's breading chicken, dicing vegetables or icing a scratch cake. "Can I help?" I often asked. "Finish your homework, then we'll see," was her stock response. Whenever she let me grease a pan or wrapped her hand over mine as we mixed batter, I asked to wear the apron with the daisies. She always left a little in the bowl for me to lick from my fingers.

At my birthday party with three of my uncles present in our living room, I took some pots and pans from the kitchen cupboard and sat down in front of them, pretending I was making stuffed cabbage rolls and mashed potatoes. Speaking about me to my uncles my father said, "I don't understand him. Instead of playing ball outside with the boys, he wants to cook inside with the women. What did I do wrong?" I put the cookware back into the kitchen cupboard and went to my bedroom alone. I had been shamed by my father.

Following supper when our extended family visited us, my favorite place was under the kitchen table with my back against the wall listening to my mother and aunts who sat and talked quietly after doing the dishes. I took my collection of Superman and Batman comic books with me. Pretending to be reading them, I was sneaking looks inside the back covers at the pictures of musclebound Charles Atlas.

I learned about creamy lime Jello salad with miniature marshmallows and, as I looked at the sketch of the bully on the beach kicking sand in the face of the 97-pound weakling, I heard my Aunt Ann say, "Well, there's Mary Bumbulis. She has the dropsy." Aunt Irene then told about Uncle George shooting off his finger when he went deer hunting "down home" in Walhonding. She said, "When I got that phone call, I just held my breath." I heard her sigh. "I wondered if his finger was all that got shot. And they just weren't telling me everything. I was on pins and needles until he walked in that door." Although my father and uncles were in the living room yelling for Jim Brown to "Run like hell!" or Larry Doby to "Hit that ball!" I never enjoyed sitting with them.

Fashion attracted me. One evening when my Aunt Viv and Uncle Mac visited us, I walked into the living room wearing my sister's maroon school skirt. I was intrigued by girls' clothes and was experimenting. I thought that I looked pretty. Uncle Mac immediately waved me away with a scornful "Bah! That's not for you. You're a boy! Take that off now! Git away! Git!" He then yelled some words in Slovak which I didn't understand. I ran to my darkened bedroom in shame, lay on the bed, face down in the pillow so they wouldn't hear me cry.

I was a misfit for much of my life but tried to hide it. I tried to conceal my attraction to other men by not calling attention to myself, and by being a high achiever in both school and work. Isolated and reclusive, many New Years Eves I spent alone watching Guy Lombardo. Although I knew that many gay men were dancing and drinking downtown at Trends or Kismet, Columbus gay bars, I feared being called a fag and losing the respect and control of my middle school students, and possibly losing my beloved job as a teacher, my chosen profession since my first day in Mrs. Martlock's kindergarten at McKinley School.

I came out of my mother's womb when she was thirty-six. Thirty-six years later I emerged from a womb of my own making, a silken cocoon I had woven with a warp of fear and a weft of loneliness. I chose, at last, to live freely. I rejected society's and the Catholic Church's prohibitions on how I could love. Big Judy's spark, which had lit a flame within me as a child, had finally ignited a more powerful blaze.

I joined gay men's support groups, began going out to gay bars, carried a rainbow flag in Columbus Gay Pride parades, and was welcomed, just as I was, as a member of the First Unitarian Universalist Church of Columbus where I met my future husband. We later retired to Arizona, and on October 17, 2014, the first day a federal district court in Phoenix decreed it, we, two men, were married by our minister on the courthouse steps.

The following morning the local paper, *Arizona Daily Star*, shouted the headline: GAY MARRIAGES BEGIN. The caption below the photo of the two of us kissing, which bled from margin to margin above the fold, read: 'Robert Gordon and Stephen Kraynak were among the first gay couples to get married at Pima County Superior Court.'

In his article the journalist, Luis F. Carrasco, noted that both men were, "dressed in matching guayaberas...." We had chosen our preferred fashion statement as we rushed from home that morning, immediately after the court order was announced on local television.

For an impromptu celebratory meal that evening we dined at Feast, a local independent Tucson restaurant, whose cuisine always challenged us to enhance our own home cooking with, perhaps, a pomegranate glaze or sweet garlic chili dipping sauce. For a belated wedding gift, I bought chef Bob an electric skillet, a needed kitchen item, which also satisfied my attraction to pots and pans.

We had waited fifteen years for marriage equality. We had resisted and won.

Our families, friends and neighbors congratulated us. Our church congregation gave us a standing ovation during the following Sunday's worship service. Poncella, our USPS mail carrier, leaned out of her

Grumman truck window when she saw me in our front yard and waved at me yelling, "Congratulations on your wedding! Be happy!"

Two years before she died, I came out to my mother. In a quiet conversation I told her, then eighty years old, that I was gay and happy with my life. "You are my son," she said. "I have always loved you. I will always love you."

***

Seven years after my mother died, I received a three by four inch black and white photo from her cousin, Annie, who told me, "This is my favorite picture of your mother. That's how I will always remember her." Facing into the sun my mother stands outside on a dirt road with a background of grass and trees in full leaf. On her feet she sports a dirty pair of black high-top boots, laced up almost to her knees. Her denim bib overalls are tucked into the boots. The overalls accent her slim waist above her slightly wider hips. A white blouse is partly visible on her shoulders. Both forearms are bare. Around her neck she has tied a scarf with white polka dots which is draped over her left shoulder. On her head which she tilts a bit to her right, is a rough textured wide brim cowgirl hat. She wears the hat on a downward slant, so it covers the right side of her head and reveals her deep brunette hair in curls on the left. Elbows bent, her slender arms reaching upward, she has tucked in her thumbs behind the overalls' shoulder straps, moving the bib slightly away from her breasts. She holds both hands open, with her palms outward and the tips of her fingers curled forward. A watch with a black leather strap is on her left wrist. The bib pocket in her overalls protrudes a bit and its flap is slightly raised as if concealing a pack of cigarettes. She has thinned and arched her dark eyebrows and lacks any lipstick or makeup. Her closed mouth smile accents her cheek dimples, and her self-assured gaze says to the camera, "Here I am. This is me."

This was the mother I never knew, my mother before there was me – my favorite photo of her: "Cowgirl Helen," my "Pistol Packin' Mama."

***

I remember now those many years ago when my mother told me, "Don't talk to Big Judy. Stay away from her." She knew the harm Big Judy had experienced for asserting her independence. My mother, herself, had been shamed for living her life on her own terms. She recognized my difference and attempted to protect me by telling me to "stay away." But how does a mother communicate this message to a child who doesn't fully understand how society can punish those who do not conform? By loving him.

***

That summer evening, two years before her death, as I listened to my mother reminisce about her life and her neighborhood, in her forlorn tone I heard, "I've done the best I could do in my life. I chose for love and made my own way. I worked, raised a family and kept this house. Now I am like this once vibrant neighborhood: old, tired, past its prime, parts of it broken or damaged and in decline. I have little fight left in me."

I had heard my mother's final confession.

I reached over and gently took her hand in mine. Turning toward her I softly said, "I love you. I love you. I love you. I love you. I love you." Ever so slightly, she squeezed my hand. In silence, the two of us sat in the old green wicker chairs on the front porch of her beloved home and gazed at this Cleveland neighborhood of West 123rd St., until sunset.

Letter To Eugene and Rosa
(on Ambivalent Belonging)
by D. B. Ruderman

My Dear, Dear Friends,

You won't believe, or maybe you will, precisely the kind of shit here in Newark, Ohio. Probably good that you didn't live long enough or stray far enough to see for yourself, to see it firsthand. A guy named Robert — he was younger than me, but he looked a whole lot older – a tough life on the street, I guess. He was on his bike at 21st street and W. Main. Someone hit him from

behind. Hit and run. Life-flighted out. Died a week after. I knew him a little bit, at least enough to say hello. He had these eyes that looked right through you like a character in a novel by Dostoevsky. He probably had some trauma, maybe meth, maybe booze, almost certainly mental health "issues." But who doesn't have mental health issues these days? All I know is he was super peaceful. It felt good to be around him even with all the camo he wore, oh, and those Dostoevsky eyes.

Related to this, I've been meaning to tell you about the city council. I guess they're a lot like any other city council, by which I mean they couldn't give 2 shits about 90 percent of the people they represent. I live in the 6th ward, which has a lot of poverty and drugs, but nothing like the 1st or 2nd wards. There's a kind of tacit agreement between almost all the people on the council, like a hate group but without the hoods, almost like a regression in time. Make America great again. Get back to some unimaginable, fictional beginning – woven through some smtory about nationhood. Rosa, if you were here, you'd probably lose your mind: zoning, housing, gentrification, vagabondage, laws against needle exchange— seriously. Remember that Dead Kennedy's song — "Kill the Poor." We should work up an acoustic version of it and play it at the next city council meeting.

There's this one woman on the council (I'm not gonna say her name, but she's one of only two women, so you can probably figure it out). She literally told my students (on camera!) that giving out Narcan, fentanyl testing strips, clean needles, etc. was enabling people, spreading addiction. When they showed me the footage, I said yeah, I guess it is enabling, it's enabling people not to die!

I don't know — I'm just tired of this shit.

I miss you of course, but I miss more than you. I miss the way things were back then, at least the way things used to seem. I have this headache, this jaw ache, this finger ache, this soul ache. I'm constantly at war with my feelings — ashamed of the fact that I judge the folks on my block — for their poverty, their rusted-out cars, their bad taste in music, all the crazy shit they drag out into their yards. At the same time, I lowkey love them — especially the kids. They run up and down the block like juvenal delinquent strays. I guess my "judgmentalness" makes me no more or less fucked up than everything else around here–turning continually away–just a hop, skip, and jump from another hit and run.

I love you like that corny 70's song says, "always and forever." I hope things are at least a little less obscure there, wherever you are, in the afterlife, the void, the land of the infinite sun.

Love on the Edge

by Stephanie Schamess

"Poverty isn't a lack of character. It is a lack of cash."
—Rutger Bregman, Dutch historian: TED Talks
https://www.ted.com · May 22, 2017

Part I: The Bottom of the Hill

Pine River.

The trip was as unnerving as I'd expected. Once I got off the highway on exit 14, I found myself navigating snaking, winding roads and going up and down hills with nothing but forest on both sides—walls of pine, hemlock, oak, and maple—for the next eighteen miles.

My nervousness was focused on the driving, but in truth its source was what lay ahead for me once I reached my destination: the town of Pine River. I had been a teacher for many years, working most recently with the children of academics at a preschool run by a prestigious college as a training ground for students majoring in education. Lynne, the principal who had hired me, had since moved on to become executive director of Pine River Behavioral Clinic, a social service agency which was one of the few resources for families in the town. A few years later, I also left the school to go to graduate school and after three years of course work, I was finally writing my dissertation when Lynne offered --begged me—to take a part-time job at the clinic as a consultant to the staff, insisting that I was the perfect person to do it.

"A couple of years ago we got the contract from the state to be the administering agency for a day care program," Lynne had said when she first phoned me. "It's free for kids whose moms are on welfare if they are enrolled in some program like school, a job training program, or a certified internship. They get a voucher from the state. We take the kids, and the state pays us." She sighed. "You can't imagine the number of dysfunctional families here. We need your input, your understanding of kids, your experience."

Pine River was a poor, depressed area whose family court judge was kept busy with cases involving domestic violence of all varieties, acrimonious divorces, unpaid child support, termination of parental rights, and the issuance of restraining orders.

I knew it had been a flourishing mill town in the late 19th and early 20th centuries, populated by Polish, Irish and French-Canadian immigrants along with the old timers of English and Yankee stock drawn to the area by the availability of jobs and cheap housing. Now, in the 1980s, the mills were long shut down, and the town was barely hanging on. The route I had taken was the perimeter of a large state forest whose many pine trees gave the town its name, and somewhere in the forest was a man-made lake, all of which separated Pine River from its neighbors: the next town was a 15-minute drive and the closest city more than half an hour away with no public transportation to either place.

I'd never actually been in the town of Pine River itself, and it was a surprise to come upon it suddenly from the peak of a hill where it looked positively quaint nestled in the valley below. But as I descended the final hill, I could see how the houses reflected the hardscrabble lives of their residents.

What Pine River did have in abundance were churches, one of which was the Congregational Church where the day care center was housed.

A Bad Start.

The head teacher, Alison, greeted me politely but not warmly. It was rest time, and the kids lay on cots, while the lunch and nap lady tried to create a soothing, relaxing atmosphere for the children while the teaching staff met with me.

At the table in Alison's crowded office, I faced four unsmiling people, two with their arms folded defensively across their chests, and the other two, including Alison, looking at one another and avoiding eye contact with me. Alison told the staff my name and informed them only that I'd been hired by Lynne to work with them. I did learn that Alison was certified as head teacher with eight years of experience; that Barbara was the assistant teacher; Sharlene was an intern in the state's training program for childcare teachers, and Renee, whose age lines and greying hair marked her as close to my age, was the aide. After I described who I was and why I had been hired, I asked each of them to introduce themselves and tell me about their roles. Their responses were brief and unenthusiastic. No one had questions for me or any desire to share their experiences with me. Given their responses, it suddenly dawned on me that Lynne might have hired me without consulting the teachers, and perhaps without even letting them know until this morning that a stranger would arrive to provide them with unasked-for-help.

I plunged in. "Lynne told me you needed help, and I'm here to offer whatever I can but I'm not here to change things or criticize or anything like that. I can't be of much help, though, unless you all let me know what you want."

Arms remained folded, eyes were rolled, papers shuffled, bodies shifted in chairs. Silence. Rest time, thankfully, was over so the meeting was concluded.

I felt obligated to Lynne to give this first visit a try at the very least. I could either leave or persist. I chose persistence. Maybe I'd do better with the kids than I had with the adults. "Alison," I asked, "since I'm here, could I take some time to interact with the kids?"

She conceded grudgingly. I had to hand it to her. "Yeah, make yourself at home," she growled, making the underlying message of 'I can't wait for you to get the hell out of here' perfectly clear.

I reminded myself that I didn't have to stick with this consultant job if I didn't want to, but at least I wanted to say I had given the job a good try.

Initiation.

Unlike the suspicious staff, the kids were overwhelmingly curious, friendly, and talkative. I was soon surrounded by six or seven children wanting to know whose mommy I was, why I was sitting in the chair, why I had a blue pocketbook and what was in it, and could they sit on my lap. Avoiding Alison's frequent glares from across the room, I sat down on the floor, grabbed a book from the nearby shelf, and started to read aloud, at which point the little girl who had climbed into my lap said, "I don't feel good," instantly proving her point by gagging and vomiting whatever she'd had for lunch all over herself and me.

Alison had the grace to be effusively apologetic. Barbara took Maggie to the bathroom to clean her while Alison offered me a zip-up house dress to replace my clothes.

It was clear I needed to leave. "I hope no one in Pine River is going to be shocked at my fashionable appearance," I said, trying to lighten the atmosphere a bit. "I'll bring the housedress back when I come for my next visit."

"You're coming back?" Alison asked, clearly surprised.

"Why wouldn't I?"

Long pause. "Because…because Maggie threw up on you." When you work with kids," she added, "you get used to runny noses and upchucks and, you know, toilet accidents. We're used to that, but you were just visiting and …"

"I think I mentioned that I worked with preschool kids for many years," I said, trying not to make it sound like a reproach. "I've been vomited on, peed on, I've wiped noses, rear ends, what have you. But it's really up to you whether you think you'd like me to work with you. Just let Lynne know."

Picking up on my frustration and feelings of failure, Alison exchanged glances with Barbara, who had joined us. "Look, we can always use an extra hand here, right, Barb?" Barb nodded.

"See you next week," I said, smiling.

Part II: The Conditions of Unconditional Love

Dominos.

I'd survived a bad situation, one that was partly of my making. Subsequent visits left me deep in thought. The long drive home became my self-imposed debriefing. It was a constant learning experience, a continual eye-opener. Sometimes I left feeling elated. Often I felt sad. Always, I felt the irony of going home to my computer to assert my expertise in child development as I typed my dissertation and coming to Pine River to discover just how limited my understanding was. I began to question a lot of the standard assumptions of the academic literature so often based on research and testing of children from the middle and upper-middle class families that I knew well.

Prior to my Pine River experience, I had worked largely with children who were wanted and loved. It wasn't that all of them came from problem-free homes. There were divorces, career conflicts in these highly-educated and ambitious families, and other issues which had negative effects on the kids. But no one in that milieu would ever have wondered whether a mother loved her child. The adage that a mother's love is unconditional, while not necessarily voiced, was an underlying assumption shared by all the families. One could hear mothers themselves talk about the joy and intensity of mother love, the enormity of being responsible for another human being. We've all read poets waxing eloquent about the innocence of childhood, the purity of maternal love. Psychologists, many of whom were cited in my dissertation, talked about the importance of a secure attachment between mother and child. Lofty words all.

But what I was coming to realize in Pine River was that love arises, is expressed, thrives or withers in conditions of comfort, financial stability, absence of trauma, security, and family stability. We enter life and go through it in the context of the conditions into which we were born. I thought of the other adage that "it takes a village to raise a child" in the context of my own upbringing surrounded by a large extended family where I was cared for and cared about by grandparents, aunts and uncles in addition to my doting parents. Many children in Pine River did not have such things.

Seventeen of the twenty families in Pine River Child Care were single-parent, with varying degrees of participation in family life by the fathers, an involvement which was not always welcome. I have no doubt that most of these mothers sincerely loved their children.

But I had to rethink my ideas about what constitutes mother love. I came to realize that unconditional love doesn't exist, not even as a reachable ideal. In Pine River the conditions of motherhood put many obstacles in the way of simply loving one's child.

The domino effect governed life in Pine River. The town's bucolic surroundings of forests and lakes provided opportunity for boating, hunting, cross-country skiing and hiking on lovely trails, but the high price paid for that was its isolation. With no public transportation, one could come and go from Pine River only by car. Work opportunities were scarce in the town itself; attempts to turn the mills into shopping malls or start a manufacturing business in small appliances failed largely due to the town's inaccessibility to varied modes of transportation.

Low paying jobs were available in the nearest town, which was about eight miles away, and better paying ones in the mid-size city that was 15 miles from Pine River via the thruway. But if a single mom woke up one morning and her car didn't start, she couldn't get to work, and her days off went unpaid, which meant she lacked adequate funds to repair the car. A mother who had to stay home with a sick child for a week risked losing her job: supermarket cashiers or waitresses were readily replaceable. One domino falling could precipitate a chain of growing tribulations and a high level of stress for mother and child alike. Some mothers just gave up. Depression was common, with the children suffering neglect when their mothers, often barely out of adolescence, simply could not cope. The overworked and burned-out social workers from the Department of Child Welfare that the staff at Pine River had to deal with were all too often judgmental and disapproving, so that the relationship between them and the mothers they were supposed to serve was frequently adversarial.

What I came to learn over time was that most, although not all, of the mothers did love their children deeply. This emerged in many ways, seeping through the layers of stress, weariness and most sadly, the underlying pain and trauma that so many of them carried. Even decades later, some of their stories which added so much to my understanding of children and families are etched into my memory.

Part III: Two Storie

The High Price of Clean Overalls.
"He can't play with us; he smells." And sometimes, "He's a baby; he stinks of pee-pee." And once, "He's poopy man; he poops in his pants."
Alison and I talked about what to do with these frequent comments about Luke, a new kid in the class. Sadly, they were accurate

descriptions of this thin, too-small-for-his-age, three-year-old boy who was enrolled in the center on one of the vouchers for children who were under Department of Child Welfare supervision due to charges of parental neglect. He was brought on the bus, arriving in overalls which had apparently been allowed to dry without ever being washed. It wasn't clear whether he was toilet trained although he did seem able to use the bathroom appropriately when reminded and encouraged by any of the staff.

"I can't force the kids to play with him. He really does smell," Alison confessed. "I have trouble being near him for any length of time myself." Apparently there was no way to reach the mother by phone and Alison was on the verge of phoning the DCW, but as always, reluctant to involve the agency, which was all too prone to place the target children in foster care.

"Maybe you could do a home visit first?" I suggested. "But for the moment I can drive over to the Carter's discount place and get some clean overalls." I was finding myself doing things on this job that I most certainly had not anticipated, but if new overalls were needed to give a kid a better day at school, so be it. Half an hour later I was back with two pairs of Carter's Kids corduroy overalls and a packet of four Little Boys' briefs with pictures of dinosaurs on them.

In the note Alison sent home with Luke, she tactfully lied and said she'd pulled the clean clothing from the pile in the church's donation box. The next day Luke returned in his newly purchased clothes, but like his old ones they were already in need of washing. Mom had either not gotten the message or was ignoring it. On my next visit a few days later, Luke had gone through all of the new clothing and it all reeked. Alison asked if I'd make a home visit with her.

Driving there unannounced, Alison said she could tell from the address that this would be bad. Lily Novak, Luke's mother, lived on the second floor of a multi-family house in poor repair owned by one of several unscrupulous landlords in the area who with blithe indifference exploited the single women who were living not just on the edge, but at risk of slipping dangerously over it.

When Lily finally came to the door, barefoot and still in pajamas, even Alison gasped. Even before we got to the threshold, we were assaulted by the familiar smell of urine. Lily looked much younger than the 17 years she'd put down as her age on Luke's admission form. Barely five feet tall, so thin she seemed to float rather than walk, her shoulder length brown hair was uncombed and her skin sallow.

"Whaddya want? You from welfare?" Lily asked, defensive already.

"I'm the head teacher at the day care," Alison said, "and this is Steffi, my coworker, and we're here because we have some concerns about Luke." Lily flinched. "And no," Alison added quickly, "we're not from Welfare. This visit is just between us."

It was obvious we weren't going to get any further than the entry, so Alison got to the point immediately. Her kind tone of voice softened her message, but she wanted to be sure that she said what needed to be said while she still had Lily's attention. "We're concerned that Luke seems to be peeing in his overalls. He does know how to use the toilet. He's good about it in day care ..." She waited hesitantly for a response from Lily, who remained stony faced. "We're just wondering if you could encourage Luke to use the toilet. Is it possible for you to wash his clothes more often? His overalls already have a urine smell when he gets to school. It's hard for him to make friends. The children comment on the fact that he ... his clothes smell of pee."

"Yeah, well, half the time the frigging toilet ain't working," Lily said. "And you think I have a washing machine? The laundromat is two blocks away. And it costs money."

"Have you talked to your social worker at DCW about that?" These are the sorts of things she might be able to help with."

"Yeah, well, I'll ask her," Lily lied. "Is that all?" We'd clearly lost her: her already-limited ability to tune in was fading fast. Visit over.

"This isn't going to end well," Alison said, by which I knew she meant that she'd eventually have to report all of this to the DCW social worker. "But let's give it a couple of weeks."

I tried to imagine how a mother like Lily could take care of a child when she was a child herself, perhaps emotionally abandoned by her own mother years earlier, coping now with overwhelming responsibilities when all the repetitive, tedious work that goes with caring for a child is made more difficult by the circumstances in which she has to live? When everything about her life confirms how uncared for, and uncared about, she is? Where does mother love come into this? Is there any place at all for it?

It was a surprising turn of events that made me realize anew how complicated loving care is. Alison's temporary solution was simply that we hand-wash the soiled clothes and keep a store of clean clothes for him to wear each day. Everyone took a turn as laundress-for-the-day, and after a few days the job began to expand, little by little, into a semi-bath for Luke. Once he was undressed it was easy to run a wet washcloth over him before putting the clean clothes on him. It was a great solution until Alison was informed by the social worker that Lily had issued a complaint against her for sexual abuse. The complaint stated that Luke came home from school talking about how the teacher gave him a bath and even washed his willy. It would have been funny if it were not for the fact that DCW scheduled a hearing to decide whether to charge Alison with the sexual abuse that was implied in Luke's unfortunate description of the activity.

Alison didn't get off totally free; she was issued a warning for performing a personal action on a child without the mother's permission.

Her solution, however, worked in ways neither of us would have anticipated. Luke's casual mention of his daily "bath" had mobilized Lily as apparently nothing else had. I could only guess what in her own childhood triggered her immediate assumption of sexual abuse. During the hearing it had been unambiguously noted that it was unlikely for a teacher to be sexually abusing a three-year-old in an open area where other staff members, not to mention parents or anyone else – including DCW social workers—could have entered any time. But Lily had come quickly to her own conclusion and decided that no one was going to abuse her child. She managed the procedure of issuing a complaint, getting herself to the hearing, confronting Alison, holding her ground, and gaining some satisfaction in Alison getting a warning for not consulting her.

After the hearing, I did a mental "debriefing" during my ride home that evening, I wondered if Lily had been abused as a child? Was she in some sense finally speaking up for herself as well as for Luke? It was all speculation. But something had motivated her enough to rouse herself from her debilitating apathy and depression to become a fiercely protective mother.

Love teeters on the edge but hangs on when it counts.

The Magic of Numbers.

Dougie was a very bright kid. He was curious and took in the world eagerly as it was presented him in the day care. On his good days, his grin was contagious, mischievous, and full of pleasure. Unfortunately, we saw it all too rarely although he did have stretches of relative calm, often for several days between his "temper tantrums" … that's what Alison was calling them, but she and I both agreed that there was a lot more going on behind the episodes. They'd always begin the same way: a real or imagined slight from one of the other kids would set Dougie off, in what appeared to be an irrationally angry outburst but still within the range of normal. He'd do the usual "time out" in Alison's office, often with me sitting there with him while he apologized profusely in between bouts of tears.

One morning, Alison called me at home. "I know it isn't your day to be here, but if you could come … it's Dougie … things are really bad."

When I arrived, Alison said, "He was pounding Tony on the back and he started shouting --excuse my language but this is what he said to me: 'You fucking cunt,' and 'I'm sick of your shit,' and 'shut up, bitch.' It was scary. He made his voice growly like he was pretending to be someone else." She shuddered. "Something's really wrong."

Dougie was in the office crying. I sat down next to him and waited, silently. After a few minutes his sobs subsided. Suddenly he asked if he could show me the numbers he knew. Taking the paper and crayon I found for him, writing slowly and with great care, he printed the numbers 1 through 10. When he finished, he held the paper up and flashed that wonderful grin.

The grin broadened as I acknowledged what a great job he'd done. "I know what to call them," he said. "I can read them to you." And he did, pointing proudly to each number as he announced what it was.

"It's for you," he said, handing it to me. I didn't address his previous behaviors with him. I was convinced it would not be productive and might lead to another episode. The behaviors indicated serious emotional turmoil, and we needed to know what was going on at home. Clearly he was a kid in crisis.

"You need to have a parent conference," I said to Alison, who agreed and asked me to join her. Not surprisingly, Dougie had another episode before we got to see Melissa, his mom. This time I happened to be at the center, and although Alison had forewarned me about the language; still, it was startling to hear those words coming from a four-year old child. The other children were still at the "bathroom talk" stage: using words having to do with their bodily functions and laughing loudly. But Dougie's language wasn't kid talk.

"I wanna do my numbers," he managed in between sobs as we again sat in the office. This time when he gave me the finished paper he surprised me by asking for another one on which he very carefully wrote the numbers 911. "Mommy taught me that. She showed me how to push the buttons on the phone. You have to do it just like that. Nine-One-One."

I wondered if this was just a routine precaution Melissa was taking and if so, whether it implied that she left him alone in the house. "Have you called it?" I asked.

"Yes, just like mommy said. She said I might have to do it when daddy had a sleepover because sometimes daddy gets mad at her and she might start screaming loud, and if she keeps screaming, I should call those numbers, 9-1-1. So I did."

I thought I was over being surprised or shocked at anything I heard on this job. But this left me utterly stunned. "Dougie, what happened when you called?"

"I told the lady who answered to come to my house cause my daddy is yelling and mommy is screaming. I know my address," he said, not without pride. "I don't know how to write it. But I can say it, it's 49 North Market Street, so I told the lady."

"And then what?"

"A nice policeman came. He let me try on his badge. Mommy wasn't screaming anymore and daddy was, I think he went to the bathroom. Mommy said I could go to sleep now and she tucked me in, but I didn't go to sleep. But she didn't scream any more that night."

I alternated between being utterly appalled and wanting to weep for this child who had to call 911 to prevent his father from … from what, I wasn't sure. Rape? Beating Dougie's mother up?

"Has daddy visited again?" I asked.

"Yeah, he plays with me, he brings me toys. But mommy won't let him have sleepovers with us anymore."

Dougie had divulged significant information, which added to what we had learned from Barbara, our assistant teacher. In this small insular town where everyone knew everything about their neighbors, such knowledge rapidly became public, and Barbara shared her recollection that as a young teenager Melissa's name came up in a court case. Melissa's older sister, Kimberley, had a serious breakdown, and when she was hospitalized, she revealed that her father and brother had been sexually abusing both her and Melissa for several years. Both Barbara and Alison also knew that Dougie's father's family had a generational history of physical abuse.

We arranged a time for meeting with Melissa, and surprisingly, Neil, Dougie's father was with her at her invitation. Dougie had his mother's blue eyes and straw-blond hair, but that appealing smile came from his lanky, tattooed father.

Melissa blanched at Alison's description of what had been going on. "Oh, my god. I had no idea. He should never use language like that. He was so proud that he knew his numbers …"

Neil broke in suddenly as if asserting everything would be fine from now on. "I been going to AA. I hit a rough spot … started drinking again," he said in a shaky voice. "Like, when I drink, I don't know what happens. I, like, just lose my head. I do stupid things …" He looked down at the floor. "I love my kid. I love her," gesturing toward

Melissa. "I wanna move back in; I wanna be a good dad; I wanna take care of Lissa," he said, his voice rising with each affirmation. "I promise, this time I'll really stop."

Melissa stiffened. "He has a restraining order, he can play with Dougie in the day if I'm home, but no sleeping over. He can't move back in until he's been sober for 6 months."

"I'm glad to hear that things are under control, at least for the moment," Alison said. "But I think …"

"Oh, god," Melissa interrupted, in a panic. "You can't … you wouldn't take him away … you won't let them take Dougie away from me?" Neil reached out and held her hand, a gesture to which she responded with a grateful smile.

"It's already in the court system," Alison said. "It's out of our control. I think as long as Neil doesn't violate his restraining order, and he stays sober, they're not likely to take Dougie. He's doing better, but he's still …" she paused. "He's still showing signs of stress, and he needs help getting over it."

Alison and I had already shared our doubts as to whether Melissa and Neil really understood the disturbing emotional implications of the position they'd put Dougie in, and we'd agreed that sessions with a trained therapist were called for. "There are people at the clinic who work with kids in a special way." Alison explained. "It's called "play therapy' and it's very helpful. We can arrange for him to see someone there."

Melissa followed through with an appointment for Dougie. Although he continued to be hyperalert and edgy some of the time, his episodes became less violent, less frequent and more manageable. Neil stayed sober for a few more months, got a job painting houses, and kept to the terms of his restraining order.

Then it was September, and Dougie joined the other kids who had reached the required 4-years-and 9 months-of-age to go to kindergarten. Alison had a little "graduation" ceremony for them and Melissa and Neil came together and beamed with pride.

In the gossip that carried news through the town it was often difficult to sort out rumor and fantasy from truth, but we were quite sure that at least part of what we heard later about Melissa and Neil was accurate: after almost a year of sobriety during which time he was able to move back in with Melissa, Neil started drinking again. Melissa got pregnant. When Neil attacked her, she ended up suffering a miscarriage along with some broken ribs, a black eye and a severe nosebleed. Dougie was removed from the home and placed with a foster family in a different town. The gossip died down, and we heard nothing more about them after that.

Part IV: Leaving Pine River

> You get a strange feeling when you're about to leave a place. Like you'll not only miss the people you love but you'll miss the person you are now at this time and this place, because you'll never be this way ever again.
>
> **—Azar Nafisi, author of Reading Lolita in Teheran**

That Time, That Place.

In 1987, three years after my arrival in Pine River, I finished my dissertation, passed the defense, interviewed for a teaching position at a local college and got the job. It was June of 1987. I'd helped Alison and her staff develop a wider range of skills in coping with children's problematic behaviors. I'd given them a lot of support in dealing with parents. I'd grown to like and admire them, and they felt valued by me in ways they were not valued by the better-educated, higher status psychotherapists and other health workers at the behavioral clinic.

I was no longer the same person that I'd been when I'd walked into the center, faced a defensive and sullen staff, passed an unwritten test by being vomited on by a three-year-old, and began to muddle my way into the lives of the families constantly on the brink of economic viability. I came to Pine River thinking I'd inspire the staff to develop creative ways of teaching, new sways of thinking about children. Instead, I found myself involved in coping with, trying to remedy, and witnessing the effects of poverty, isolation, and lack of a truly functional and well-coordinated safety net. Witnessing these sometimes quotidian and sometimes disastrous experiences brought home to me, vividly and intensely, what it really means to "live on the edge." Even more than that, it made me examine my assumptions about mothering, what it means to love and to care for one's children in the face of constant obstacles and underlying trauma.

Lily's transformation from a depressed, neglectful mother to a fiercely protective one opened my eyes to the resilience that is possible, and even more to the often-unpredictable conditions under which love either fades or blooms. I pondered on the convoluted relationship of Melissa and Neil: did they love one another? I believe they did, as deeply and faithfully as each was able. Did they love their child? I believe they did, very much. And he loved them. I had come to see that, against all reason, we can love the thing that hurts us. Holding on to the memory of how it feels to love and be loved, we forget for a time the pain that came with it. And so we go back for more.

But I learned also that love does not conquer all. The web of loving care between the two parents, parent for child, and child for parent can survive the baggage of past trauma, can withstand rage, rejection, despair. Just not forever. Each assault on the fragile threads sustaining the bonds of love makes a deeper notch, weakens the thread until it is beyond its capacity for repair.

Years later, I still marvel at the resiliency—the capacity for perseverance that these families had. I don't want to glorify or romanticize it: It was a harsh life, and the scars were deep and lifelong. Love persists against great odds but sometimes it isn't enough. It takes a village to raise a child but a village where everyone is struggling is not a reliable support.

And yet … and yet …at the center, children played, built houses with blocks, painted dinosaurs at the easel, made pretend meals from play doh, remained wide-eyed and curious as they listened to stories, giggled, fought, made up, and managed to learn their letters, numbers and colors before they went on to kindergarten. The teachers at the day care center worked long, hard days but retained their patience, kindness and affection. Many of the parents—mostly mothers, to be sure–somehow found the emotional and physical energy to do what loving mothers in Pine River were supposed to do: keep their kids clean, get them to day care on time, teach them how to behave nicely, and above all, try to give their kids the love that too many of the mothers themselves had never experienced.

I miss them all.

A Survey Course in Victorian Lit

by J. Martin Pfau

All the Kaiser's complaints
are quaint,
every Victorian victory
a boor.

After Europe pillaged the world,
the reserves of time
it afforded were spent
to advance the abattoir.

The sun never set on England,
until she built
her own darkness.
Seventeen million dead
by two grandsons
of Queen Victoria,
in one world war.

Men were driven mad
by a punitive peace,
ordained by the titled
and the wealthy,
who had never walked
with bayonets high,
who only tasted mustard
on their sandwiches,
and would soon begin anew,
feeding 71 million
more into the machine.
Nein, nein, nein.

Into the valley of death

Rode the six hundred.
What of the 11 million
who rode trains
into the Shoah,
to become the industrial smoke
that chokes us still?
Nothing Christ
or Voltaire ever said,
ever mattered.

I should give a fuck
what Mr. Darcy decides.

Anthropogenic Futures

by Joseph Randolph

The bus smelled like prepubescent heat death: a noxious cocktail of Axe body spray, the kind of hot plastic that might have been molded in some dystopian factory where ergonomics counted as a discarded rumor, and the stubborn tang of chips ground so deeply into the vinyl seats that they had merged with the upholstery. The whole vehicle resembled a failed biosphere experiment, an outgassed containment dome from a long-abandoned moon colony where someone had tried, and utterly failed, to simulate joy. Only the hellish, elastic vacuum of a 90s childhood could forge that kind of scent, which lingered above the seats like the ghost of all the other kids who had passed through, their sticky fingers apparently permanent.

Sora sat halfway back, wedged between a boy submerged in his "noise-canceling" TikTok wormhole and another boy entering his private dairy-induced crisis. The first had his volume pushed to a level any tribunal of sane adults would classify as auditory self-flagellation: an algorithmic hellscape of engineered stupidity spilling from his headphones, strobing like a dying star, content curling inward and spitting out signal like Hawking radiation from the slow-motion homicide of cultural meaning. The second, after twelve minutes of travel, had already asked six times, with the steady panic of someone whose soul had begun to mistrust its container, whether it was "normal to feel carsick in a bus if you drank milk really fast." The question carried a slight tragic charge; it hovered between Sora and the boy unresolved, as though his inner world were unraveling in increments, his body struggling to reconcile motion and digestion, some cosmic glitch in the Matrix playing out in his stomach. Sora held back the lecture forming in her mind—humans as fundamentally lactose-intolerant creatures staging a daily revolt against their own intestines, the Enlightenment just the larger and more confident version of the same mistake—and decided the boy deserved a smaller burden for the morning.

Two seats ahead, another kid hunched over a cracked phone screen, watching the same five seconds of a rap video on repeat: some local artist botching a backflip during a parking-lot shoot, hitting the pavement with a thud just off the beat. He kept rewinding manually, thumb tapping back with the regularity of a nervous ritual. Over and over: the same flex, the same stumble, the same grainy impact. It had passed the point of comedy and turned into something quieter, almost devotional—a looped rhythm that steadied him, as if the predictability of that small disaster offered a form of order the rest of the day withheld.

Sora's eyes were closed, not because she was asleep, or even pretending to be, but because she'd long since learned that sometimes the only way to endure was to perform a kind of mental triage—an internal audit of sensory input, each fragment of noise and movement examined like entries in a ledger, half of them stamped with a grim little "return to sender." Her phone ticked once against her thigh. A text from her sister, Grace: "Come by this weekend, take Paul and Susanna to the park? They miss you." Sora stared at the screen, thumb hovering while fatigue inside her bones deepened like a tide slipping away from shore and revealing rock. The answer arrived before she typed it. She would stay home. It wasn't that she didn't love the kids. That wasn't the issue. The body simply chose another ritual: a bed, a little weed, and a mind allowed to wander until it reached the quiet center of nothing in particular.

Up front, the driver monologued into his CB radio with the weary intensity of a man who had argued with machines for three decades and believed he was losing on points. His voice carried the slow, ringed sorrow of a long-filed grievance transmitted through thirty years of bureaucracy, like a complaint that kept returning unresolved. At the back, a cluster of eighth graders worked their way through what could only be described as a diss track about mitochondria, voices rising and falling in a blend of adolescent bravado and the strange, untapped potential that clung to any topic once a rhyme scheme took interest in it. It was bad science but good theater.

The boy with the milk problem, as persistent as his confusion, began a tuneless, off-kilter murmur, like a broken refrigerator attempting song. The sound fused with the TikTok spill beside her—an onrushing tide of hyped soundbites, looping like some apocalyptic dopamine centrifuge that had seeped into the shared bus consciousness. The racket turned the world into a single crowded corridor where distraction and a faint whiff of biological regret moved together, every clipped phrase and overproduced beat reminding her of things eaten too fast, thoughts driven too hard, experiences left forever half-processed.

She could feel her pulse in her molars. Never a good sign. Her neck ached in a way that felt ancestral, as if several generations of women had ridden this same bus and passed the ache forward like jewelry.

By the time they pulled up to the museum—a squat, brown-bricked structure that looked as if an AI trained exclusively on 1970s office parks had been allowed one attempt at culture—Sora's mind felt lightly poached. The kids spilled out, half-feral, their joy a blend of genuine excitement and the lawless energy that emerged whenever the institutional leash of school slackened for more than thirty seconds. She delivered the usual speech—stay in groups, avoid touching anything, remember you represent the school, all of that—already aware that the words would slide off them like rain from a newly waxed car. No one listened. She didn't expect them to. Their attention had other loyalties. Her job, today, involved walking behind those loyalties and making sure none of them fell off a mezzanine.

Inside, the museum was mercifully underpopulated—a few retirees moving at the speed of contemplation, a dad and his toddler whose meltdown in the lobby had already reached biblical proportions, and her students: this roving, hormonally confused tide of noise and motion, absorbing nothing, devouring everything. Sora stationed herself near the coat check with the clipboard raised, the picture of administrative purpose, while every part of her concentrated on occupying a single square foot of silence. Her feet hurt in a way that steered her mind toward mortality—less an image of final breath and more the daily attrition of joints and cartilage, the slow, bureaucratic decay of standing still in public spaces while other people learned almost nothing.

Wolf—who had, critically, chosen that nickname for himself—hovered a few feet away, applying roughly the same level of interest to an ancient vase that a sleep-deprived raccoon might grant a recycling bin. His gaze drifted somewhere past the museum walls, yet his hands stayed busy: one wandering up to scratch his nose, the other burrowing into his pocket as if searching for loose change or absolution. The S.P.A.N. badge on his lanyard—officially the Student Predictive Awareness Network, a behavior-risk sensor trial, unofficially a jittery tattletale—blinked yellow twice, misreading his slow, private excavation as a sign of looming crisis. Sora watched the badge with the same resigned attention she reserved for falling leaves and public Wi-Fi disclaimers, and then his finger emerged, subtly yet unmistakably coated in whatever secret lay inside his nostril. Without a flicker of self-awareness, Wolf wiped it across the bottom edge of the urn's display case, a slow, casual swipe, as if this fine piece of antiquity were a McDonald's countertop and the world existed to accommodate his momentary need for a napkin.

Sora stood there in a precise mixture of horror and amusement, suspended between the professional obligation to correct him and a quiet appreciation for the innocent blasphemy of the gesture. The act carried such deep absentmindedness that it felt less like misbehavior and more like a bodily reflex, a small, unconscious rebellion against the museum's carefully curated order, a reminder that the human organism handles its own secretions first and culture second. His face remained blank—no smirk, no challenge—almost peaceful, as if he had entered a trance and was sharing a private, wordless message with a centuries-old relic. Of course the urn would understand. Objects that survived empires probably knew about boys like Wolf. It was always the quiet ones who rearranged the timeline in ways no docent could anticipate.

She let the moment pass. The gesture was disgusting; it also lacked intent. Wolf wasn't trying to make a statement. He had no desire to provoke the museum or critique history; he simply drifted through both with complete indifference. He existed as he was, careless, unconverted, and somehow the whole scene turned absurdly close to poetry—a boy, a relic, a smear of organic matter bridging centuries, the museum's fantasy of reverence punctured by a single, absentminded finger.

Eventually she wandered. Close enough to keep any liability clause asleep in its folder, yet far enough that her own students slipped out of her direct line of sight. District policy would count this as a violation; the laminated field-trip guidelines, with their passive-aggressive bullet points and clip-art exclamation marks, demanded constant visual contact, as if the human eye were a surveillance camera that never blinked. Still, an aide moved with the group—a competent one, by the gentle standards of the profession—and another teacher traced the perimeter of the herd like a sheepdog who understood the futility of barking at every stray impulse. The students had adults; they had supervision, at least in the technical sense of the word. Sora composed the justification even as she walked: the paraprofessional needed practice, autonomy required distance, and adolescence, like literacy, only developed when someone stepped back long enough for confusion to try its legs. Everyone broke the rules. Survival depended on the elegance of the explanation afterward.

The museum lighting sagged toward dusk in a carefully engineered way, each recessed bulb working to manufacture reverence, to summon that mild, gooseflesh awe visitors were expected to feel in the presence of bones and artifacts and anything old enough to whisper that their own lives would end. Sora moved straight through the taxidermy exhibit. The bear, frozen mid-roar in eternal ambush, held no claim on her, and the bobcat suspended in its permanent leap, mouth pinned open in a snarl that had lingered so long it now looked vaguely embarrassed, resembled a constellation no one believed in anymore— stuffed into myth and pinned to a sky that no longer hung overhead. She drifted past the mineral cases, the geodes split open like geological confidences, their glittering guts exposed under halogen interrogation; past the reconstructed mastodon skeleton, forever a little too tidy, too rational, a myth paraded under Enlightenment hubris, stripped of omen and handed over as bone, a monster carefully trimmed of its mystery. She slipped by the paleobotany diorama where someone— with access to both funding and a private sense of humor—had placed tiny, manic ferns in brittle fake soil, arranged as evidence of a world already gone. The diorama read like an elegy staged for no one in particular: Venus in retrograde, sung through ferns.

She drifted until the early hominid display materialized before her—a glass case embedded in the wall like a concealed reliquary, its stingy lighting issuing a kind of tacit caution, as though illumination itself had grown selective and preferred to leave certain truths half-veiled. The entire installation carried the atmosphere of a shrine that refused worship, an alcove reminiscent of the Primum Mobile—motion imagined within silence, intention suspended beyond language. She held herself still, almost ceremonially, since stillness felt like the only honest physical response in a room arranged around the remnants of former bodies.

Four figures stood inside, grouped in an awkward crescent rather than the straightforward, triumphalist line usually assigned to progress narratives. Australopithecus crouched into its lurch, an ancestor startled into presence. Homo habilis, slightly more upright, presented the earliest glimmer of purposeful manipulation, some first desire to shape the world lodged behind a sloped brow. Homo erectus, longer of limb and steadier of stance, leaned into the whisper of advancement with the fatigue of one who already understood cost. And then Cro-Magnon—third from the end if counted from the past, second if counted from the present, the hinge between origins and aftermath.

She did not precisely look at them; she entered instead the beam of their collective attention, or perhaps only his—the Cro-Magnon, whose meticulously replicated eyes met hers with a fidelity that invited questions about the sculptor's private obsessions. Not in that dead-eyed mannequin way where the blankness becomes a screen for your own projection, but something stranger—a precision of posture and angle, the tilt of the head, the barely parted lips that weren't quite emoting but weren't neutral either: a stillness like the fixed stars, ancient and unblinking, not watching so much as enduring. Like the figure wasn't just looking but registering. As if evolution itself had paused at this particular junction, taken a long, unhurried inventory of everything that came after, and decided—quietly, without malice, without even really caring—that this was probably the best it was ever going to get. Maybe that was what hope turned into, eventually. A face like his, looking back and not saying no.

Wide cheekbones gave the figure a sheltering quality, while the deep-set eyes and heavy brow shaped an expression acquainted with knowledge yet freed from commentary. The mouth neither smiled nor hardened. It simply existed—alert, present, possibly resigned. Here stood the face of someone who had glimpsed something immense and opted for silence as the only faithful translation. Sora recognized that exhaustion intimately. Each morning required its own ritual of continuation, and improvisation carried the rest. She stood there, breath shallow, suddenly attuned to the heat of her coat on her shoulders, the vascular tides rising and receding in her hands, the way her thoughts circled and caught like strands of hair around a drain. Some severe comfort emanated from that face—not through familiarity, since familiarity had no place here, but through its absence of irony. A face uninterested in commentary, metaphor, or interpretation. Flesh articulated by bone. Bone shaped by weather. Weather untroubled by interpretation. He seemed built for a world where language had never formed, and thus no grief accompanied its absence.

Her phone slid into her hand almost without intention, and she lifted it, posture unchanged, snapping a picture with casual imprecision. The camera caught the figure in a crooked blur, a minor act of documentation devoid of artistry. She didn't check it. Didn't care. She typed "you in 6th grade" and sent it into the world without punctuation, confident the intended recipient would understand the gesture as a shared fragment within a private orbit—one of those slight occultations that bind two people who move through the same symbolic weather. The image, already buried beneath newer messages, looked older than the moment it recorded, as if its meaning depended entirely on being remembered by exactly one person. A thought followed, quiet and unforced: extinction begins wherever ritual stops. An ending forms through absence rather than judgment. The gods never punish; they drift when attention falters, leaving names unremembered.

She remained rooted before the glass for another full minute, perhaps longer, matching herself against the figure's patience and discovering how quickly a living body negotiates with its own stillness. A communion formed across millennia, mediated by tempered glass smudged with fingerprints and the heat of countless exhalations. The Cro-Magnon hovered inside his eternal present, sculpted into vigilance, and Sora hovered in hers—over-warm coat, feet swollen from too many hours pacing institutional linoleum, tendons along the backs of her knees stretched into thin, quivering ropes, some interior rigging frayed to its last workable strand. That was the thing about being tired. It wasn't dramatic. It just spread.

She didn't move. Didn't need to. Her knees had begun their small, autonomous negotiations. There was something almost sacred in the standoff—a recognition that none of them, not the *Homo sapiens* nor the wax replica of his prehistoric cousin, had anything new to offer the other.

Her teeth found her thumbnail. Stayed there.

Somewhere outside the room, a shriek tore through the museum's engineered quiet—high, sharp, nasal, the registered sound of modern inconvenience rather than the diaphragm-deep alarm of genuine danger, the cry of something mislaid or fumbled: a phone, most likely, or a friend whose attention had wandered irrevocably toward a vending machine, or the last margin of patience required to endure this sprawling, bureaucratic mausoleum of human curiosity with its deliberately confusing signage and its floorplan designed less for navigation than for slow psychological erosion. The moment buckled and slid away; whatever fragile equilibrium had formed between her and the waxwork ancestor surrendered to the present in an instant, and the future re-entered the room in its habitual form—loud, foolish, sticky, barging in with juice on its hands and no awareness of what it interrupted.

Sora turned, slowly, without theatrical intent, simply because her body had adopted an economy of motion over the years, the calculus of long days and longer weeks teaching her that every gesture drew from a limited account. She stepped back into the corridor and its disciplinary gleam of institutional lighting, into the pedantic glow of touchscreen kiosks that cycled endlessly through facts almost nobody would read, looping videos of kelp forests and erosion patterns and the lifecycle of plastic, one of them narrated by an outdated build of VoiceCompanion—version 9.8, the one with the faint glitch that added a soft "we tried" after every major extinction event, as though the software experienced private regret.

To her left, a low-lit room floated behind a glass divider, a kind of aquarium for attention. Above the entrance, a wall display rotated through a carousel of sponsored tags: PRESENTED BY ENVIRONWARE™ + SIBYL™ AI SYSTEMS. QR codes sprawled across the floor like a second species of lichen, half of them scuffed into digital purgatory by countless sneakers until their links split and rerouted to conflicting URLs. Even the staff cycled through shifting explanations of the pods themselves. The official acronym changed with each grant cycle—Simulated Inquiry-Based Youth Behavioral Learning during one funding window, Somatic Interface for Biome Evolutionary Lore during another—yet every rebrand promised the same hazy miracle of "empathic future modelling," a phrase that felt less like pedagogy and more like secular divination. Some kids claimed they met God in there; others treated the pods as highly funded vape dens.

Laminated placards with their apologetic fonts—forever pitched between the authoritative and the condescending—slid along her peripheral vision, just additional nodes on an overstimulated circuit. The sound thickened: that bright, needling dissonance produced when middle schoolers receive more autonomy than protein, their bodies jittering and ricocheting through the space like agitated molecules in a gas cloud, slamming against the boundaries of adult supervision and bouncing back into whatever impulse currently held the wheel.

She kept her gaze forward. Some inner certainty already carried the knowledge that the Cro-Magnon remained behind her, still and available, less a watcher than a fixed point—an unblinking presence capable of holding space in a way reserved for the dead and whatever counts as immortal.

The corridor narrowed behind her like a throat committing to a swallow, closing over the hush and that brief interval of stillness, as though the building had grown tired of permitting silence and resumed its true function with a kind of Saturnine descent, dropping from the outermost sphere of reverence into the low orbit of institutional burden. The shift resembled less a return to duty than a demotion on an existential scale she could hardly name, a slide from one register of being into another lower, stickier tier where the atmosphere carried faint notes of cafeteria pizza, cheap sanitizer, and every serious question drowned beneath layers of explanatory signage. A divine arrival in this place would likely trigger a flurry of emails from the exhibit department followed closely by a visitor survey, a wall placard, and a slogan: "Scan here to learn more about your role in the Anthropocene."

She moved toward the sound—the jagged, flayed-edge frequencies endemic to children in public spaces where emotion functions as both sensation and weapon, deployed like ordnance. Shrill demands for snacks, shouted negotiations over exhibits, preverbal screeches in which joy and complaint fused into a single, restless waveform. Yet deeper in her attention something held fast, some small tensile thread still anchored to the Cro-Magnon behind glass, short of obsession, weaker than preoccupation, closer to a retinal afterimage stamped on the inside of the skull, the lingering burn of that face: steady, unyielding, present in absence, like the ghost of a stare that had resisted blinking for thirty thousand years and had somehow still managed to register her. The image settled under the subcortical loom of conscious thought like a dropped stitch in a tapestry she had never chosen yet felt, absurdly, claimed by—a pattern older than cities unspooling beneath the grid of modernity, her own life just one brief combustion across its surface.

By the time she reached the Hall of Marine Invertebrates, her group had completely atomized; what had once traveled as a cohort of eighth graders held together by institutional inertia now drifted as small constellations and solitary particles, each body following its own vector of curiosity, boredom, or private drama. Somewhere between the giant squid model—its tentacles frozen mid-undulation like the folds of a particularly violent bedsheet—and the looping video of coral bleaching, a time-lapse that offered education with the emotional cadence of slow euthanasia, she spotted the milk kid.

He lay flat on his back beneath the cross-section of an isopod, arms crossed neatly over his chest like a vampire at peace with mortality yet still resentful of the décor. When he saw her, he raised one hand in a lazy, open-palmed wave, the sort of acknowledgment you might give a figure from a dream, his face washed in that glazed half-smile that suggested mild dissociation from the entire enterprise of waking life. She nodded back with the same small affirmation she had deployed a dozen, perhaps two dozen times already that day, a gesture without volume or judgment that translated roughly into: *as long as flames stay absent and blood remains inside, this situation lives below my intervention threshold.*

Her gaze slipped beyond him—past the placards with their focus-grouped typography, past the recycled atmosphere tinged with salt and institutional cleansers—to the octopus reconstruction suspended overhead. Its arms radiated in all directions with an order that felt older than mammals, older than bone itself, the entire structure hanging there like a biochemical mandala, a prayer wheel fabricated from silicone and steel, radiating a dignity that persisted in spite of the exhibit's theatrical staging.

Memory surfaced: not this octopus, yet a cousin in image, moving on a television screen years earlier in the sagging gloom of her apartment while her body staged its own quiet mutiny. She had been sick in the low, grinding way that never convinces anyone to send flowers—head congested, energy leeched away, throat rubbed down to rough grain. Her cycle had joined the party, layering cramps over the illness until the whole experience resembled some minor medieval affliction, the sort of thing a nameless pilgrim might drag through a Chaucer tale, minus the jokes. She sat slack-jawed on the couch, a half-eaten dinner sweating on the plate beside her, fork stranded mid-air, as the octopus on-screen manipulated a jar lid with excruciating patience, unscrewing it millimeter by millimeter like a small, exhausted god of persistence. For more than an hour she barely shifted. The voiceover, delivered in that soft paternal register favored by nature documentaries, described the creature as "an alien intelligence from our own planet." Her faith skipped the traditional deity and lodged itself, briefly and wholeheartedly, in that narrative tone; voiceovers enjoyed the privilege of finishing their sentences with orchestral accompaniment. The music swelled on cue, the familiar crescendo manufactured to summon awe, and she felt herself lean toward it.

Explanations lined up automatically—fatigue, hormones, too much time alone—and for one unstable second, inside a body running a low fever and quietly bleeding, something tightened in her throat, as if tears were warming up backstage. The feeling didn't settle into any tidy category. Words showed up late and unhelpful. What remained lived somewhere between guilt and awe: guilt that this impossible intelligence moved through the world mostly as a novelty act, brilliance briefly admired and then filed away, and awe that she, even in this half-sick, half-distracted state, could still feel the unfairness of it. Then came the dull, reliable knowledge that none of this mattered to the octopus. Her throat loosened again. She turned off the television and sat in the dark, the image of the jar and those slow, deliberate arms still running on the inside of her eyelids long after the room had gone quiet.

Something in her shifted. Not emotion exactly—emotion had clocked out—but a small electrical acknowledgment under language, a nerve firing that reminded her she was still here, inside this particular body, in this particular moment, attention hovering in that half-state between zoning out and actually paying attention. It felt like a scratched CD that keeps playing, skipping just enough to show you the damage while the song stubbornly continues. No revelation arrived. No storyline declared itself. Just a quiet mechanical click somewhere beneath awareness, the system catching and moving on. That was enough. Things wore down. Things kept going. She trusted entropy more than breakthroughs.

She let herself sink along that current, deeper this time. Past exhibits sealed behind bulletproof glass, past labels set in fonts that strained for authority—too rounded or too angular, as if the type itself asked deference from passing eyes. Past a volunteer explaining photosynthesis with the rhythm of a liturgy long outlived by its priest, his words unraveling into the room's murmur before they could reach any child's inner world. In the next alcove, the AI docent projection stuttered mid-sentence, mouth looping around "cyanobacteria" while its eyes recalculated, caught between a slumped boy and a motionless aide. The program froze, corrected, and started the line again. The boy stood beneath the glitch, eyes glazed in that proprietary digital stupor, mind already elsewhere, knee-deep in virtual circuitry, assembling some elaborate Redstone trapdoor in Minecraft. His face carried the distant, emptied look of someone who had set his body down in a public place and wandered off.

A hangnail yielded under her teeth with the clean surrender of old paint flaking from a window frame. She wiped her thumb across the side of her coat without looking and drifted past it all, past the faint synthetic smell that hung in every public building, the default setting of lemon, wax, and a chemical note that suggested cleaning rather than cleanliness. It pulled up whole rooms at once: middle school auditoriums, municipal hallways, the quiet dread of institutional corridors. The smell of being managed. It hit her in the teeth. Memory lodged there, for some reason. Paper towels that never quite dried your hands. Long afternoons waiting for something that never arrived.

She descended a stairwell that folded back on itself in a way that felt self-conscious, as if an architect had attempted to compress space into a smaller blueprint, lost interest halfway through, and abandoned the project to fend for itself. Each step answered her weight with a faint, chalky fatigue particular to places worn down by generations of field trips and civic obligation—stone smoothed away from elegance into resignation. The railing and risers carried the signature of some long-ago public works initiative, one of those high-minded 1930s projects that raised museums as temples to civic virtue and knowledge as shared inheritance, before the buildings were metabolized into backdrops and every corridor began to resemble a debased spandrel of what Piranesi believed a museum could contain: understanding rendered architectural, preserved after the understanding itself had thinned. Those men were dead now. Their buildings remained, instructing no one in particular, though she couldn't quite tell whether that judgment belonged to the place or to the afternoon she was having.

The further down she went, the louder the HVAC system complained, rattling against itself with the bronchial rhythm of old infrastructure, like a throat forever attempting to clear and always landing just short of relief. Somewhere in the building's subterranean gut, where daylight existed only as rumor and all illumination arrived prepackaged in LEDs and screens, she entered a room labeled "Anthropogenic Futures." The phrase read like a diagnosis. The sign alone produced in her the small, stubborn impulse to sit on the stairs and decline, with the mute resistance of a tired animal, any further participation in moral instruction.

The gallery was empty. Just her and the exhibits: a deliberate arc of semi-immersive pods, each devoted to a version of Earth's tomorrow—Post-Pollution Recovery, AI Coexistence, Subaquatic Civilization, one more terminal scenario with a focus-grouped name. Speculative futures lined up like a product range, urgent and theoretical at once, their precise labels acting as insulation against the fact that probability favored at least one. Fate felt diagrammed here, as if some melancholic disciple of Manilius had repurposed astrological tables to plot civic decline against planetary ascent.

She chose a pod at random. The titles had already blurred in her mind, their engineered optimism and dread colliding until both faded into white noise. Any capsule would deliver the same sermon in a different accent. Inside, the space formed an oval—curved walls, wraparound projection, engineered light. The climate controls had been tuned to suggest a particular future atmosphere, though whether the designers aimed for tropical, industrial, or late-industrial was obscure. The air tasted sweet and mineral-heavy, faintly ionized, reminiscent of blood after a bitten tongue. She sat. She had no stake in the future. Just the sitting part.

The simulation started without warning. No fade-in, no gentle voice easing her in, just a hard cut to a child's voice pitched in that carefully engineered middle zone—neither boy nor girl, neither warm nor cold, just neutral enough to sound inevitable. Of course they'd picked a child again. Children always made the stakes feel higher than they were. The voice sat in an odd range—too smooth to be real, too imperfect to be obviously synthetic—and delivered short, declarative lines over images that moved with the patient insistence of time-lapse: jellyfish rising through currents where birds used to trace their routes, cities sinking under slow blankets of green, vines working their way into the empty eyes of high-rises, server racks blinking out one by one as the sea reached them. Lights going dark. One after another. The network winding down to a rhythm that felt mathematical and indifferent. Systems didn't fail. They simply reached their end state. She found herself believing that, not as an argument, just as a fact that settled.

The whole thing worked like anesthesia. Edges softened. Friction disappeared. Her body followed along, skin less boundary than suggestion, the self starting to feel like something that could be thinned out gradually by the right combination of sound and light. Not a ritual, exactly. Just engineers who'd figured out how to aim spectacle directly at the nervous system and wait.

The voice said, in that steady, flattened tone: "The future will not remember your name. It will not forget you either. It will metabolize your choices into sediment, heat, and story." It sounded true, but so did everything when she was tired.

Without fully understanding the impulse—without any conscious debate—Sora bit the inside of her cheek, hard enough to send an electric jolt across the soft interior of her face while the skin remained unbroken, a small surge that reasserted the borders of her body. A quiet, animal refusal. She clamped her fingers against the molded sides of the seat, fingertips pressing into the faux-leather ridges, and for a moment the room snapped into focus: the engineered scent that hovered between metal and violet; the low, continuous drone of the projector; the faint churn of air through tired ducts. Her teeth met with the firmness of a door wedged shut against a draft. She focused on the jaw. It was the only part still doing its job. Somewhere in the system's imagined logbook, if such a logbook existed, a line would read: user declined full absorption. And as jellyfish pulsed across the projected sky and the child's voice continued mapping out its sequence of inevitable tomorrows, she found herself thinking that endings, too, were staged—some with better lighting than others.

When the simulation ended, the door hissed open, less in the spirit of spectacle than as a tired exhalation from the building itself, releasing Sora back into the larger system. She remained in the seat for a moment, jaw clamped, attending to the dull ache where her teeth had met the inside of her cheek, the small, throbbing proof that some portion of her remained outside the exhibit's digestive tract. Then she rose, rubbed her jaw with the back of her hand in a motion so practiced it barely grazed awareness, and stepped through the frame—back into a world of light and signage and administrative burden, back into the farce that passed for ordinary life. Familiarity conferred a strange, minimal mercy.

She climbed the stairwell that twisted through the building like an occlusion in its nervous system, a kink in the line between intention and execution, and emerged into the high-traffic artery of the museum where reality resumed its usual costume: unruly children, laminated floor plans, the low-grade chaos of supervised freedom. A boy tore past her, lungs fully engaged, wailing about the gift shop as if retail shelves housed salvation. Nearby, another stood with both arms wrapped around a plush trilobite, holding it to his chest with the grave tenderness reserved for things whose fate feels prewritten. Some things were easier to hold than to explain.

Sora's thoughts returned to the Cro-Magnon—not the face itself but the steadiness it lent to the room, the sense that something had been holding its place long before her arrival and would continue without reference to her departure, the ballast pressed into that alcove and the quiet, unspeaking agreement that had formed in its presence: You'll keep going. That was the whole thing.

She found her group near a wall-length diagram titled "Adaptive Pathways in Primordial Environments." Plexiglass arteries branched across the panel into color-coded filaments—red for instinct, blue for tool-use, green for social regulation—each line converging on a box labeled "Cognitive Economy, Approx. Now." The docent narrated the chart like a bus route destined for permanent emptiness, pointer gliding along the arrows with the careful affection of a bureaucrat updating a flowchart that would outlive her job. A kid asked what came next. "Lunch," Sora answered. The word slid into place with disturbing precision. She repeated it, louder this time, with the firm intonation of someone mic'd for a nature documentary, cueing the herd to migrate. They listened, or something like it—the group, the day, the long, blunt arc of time all shuffled forward under the pressure of inertia. She said it again, and the field trip resumed its scheduled shape.

At lunch she sat across from Elijah, who explained through mouthfuls of fries that dinosaurs still counted as present as long as chickens were still alive. "They never really lost," he said. "They just got smaller." Sora told him that was one way to survive: make yourself too ridiculous to kill. He grinned, squinting at his straw like it might confirm the theory. "So... if something keeps shrinking, does that mean it's winning or giving up?" he asked. She said, "Depends who's keeping score." He thought about that for a long time, then nodded, serious as prayer. "I think chickens are winning."

Sora smiled to herself. Maybe they were. The T. rex hadn't vanished—it had just learned to eat corn and live behind chain-link, traded thunder for endurance. Survival had shifted its emphasis; glory ceded the stage to persistence with feathers. The meek inherited fewer kingdoms than sermons promised; domestication simply outlasted drama. The line landed as comedy at twelve and as indictment at thirty.

She sipped her coffee—burnt, beige, passable—and stared at a poster explaining the carbon cycle, each arrow looping back into the next with bureaucratic cheer. The diagram felt personal in a way the authors probably hadn't intended.

After lunch, the day resumed its slow centrifuge. More exhibits, more performed engagement, more fingers rapping on glass and asking whether extinct creatures might exist "but, like, in secret." The museum resolved into its own genre: dioramas, infographics, the occasional animatronic twitching in place like a mascot still waiting for its cue. Time advanced in uneven bursts—bathroom breaks, water fountains, a brief interlude in which three boys insisted they had become lost despite maintaining constant proximity to the same room. She didn't bother correcting them. Let them be lost. It built character.

Eventually the docent reappeared with the final clipboard, and the group reassembled by the exit like debris circling a drain. A few kids wore new hats. One clutched a rock whose origin remained mysterious; the universe produced contraband even inside curated spaces. No one knew where the rock came from. Someone would notice, eventually.

They boarded the bus through the usual chaotic gradient—eager faces, bored faces, expressions already moving toward mischief around the edges. The same songs spilled from the same phones. A novelty whistle had entered the ecosystem. Seat negotiations flared and resolved, alliances formed and evaporated at the speed of a group chat. Sora moved through the aisle like weather, present everywhere and responsible for almost nothing in particular.

She didn't bother inserting herself into the flow. Instead, she chose a familiar seat, folded her hands in her lap with palms pressed down in a posture that resembled intention, and let the motion of the bus set the cadence of her thinking. The low hydraulic sway, the engine's steady vibration traveling through the seatback and into the spine, worked a quiet, repetitive massage on whatever parts of her nervous system still responded to rhythm. The movement filed the edges of thought without altering what they were.

Her phone stirred. A reply from Jim: "Lol. Tell him to give me my brow ridge back." She laughed once, startled by the sound, like a coin dropped into her hand by an unseen passerby. The noise vanished into the bus's general roar. No one turned. The day already felt half folded behind them, the set coming down mid-performance.

The bus shuddered in that muted, spinal way that belongs more to tissue than to machinery, as if some bored, low-level deity had begun redrafting her nerve network from the inside, tightening and loosening circuits without consultation. Sora sat slouched in the seat, her body already knew by contour, the same angle of discomfort met with the same practiced resignation, and watched the landscape scroll past in a sequence of dull frames that suggested the world had entered reruns: parking lots veined with cracks, chain-link fences bowing under the effort of pretending to matter, power lines drooping like exhausted clauses stretched too far across the sky, billboards shouting their imperatives into the open, one of them decorated with a pair of blue cartoon eyes floating above a peeling slogan—"YOU DESERVE TO BE SEEN." One eye had fallen away, leaving the other to stare alone over the access road.

Her mind, tired of making meaning, latched onto a sound-memory: potatoes in a microwave. Not the beeps or the current charging through wires, but that soft, wet *thump* at the end, when they yield under their own steam and slump inward, starch drawing tight in a quiet little surrender, a small, damp exhalation where heat meets matter and convinces it to change shape.

Stacked

by Stephen Haven

So easy to forget that the Deck of Independence
calls on the "laws of nature and Nature's God."
God as arbiter, maybe overseer, even as BJ Franklin,
our seminal inventor, nudged the language closer
the way of Nature, and won the general consensus
for the more temporal *"self-evident"* relative to
Jefferson's *"sacred and undeniable"* in an early draft.
But on the question of equality poor boy BF
couldn't shoo trust-funded TJ from the absolute notion
and the bloody aftermath. "All men are created equal"

won the day, even as BJ hoped to temper it with the
more pragmatic *"All men are born equally free"*
acknowledging what he knew about social status
and money. In more obvious guises, Franklin doubted
the dreamy absolute in the inkwell of his partner
even as he allowed for its ubiquitous presence
in terms of vanity, ignorance, foolish opinions,
pretensions to truth, other human foibles, unavoidable
spectacles, I should say, with all due respect
for BJ's inventiveness, for none of which he ever took
a patent. But neither one of them listened to Abigail,

the simple task she asked of her husband:
"Don't forget the ladies." Among the many others,
women were appendages of their husbands. Egality
sticks in the craw of the country, an idea so lofty
it couldn't ever actually be true, but who's to say
it might not wean that way again? We will need
a chunk of virtuous black bread, with salt and butter
to swallow those fishbones and breathe again

a song of joy and sisterhood. As Lennon or Lenin
once dreamed of it. You can pick your poison,
Vlad or John or Ben, the youngest son, child of

a simple candle maker, a millionaire by 30, wearing
a tradesman's apron to magnify half-hidden power.
All his life he wondered what to make of the way
he was indentured by his brother. Like Jonah, swam
from the father, and from the beast, which in this case,
his flight by water, was the city of Boston. He secured
his fortune as a writer, a master printer, then sent his
journeymen franchising out to other cities to rid
Philadelphia of the competition, stocked their shops,
took 33% of their revenue all over the country, until his
largesse was repaid. In this way he raised many families.

The sweet spot was always where he profited handsomely
for the good of the country. He was all over the fence
as president of the "PA Society for Promoting
the Abolition of Slavery," what with the seven he "owned"
his entire life at home. In the Deck of Independence
it's simple math: Signatories 56, slaveowners 41.
55 and 25 at the Constitutional Convention.
And still that absolute spirit presided over everything
as Jefferson put it: *Natural rights, Nature's God,*
call it what you will, maybe even the song of freedom.
"With a firm reliance on the protection of Divine Providence"

slips in at the end, though Franklin was a Deist, lacking,
in that belief, the concept of an interactive God
and a communal morality he otherwise preached,
as if God took off for darker, distant dimensions,
leaving little more to say but only after he set,
to teach us, the whirling dervish of the Universe.
Complicated BJ daily prayed to a higher rational power,
wanting it both ways. As for Jefferson? A Christian minus
the miracles he cut out of his family Bible. When they put

their heads together, with input from the others,
when they gained the confidence of all the landowners,
the Egalitarian Myth of Man danced somewhere
among our twenty-first century billionaires.
It hovered in the West, and for the longest time
bared its white young neck. But before the shooters
stared down their scopes, their silencers, before
the whoosh, the bucket, all the rest, as if he were
a block editor crafting the only text that mattered,
a hooded man spat on a grindstone, sparked his fat ax.

Waterfall After Rapids

by Jim Hodnett

The first time Liam entered Mean Grounds, he thought it might become a sanctuary for him. The baristas, who worked beneath the coffee shop's motto painted in large lettering on the wall behind them—"Mean Grounds for Nice People"—were pleasant and efficient. The emporium's furnishings were clean, white, and geometric, and the north-facing exterior wall was almost all glass, bathing the establishment in soft, indirect light. There was always low-volume, soothing music on the sound system (today it was jazz crooners), and the silent and captioned flat TV screen at the end of the counter typically played innocuous romcoms or colorful animated features. The patrons, who were mostly young, hip, and prosperous looking, were usually quiet and amiable in their interactions, if they had any. Most stared intently at laptop screens or read books.

So it was a shock for Liam to see her walk into these environs, that sad-sack woman he had encountered several times pacing the downtown sidewalks, always wearing the same bulky coat over hunched shoulders, even in warm weather. She typically carried a cloth bag full of snacks and other supplies as she strode with weight-shifting steps. The angry words she would yell at passing traffic sounded Asian. Liam wasn't sure which language, but judging from her appearance, likely a Chinese dialect.

Her voice was guttural, and her pronunciation sharp, making her syllables sound to Liam's Western ears like hatchet strikes—chop! chop-chop-chop-chop! chop! chop! The assaultive phrases were often concluded with drawn out nasal intonations—yowls that ascended nearly to a screech, then plummeted to a low-pitched moan. The yowls after the chops reminded Liam of a waterfall after rapids—or anguish after anger.

Sometimes she would direct her abuse at people rather than cars—for instance, patrons of a sidewalk café. Liam had been one of those patrons the first time he saw her. Alarmed, he considered calling the police to report a mentally ill and potentially dangerous person. But when he noticed that the other diners ignored her, unfazed as they sipped their coffees or took delicate bites from their pastries, he followed suit.

He had not recognized "The Shouter"—that was what he had come to call her—when she entered the coffee shop. When she was at the counter, he was aware only of the back of an inconspicuous woman giving her order in English and, in a soft, polite voice, responding "yes, please" when asked if she wanted room for cream. She had bowed slightly and said "thank you" when she received her coffee, clasping it with both hands.

But Liam did take notice when she sat down at the two-top table next to his. *Oh, Jesus,* he thought, *it's her!* He looked around the shop to see if there was another table he could move to, but all were occupied. With a deep breath and resolute intent, he encased himself in an imaginary, impregnable bubble, staring at his laptop screen and steeling himself to pretend she was invisible and inaudible. Yet, he could not help watching from the corner of his eye as she pulled something from her bag and placed it on the table in front of her. It was about the size of an old-style cell phone, and that's what he assumed it was, particularly when she flipped it open and began talking to it in her native language. Her voice was emphatic, but not aggressive. She would pause intermittently, as though listening to a response and then reply to it although Liam could hear no sound coming from the device. It was not until The Shouter pulled some lipstick from her bag and began applying it that he realized she was talking to a compact case, talking to her own image.

After five minutes or so, she put her compact away and pulled a bag of chips from her bag, munching and crunching noisily. Soon after that, she turned to the two men occupying the table on the opposite Liam. Without warning, she shouted at them in her chopping cadence, eyes round with apparent indignation. The two men, dressed casually and of an age that bespoke retirement, neither turned their heads nor paused their friendly, light conversation. Nor did anyone else in the coffee shop pay The Shouter mind, not even the baristas, who might,

Liam supposed, have been concerned about the comfort and welfare of their customers. Clearly, The Shouter was a known quantity here as she was elsewhere downtown, a person best not acknowledged.

After her outburst at the two older gentlemen, The Shouter seemed to settle down, chewing her potato chips and rocking in her chair, but uttering no words. Liam relaxed and became absorbed in his email correspondence, nearly forgetting her presence. He took periodic sips from his Americano and occasionally pushed back collar-length, brunet hair from his face. His hairstyle, combined with a full, trimmed, dark beard gave him a Biblical vibe. When he first adopted the style a year ago, friends called it his "Jesus look." He enjoyed the irony of that and settled comfortably into his new appearance, a departure from the corporate, clean-cut look of his college years and twenties.

His concentration was interrupted when the door to the coffee shop opened, and a middle-aged man walked through wearing a red baseball cap and a T-shirt that demanded to be seen. It was black and declared in large white letters "JESUS ..." Underneath those characters was a Nike-like swoosh, also white but with three black crosses printed inside it. Below the swoosh were the words "... did it!"

Oh, God! Did someone put up a sign out front announcing, "Kooks welcome! All drinks half-price!" And what was with this trend of wearing one's religion on a T-shirt? Just a few days earlier he had passed a brawny, greasy-haired man on the sidewalk wearing a sleeveless T with the message "Jesus, the Ultimate Deadlifter!" emblazoned on it. It had unsettled him, made him feel as though he had encountered an alien, a being both inscrutable and mildly threatening.

Liam watched as the swoosh man strode with chest out to the counter and delivered his coffee order at a blaring volume. He seemed oblivious to the subdued atmosphere in the shop—the murmured conversations, the heads-bowed postures of most of the patrons as they absorbed themselves, like Liam, in the screens of their devices. The noisiness of his presentation overpowered the voice of Sinatra singing "Fly Me to the Moon" on the sound system.

Liam rolled his eyes and returned his attention to his laptop, only to have it interrupted a few minutes later by a voice full of bombast.

"Excuse me, sir. Okay if I sit here?" Startled, he looked up to see Swoosh Man hovering over the chair opposite his. The man was smiling and holding a paper cup of coffee. Liam looked around the room and saw that the chair that Swoosh Man was coveting was the only empty one in the shop, other than the one opposite The Shouter, but she had claimed her table's entire surface with her paraphernalia and, at this point, her sleeping head. He had no option but to reply, "Sure."

"Thanks," said Swoosh Man, setting his coffee on the table and extending his hand as he lowered his butt into the chair. "Name's Chuck."

"Liam." He shook Chuck's hand then returned his gaze to his laptop screen.

"Liam? That's a fine name! Irish, are you?"

"Not particularly." He did not look up when he answered.

Chuck responded to the rebuff with a momentary frown of defeat but recovered quickly. "Yeah, we're all a mixture here in the good ol' U.S. of A., aren't we? Well, except for those criminals coming across the border—and the Muslims, of course, and …" He nodded toward The Shouter and lowered his voice, "her kind."

"Hmm," said Liam, feeling a flame ignite beneath the skin of his cheeks. A pause ensued, during which he could feel Chuck's gaze and smile aimed at his forehead.

"So, Liam, have you heard the Good News?"

Liam set his jaw and pressed his lips together before looking up and staring at the grinning zealot across from him. How often had he heard this same inane question during his tortured evangelical youth. "Yes, I have," he answered, ice in his voice. "Seems like most Americans are finally waking up to that fascist, pedophilic, senile con artist in the White House. With any luck, he will be voted out or impeached soon, or—better yet—drop dead of a stroke." He pointedly returned his gaze to his laptop screen.

Chuck sat with eyes wide and mouth open before offering in a timid voice, "Well, actually, I just wanted to tell you about Jesus Christ and how he died for your sins, so you can spend eternity in heaven with Our Father and Our Savior and the angels. I didn't say a word about Trump."

"Trump, Jesus—same thing to you guys, aren't they?" Liam kept his voice cool and quiet, so as not to draw attention. "And anyway, if heaven is full of evangelical Christians, I'd rather spend eternity in hell. At least the company would be more interesting—Buddha, Gandhi, Confucious, Socrates, Einstein, Jesus himself."

"Jesus isn't in hell!"

Liam drew a breath and stared at Chuck with an unrelenting gaze. "He was a pacifist, a champion of the downtrodden and oppressed. What's that got to do with evangelicals? You're all about making money, driving big cars and hating anyone who doesn't have the same color skin or set of beliefs."

"That's not true. We just want to keep America what it's always been, a Christian nation founded on Christian principles. That's why God has blessed us, made us the greatest and strongest nation on earth."

"As a matter of fact, America was founded quite intentionally on secular principles, including strict separation of religious authority from government authority. And if your god has blessed a nation that enslaved one race of people—cradle to grave, multiple generations— and nearly wiped another off the face of the planet, then he is one fucked up god. Meanwhile, we've colonized other people, stolen land from our neighbors, exploited immigrants and raped the environment. And all that is what your god rewards? Approves of?"

Liam's voice was gaining volume, and people—the same people who showed no reaction to The Shouter—began to glance in his direction with raised brows.

"So, you're an America-hater?" asked Chuck.

"On the contrary. I love my country. It's made enormous contributions to the world, to science, to the arts, to humanity itself. I just don't buy into loony mythology about America, any more than I buy into stories about talking snakes and virgin births and resurrections from the dead, at least not literally." Liam's voice had risen even louder, causing sideways looks and frowning faces in his direction. Even The

Shouter had woken up, staring at the two of them with an expression of wonderment.

"You're making fun of my religion," said Chuck, raising his chin and sitting up straight.

Liam took a few shaky breaths. How had he allowed himself to become so riled up? It was as though Chuck had found a hidden fuse to light or a trigger switch at the base of his brain. He felt the heat of shame as much as anger now. "Look," he said, lowering his pitch and volume. "I just want to drink my coffee and do some work. Sit here if you must, but please leave me in peace."

"Well, I think you're very rude. I was just trying to be friendly."

Liam opened his mouth to respond, intending again to say something cool and deliberate—boundary-setting. But at that moment, The Shouter rose from her chair and jabbed her finger in Chuck's direction. Her eyes formed into circles. They vibrated, almost spun, as she bellowed her staccato cadence, louder than Liam had ever heard it. Her face contorted and her teeth gnashed as she let loose her long string of chops and yowls. This time, everyone in the shop, already attuned to the tension between Liam and Chuck, stared at her with tense, frozen expressions.

Chuck pushed back his chair with a screech and stared at The Shouter with astonishment. He stood up, scrambled a few steps backward, knocking his chair on its side as he did. It hit the tile floor with a calamitous rattle. Chuck looked around, seeing disapproving faces from all, then hurried toward the door as The Shouter continued her chastising stream of staccato syllables in his direction. He glanced back as he exited Mean Grounds as though to make sure she didn't follow him. He had left his coffee on the table.

When the door closed behind Chuck, The Shouter became quiet, as did everyone else in the shop. The only sounds were the hiss of the espresso machine and Michael Bublé singing a jazzy cover of Patsy Cline's "Crazy." After a few moments, a barista walked from around the counter and picked up Chuck's chair from the floor and returned it to its place under Liam's table. He grabbed Chuck's abandoned coffee cup. As he did so, he made eye contact with Liam and gave him a cryptic smile.

Around the room, patrons exchanged smirks and shoulder shrugs. "Well, you don't see that every day," said someone. "Too much caffeine, maybe," added someone else. Some more chuckles and head shaking, and then they returned to their screens and muted conversations, as though seeking a higher, more soothing reality.

The Shouter sat down and began rocking. Liam hid his face in his hands for a moment, then shut his laptop and packed it away in his satchel. *No more work to be accomplished at this point,* he thought. As he stood to leave, he turned to The Shouter, who had stopped rocking and was staring into middle distance. "I don't know if you can understand me," he said, "but thank you."

She looked up at him when he spoke and stopped rocking. Liam could see a shift in her face, a light in her eyes, blankness lifting from her features. Clarity, sensibility. "Oh, no problem," she said. "He was pretty annoying, huh?"

Nothing The Shouter had ever said or done shocked Liam as much as those words. His response was stumbling, vulnerable. "Yeah … Yeah, he was. I-I hope I wasn't annoying, too. I can get kind of … well, passionate about things. I …" But before he finished his speech, The Shouter's face reset. The vacantness returned. She looked away. She was gone. "Well, goodbye," he said. She did not reply.

Just before he reached the exit, he heard her. He turned around to look. At whom was she directing her invective now? To Liam's dismay, it was he himself. She was shouting at him, wagging her finger with each denouncing chop of her speech. Liam sighed as he looked at her and nodded his head, as though he deserved her censure. He adjusted his satchel on his shoulder and pushed wearily through the coffee shop door.

And then he heard it, felt it—the yowl, the waterfall, the anguish.

Indian Boarding Schools

by Michelle Tackla Wallace

I shiver in a railway car,
in the faceless night,
I see land we leave, families
grow small, as we go
to the place *of forgetting*
who we are, forgetting who
we are, forgetting
who we are.
The great iron beast
sometimes called
       government
    or at other times,
  religion,
trades our clothes and names
for corn and 973 child graves.

They beat our selves
out of us like our own skin
stretched over us, our earth tongues
washed clean with bitter lye,
our bodies stripped as white canvas:
they can draw us new eyes
in the place of *forgetting*
who we are.

You can take me there—
but not my song:
I am a ladder of the wind.
I am a brown river,
whisper of nettles,
wolf cry in the pines,

I am spirits intertwined.
I am a red stallion
still running free.
I am a red balloon
slipped from a child's grip.
I am a slip of a child's spirit
from its body.

Drunk on Love

by Thomas Dukes

Old joke: What do Baptists say to each other in the liquor store?
Nothing

We took a holiday from childhood
On Easter, Christmas, two or so other days,
Sharing Daddy's whiskey shot,
Aunt Ruby's muscadine wine
Almost too sweet for words—
Aunt Poppyseed's sangria sent us
Into a Carolina tango.

Pound cakes soaked in rum,
Fruitcakes drenched in brandy,
Plum pudding set ablaze:
All custom and ceremony.

I have tasted wine
Mama announced with the scorn
Baptists reserve for the unclean and stupid.
Still, she cut our tipsy gifts with the good knife
And a reverence Depression babies
Kept for food: even she took a fork.

We'd return to sober life
And school every Monday,
Our parents to work.
None of us became drunks:
Other problems chose us.
Still, we'd tasted sin--
Who wanted Eden, after all?

A New Day at the Taliban Café

by John Kachuba

Apparently, Brandon will live.

I remember the attack--falling to the sidewalk, the mob closing around my nephew just as I lost consciousness--and I am amazed that the doctors can tell us that he will live. Sick at heart about the whole thing, yes, but amazed and grateful. Let me tell you what happened.

My name is Al Kaydah. Please, I know. Don't say it. I'm Armenian, and a lapsed Christian-Armenian at that. Not Afghani. Not Iraqi. Still, what a pain in the ass since September 11. I'm sure you can imagine.

I knew *bupkus* about terrorists, Bin Laden or otherwise. Living in New York, my life was stressful enough without terrorists, I'm sure you know what I mean. I was busy slicing sesame bagels for the breakfast crowd when the Towers came down. Our deli is all the way over on Delancey, near Little Italy, so I never saw a thing, except the brown dust cloud rolling through the streets. My brother Armand saw the second plane as he came up from the E line at Chambers Street. A terrible thing. He's still in therapy. Think of it—had he not spent the previous evening with his girlfriend, instead of his wife, he would have been at work on time the next morning. He thinks God sent him a message, but I wonder, what message would that have been?

Two weeks later, the suits were in the store. Two sides of beef wearing Ferragamos. They flashed badges, but I don't remember their names. Smith and Wesson we'll call them.

Let me explain something. When I said *Armenian*, I meant Armenian-American. I'm a citizen, born here, like my parents, like you. My grandfather came to America around 1900 to escape the Turks. You see, there've always been terrorists. Nothing really has changed in the world; we've just learned we're not immune to it all. I grew up in Queens, went to high school there, spent two years at Columbia before winding up in the family business, so I'm not some foreigner afraid of losing his green card or being hauled off to one of Alberto Gonzales' gulags, but I do have a New Yorker's healthy sense of caution when dealing with the cops and it was on full alert the day Smith and Wesson dropped in.

Business was slow, the neighborhood just beginning to recover from the "disaster"—an inadequate word, I know, but what word works better? What would you call it? It was close to noon on a Saturday. My sister's boy, Brandon, who frequently helped after school and on the weekends, was pushing a mop across the wood floor. A handsome kid, Brandon, but a little slow mentally. Old man Spinelli, God love him, sat at his customary table, gumming his customary pastrami on rye. He pulled the plate closer, hunkering over his sandwich, eyeing the men warily as they walked by. The few other customers milling about didn't pay them any attention.

The men approached the counter. Manny, the Colombian kid I had hired only the month before, cut me a look as if he were ready to bolt, but I shook my head no.

"Watch the counter for me," I said. I came around from behind the meat case, wiping my hands in my apron. "Help you, gentlemen?"

They flipped their FBI badges just like cops do on TV and I wondered if they practiced that wrist flick.

"Are you Mr. Kaydah?" said Smith. Or maybe Wesson.

I answered that I was.

They asked if there was someplace we could talk in private, so I brought them into the storeroom, reassuring Manny once again that everything was cool. The storeroom did not make a comfortable conference room, crammed as it was with cases of olive oil, sardines, and delicacies such as pickled pigs' feet and beef tongue and redolent with the fragrance of gorgonzola, goat cheese and Raid. I took the only seat in the room, a metal folding chair. Smith, a blue-eyed, sandy-haired Viking, sat on an empty soda crate while Wesson, a blue-eyed, sandy-haired Viking, leaned against the wall.

"You have a very interesting name," said Smith.

I sighed. "Tell me about it."

"What does it mean?" asked Wesson.

"Al? It's short for Albert, my father's name."

Smith made a sour-pickle face. "No, he means your last name. What does it mean?"

"Oh. Damned if I know. I guess it's Armenian for something, but I don't know what," I said, crossing one leg over the other. "I don't speak the language."

"You don't?" asked Smith.

"Nothing more than a few choice profanities."

The two looked at each other for a moment and it must have been like seeing their reflections in a mirror. I could hear the gears whirring in their heads, could smell the circuits burning. Wesson folded his arms across his chest and adjusted his position against the wall. Smith tugged on his tie, a red silk number with little smiley-faces on it. Neither spoke. I knew what they were doing, they were giving me that old *we're-thinking-that-you've-done-something-wrong-we-may-not-know-what-it-is-but-it's-something-and-we're-going-to-get-it-out-of-you-one-way-or-another* look and, damn, even though I was on to their game, it still made me nervous. Reminded me of my SDS days at Columbia, the cold sweats I got knowing that, even as we stormed the dean's office, the crowd was laced with undercover cops.

Finally, they spoke, asking me questions about the business, my customers, my employees, the neighborhood, what was going on at the deli on September 11, and a lot of other crap that I can't remember. I answered their questions as best I could.

They must have been at the deli an hour at least. When we finally emerged from the storeroom, Manny's face turned a couple shades paler. He was sure they were hauling me off to jail for something. Manny had his own history with the police that left him with a limp and just a little paranoid. He was surprised when the agents left without me.

"Are you all right, boss?" he asked.

"Yeah, sure. They just wanted to talk."

Manny twisted the gold stud in his ear lobe. "Shit, that's what they always say." He turned back to the meat slicer where he was shaving a roast for Mrs. Perlman, extra thin, just the way she liked it. "Watch your back, boss," he whispered, so Mrs. Perlman wouldn't hear.

"You worry too much, Manny," I said.

Brandon, God love him, had been oblivious to the whole thing, spending his time leaning on the mop, ogling the girls passing by the window. Kids.

But that night, back in Queens with Nancy, I did begin to wonder what the feds wanted from me. As I brushed my teeth, I saw myself in the mirror like I never had before. The thick black mustache and wavy hair, the olive complexion, were now prominent and somehow sinister features of a face I had grown to appreciate over the years as being, if I didn't say so myself, rather handsome in an Omar Sharif sort of way. But now I had my doubts. I rubbed my chin, stubble scratching against my fingers, and looked again.

"My God, I'm ethnic," I said.

Nancy was already in bed, propped up on a couple pillows, deeply engrossed in a Sue Grafton mystery. *U is for Ukulele.* She didn't pay much attention to me as I climbed in beside her and rolled onto my side.

I tried to sleep but my mind kept replaying the conversation at the deli. I couldn't lie still.

"Are you all right, Al?"

"I'm ethnic."

"What?"

"Ethnic," I said, turning to her, "you know, like an immigrant."

"Jesus, Al." She set her book down. "What are you talking about? You're no immigrant."

"Really." I pushed my face closer so she could get a good look. "What do you see?"

She laughed. "I see you, a moron. What am I supposed to see?"

"Never mind." I turned away, closed my eyes. What could a seventh-generation WASP from Westchester know about ethnicity?

The neighborhood slowly started to come to life while the cleanup at Ground Zero continued. As twisted metal and broken glass were hauled out of the site by the truckload, Americans were gradually throwing off the shock of the attack and returning to their lives as they knew them, whatever that might mean. The President was on television, starring prominently in commercials for Disneyland, urging us all to go out and spend, spend, spend. Ride the Mouse for America. Show the terrorists we would not be defeated—they would have to pry the VISA cards from our cold, dead fingers.

Business at the deli picked up again. I hung photos of New York firefighters and policemen on the wall as tribute to their heroism, but what I really wanted to do was figure out a way to post the day's terrorist alert color in the store as something of a public service. I thought maybe a plastic pennant in the day's alert color above the meat case. Green for no threat, red for kiss your ass goodbye, and the rainbow in between. The problem was that I never could find out what the color of the day was and none of my customers seemed to care anyway. After all, this was New York. ADD New York. I thought it would be a whole lot easier if the NBC weather guy included the day's terrorist alert level with his forecast: *For those of you heading to the Jersey shore today, there is a 50% chance of thundershowers in the afternoon followed by a 2% chance of being hit by a hijacked airliner. And if you're flying to Europe, watch out for those pesky Stinger missiles.* In any case, I gave up on my idea.

I managed to push memories of my visit from Smith and Wesson to the back of my mind so I could concentrate on the day-to-day activities of running a business but, as the war in Afghanistan plodded along, I began to feel uneasy.

The Internet was full of rumors about people of Middle Eastern descent being rousted out of their homes by the FBI and spirited away to unknown locations, held incommunicado without being charged with any crime. Some of the newspapers carried similar stories, although buried in the back pages. At Columbia, I had flirted briefly with the idea of becoming a lawyer, and what little I learned about the Constitution told me that these detentions were, number one, bullshit, and number two, terrifying. No one could find out who the prisoners, excuse me, "detainees," were, where they were being held, how they were being treated, even their exact number. What was certain was that these detainees, citizens and aliens alike, fitted a certain profile that Gonzales & Company decided was unfriendly, a profile that I feared could include me, the Ethnic. It was a strange and unsettling feeling, maybe you felt it too, walking my city streets, the fear and suspicion surrounding me thick as fog. Maybe everything had changed after all.

And wouldn't you know it, at about that time, Smith and Wesson returned? If I had been a little nervous during their initial visit, I was anxious now, what with the paranoia fostered by the government hanging in the air. Manny sensed my fear and stuck close to me, a large carving knife in his hand. That's all I needed--two FBI agents filleted in my deli by a mad Colombian.

"Manny, please," I said. "It's all right. Watch the counter."

He backed away, keeping an eye on our visitors, and I was sure that if they so much as looked at me funny, Manny would carve them up as easily as he did the roasts for Mrs. Perlman.

"This way, gentlemen," I said, once again ushering them into the storeroom.

Smith and Wesson didn't waste any time.

"Mr. Kaydah--" Smith said.

"Please, Al," I said.

"Al, the FBI could use your help."

I fumbled in my shirt pocket for a cigarette but didn't say anything.

"Actually, we're looking for a lot of people to help," said Wesson. "Have you heard of the TIPS program?"

"No."

"It's an idea of the Attorney General's," said Smith. "He's asking for volunteers in the war on terrorism."

"There's a war?" I asked. Smith ignored me.

"The Justice Department is asking people who interact with the public daily to keep their eyes and ears open. Mailmen, cable TV installers, meter readers, like that. We're asking that they note any suspicious activity and call it into us on a special number set up just for that purpose."

"Kind of like an informer?" I asked, finally lighting my Marlboro.

"More like a good citizen helping in a good cause," Wesson said.

I took a drag off my cigarette. "All right. Say I'm a cable guy in someone's house. What am I supposed to be looking for? Guns?

Bombs? You don't think those things would just be lying around in plain sight, do you?"

"Not very likely," admitted Smith. "We're thinking the clues would be more subtle. Maybe you see a phone bill on the table with a lot of calls to some Arab country. Maybe you note the presence of the *Koran* or some other suspicious foreign books, couscous or hummus in the kitchen, things like that."

"Gentlemen, I sell couscous and hummus. So, I would call those things in as possible terrorist activities?" Wesson nodded his head. "Aren't you afraid of getting swamped with calls?"

"We'll handle it, Al, don't worry about that," said Smith.

In truth, I didn't care much about whether they could handle it. I was more concerned about turning a couple million of my fellow Americans into spies. I already looked Ethnic and somewhere in the house, a copy of the *Communist Manifesto* from my Columbia days was lying around growing mold. Would someone turn me in? What about old man Spinelli? Mrs. Perlman?

"What is it you want from me, exactly?"

"Nothing much. Just keep your eyes and ears open," Smith said.

Smith liked to say *keep your eyes and ears open*, I noticed. "But why me? Don't tell me it's because of my name." They didn't tell me anything, only looked at me as if I just didn't get it. "You've got to be joking."

"We think it's worth a shot," said Wesson.

"Maybe I should change the name of the store. Call it the Taliban Cafe. That should bring them in, don't you think?"

"This is no laughing matter, Al," Wesson said. "National security may be at stake."

"And you're leaving it up to me? God love us, we're in trouble."

As I expected, nothing happened. A year passed and the suits never came back although I sensed that they were never very far away. The rubble had been cleared from Ground Zero and plans were already in the works to rebuild on the site. Old man Spinelli still came into the deli for his pastrami sandwich, Mrs. Perlman for her roast. Brandon still swept the floors after school. And then the President invaded Iraq.

Just like that. Never mind that even the CIA didn't believe the Iraqis had anything to do with what was now simply called 9-11. God spoke to the President, told him Iraq was the evildoer and that was that. Don't ask me to explain it, I'm Ethnic. I tried to laugh it off, the absurdity of it all—a Connecticut-born Ivy Leaguer, pseudo-cowboy, ex-drunk, ex-druggie, AWOL reservist, born again Christian throwing the might of the most powerful army in the world against a sand pile— but the humor wore thin when people started dying.

It seemed a day didn't go by without hundreds, if not thousands, of people marching in the streets of New York, protesting the war. They were loud but peaceful. Soon, there were handfuls of flag-waving supporters of the war on the streets as well, and the mood between the two groups turned ugly, even by New York standards of etiquette. I felt uneasy in the city, more so than the days after 9-11. It was a visceral emotion, palpable as any tumor.

The evening news only made it worse. Nancy and I tried not to watch too much of it, but it was like a car wreck, difficult to turn away.

"Everyone hates us," Nancy said one night, as we watched a montage of anti-war protests from around the world. Fists pumping the air. Banners in languages I could not read.

"Yes, but we hate ourselves, too," I said, just as the image changed to show a group of war supporters taunting peace demonstrators in San Francisco, getting right in their faces, spitting, cursing, calling them traitors, un-American, Saddam lovers, communists, Boy Scouts, anything that came to mind. "It's hard to believe that one man could cause so much conflict in the world."

"They say he executed his own son," Nancy said.

"I wasn't talking about Saddam."

We watched an interview with Iraqis living in Detroit and heard how fearful they were to leave their homes, go to work, send their children to school, or even to pray at their mosque, fearful of their neighbors. The reporter said the FBI was in the process of interviewing hundreds of them, for what reason, no one seemed to know. But I knew. It was because they were Ethnic.

"I can't watch this anymore," Nancy said. "I'm going to bed." She took her empty teacup into the kitchen. "Are you coming?" she said from the doorway.

"In a minute," I said, but I stayed longer than that. With the sound muted, I watched the violence of the war in Iraq, the explosions and clouds of smoke, the injured women and children, the angry people in the streets. The images were horrible enough; I didn't need sound.

The next day was Saturday. As was my usual custom, I walked the three blocks to my sister's house to pick up Brandon. Together, we'd take the subway into the city. Brandon was tall, dark, the fitting product of my sister's union with her swarthy Sicilian husband. He loped along beside me as we headed for the train. Funny, even then, with all that was going on in the world, I did not see Brandon as I saw myself, as Ethnic, and so was completely blinded to the fact that others might see him that way.

My recollection, even now, of what happened when we got off the subway and encountered a Support Our Troops demonstration only a block away from the deli is still hazy, as if seen through gauze. I remember a man's face, round, pig-like, screaming obscenities at us as we tried to make our way past the protesters, a dozen or so American flags poking up above the crowd, one of them leveled at us like a spear; a woman's voice yelling at us to go back where we came from and I knew she didn't mean Queens; someone jostling me; stumbling, falling to the sidewalk, Brandon coming to help me, the mob—and it was a mob now closing around him, and someone looming large. A man with a lead pipe? A cop with a nightstick? And then only blackness. I remember slowly opening my eyes, a policeman bent over me, his hand beneath my head, and seeing far above him a flag waving from a pole attached to the building. It rippled brightly in the sunlight, and I could not look away.

Essay Ideas

by Linda Davis

I ran into Nancy while walking my dog Rudy. You don't need to know Nancy's name because she's just an acquaintance and will not likely be in the rest of this story, but it's a good name and, if I ever have a cat again, I want to name her Nancy. She asked me about the kids, partly because I have difficult kids and everyone asks about them, but also because there's not a lot of other things to ask me since I'm a fifty-year-old married woman without a paying job. "Funny thing about kids," I told her. "When one is doing well, it's a given that something bad will happen with another, like some sick whack-a-mole game of you vs. your kids." I'd been pondering ideas for a prestigious essay contest that would surely lead me on the road to established writer, and just like that, I'd landed on my first prospect: "Kids and Sanity: Oxymoron?" And what of those who only have one child? These are just some of the topics I would cover in that essay.

Nancy, like her name, is nice and pressed to know the details. I told her how our middle son—the "easy" one—had racked up an enormous credit card bill buying his friends tickets to *Hamilton*.

She laughed. "Whoa. At least he didn't spend $300 on heroin."

"My thoughts exactly." It was true, everything with my kids was graded on a worst-case-scenario scale to make me feel better.

At that moment, there was a sound across the street and I saw her: a young girl with a bald head, laughing with a friend. "Okay, I'm done complaining."

Nancy laughed. She's an ex-writer, who, tired of the hustle, gave it up for great tips. If the shifts weren't so long, I would consider waitressing again. I loved being on my feet, the choreography of serving multiple people their meals. Anything for a break from mothering. Custodian. Retail.

After I left Nancy, I crossed the street towards home when I spotted it: my husband's car in the driveway. "Shit," I said or thought.

I forget which. As his own boss, George came and went as he pleased. But dammit, how dare he trespass on my time? I only have a few hours to myself every day, and I guard them with my life. It'd be one thing if George was quiet. But no. He has Only Child Syndrome: a desperation to connect every second of the day. The number of times I've thought of things I wanted to discuss with him, only to have them knocked out of my head whenever he walked in the door, talking. I shuttled a very confused-looking Rudy into the darkened basement that smelled like detergent, dirt and mold so I could avoid George. After all, I was working. This *was* my job: to find something, anything, to help my autistic son's soul crushing anxiety; to mend, as best anyone could, the gaping hole in my adopted daughter's heart; and now, to sort out my middle son Julian's spending spree. It didn't look like it, but I was hard at work.

After only a few seconds of waiting quietly, I heard my husband's footsteps above me as he walked down the stairs to his car. I peered through a splintering in the wood, cause, really, there's nothing better than spying on one's family—seeing them out in the world—when they don't know they're being watched. My husband: good looking, meticulously dressed, and in freakishly good shape, all of which added up to a hell of a lot of pressure for me. I refuse to be the wider person in the couple you see from behind.

Rudy and I then went upstairs where I plotted out my errand course before heading to the car. More than anything else, my primary job for many years had been cab driver. Typically, I averaged twenty shops and fifteen appointments a week. I hate driving. Whenever George and I are in the car together, he always drives, which is the least feminist thing about me.

One of my favorite songs was playing on the radio in the car. I once won a contest at WBCN in Boston by choosing ten of my all-time favorite songs. I knew when I mailed it in that I would win because it was so eclectic and might have included The Hollies and Vicky Sue Robinson. The disc jockey on my NPR station and I have similar tastes, and I know if I wasn't older and didn't have difficult kids, I would be working for him. Now that's a job I would enjoy. I don't understand why 90% of radio stations play the same ten songs ad-nauseam. It's an essay, for sure. "Popular Radio and the Sheep that Listen to it." Too harsh? Maybe Elvis Costello should write it? If you didn't understand that last line it's because it's an inside music joke that goes to my point of why I should work at the radio station.

The errands ate up a few hours of my day. When I got home, Rudy jumped up and stared at me with the plea: walk? in his eyes, I had no choice but to leash him up for walk number two. The thing with dogs and people is that it's very much a match of wills, and mostly, I don't let him run things. But the morning walk had been shorter than usual, so guilt had settled in. Guilt rules so much of my life. There's always a kid, a dog, or a husband to take advantage of that. So, be strong, I told myself. But dogs' lives are so damned short. As a cat person—read independent—I'd had no idea. It wasn't until I thought of the dog as therapeutic for my kids, especially Noel, my autistic son, that I conceded the pet war that pitted me, cat woman, against the four of them. But Noel liked to ride the dog, which Rudy didn't like. And now, there was little therapy going on, and one more body utterly dependent on me. Another slice of me cut up and served to my family. On a good note, I liked walking.

Rudy and I walked across a bucolic green lawn banked by a huddle of "unhoused people," as NPR refers to them. If I worked in city government, I would implement a program that would benefit two problems: homelessness and, another one of my pet peeves, litter, by rewarding homeless people per bag of litter they picked up, like bottle rebates. If only I could turn that into a job, or an essay, as in: "Litter Does Not Glitter, Only Cleanliness Does."

At the dog park, I spotted a woman I suspected didn't like me. Despite that, I walked close to her, trying to think of something to say. I'm a peacemaker, and social grievances unnerved me. She wore a 'mixed messages outfit:' camouflage jeans and a beret. I'd heard she went to Stanford, which made her dismissal of me worse because I like smart people. But other than telling her about the places I used to work before I had kids, what did I have to talk about? I'd worked at Redford's film company! And Universal! The *LA Times* Syndicate!

Harper's Magazine, for god's sake! I had things to say! But wait, that had been 15, 20, 22, and 25 years, respectively. Who was I kidding? I could talk politics, although sometimes that went horribly wrong given how emotional I am. Even as I write these words, my rage and disappointment of not having a woman president—twice!—has re-surfaced.

"What do you think of Oprah for president?" I said to Stanford.

"Is that your dog pooping?" she pointed to Rudy.

"What? Oh, thanks. Be right back."

By the time I'd finished cleaning up after Rudy, Stanford had left. Good, I thought. I probably wouldn't like her anyway because of those camouflage jeans. I refused to buy clothes, lunch boxes, anything that used war as a fashion statement.

An hour before I picked up the kids, I tried to work at the coffee shop. I say 'work,' but it's a joke since I've been paid $1000 in the ten years since I got my MFA in writing. 2016 had been on track to be the best year ever. In addition to President Hillary, I'd written a novel that I knew for certain would get me an agent, a big five publishing contract, and possibly a movie deal. My book had everything: suspense, humor, politics, endearing characters, and even some feminist overtones. All year, I carried the secret within me. My laptop: a veritable treasure trove that I protected with my life. Whatever problems the kids had, I could handle *because* of the book secret within me, like insulation against the storminess of our lives. I can't tell you how much I looked forward to 4:30 a.m. when I could be alone with my treasure, and no one needing me. When Hillary lost, I knew for certain my book dream would come true, since I hadn't gotten my way with Her; that's how optimistic I am. Sadly, after too many rejections, the book didn't get past step one. And then Noel's anxiety got so bad, he lost five, ten, twenty pounds. And then what, what, what? Donald Trump and the dismantling of democracy, more book rejections and Noel slipping even more. That's what. Another essay: "Hillary, Kamala and Me: Competent and Jobless!" Except that they both had a book deal, and I didn't.

My husband called. I felt bad about having hidden from him earlier, so I answered. "Would you carry pepper spray?" he asked. Apparently, he'd seen a homeless person that morning that scared him so much he wanted to arm me. Adorable, right? "Happily Ever After the Fact." That's the name of the essay I want to write about marriage. It was hard to feel lucky in the moment with difficult kids, and little of me left. Then he mentioned the dates of his UK trip. "Jerk," I muttered. I always felt insanely jealous that he got to fly business class to Toronto, Spain, China, away from the family, for a week.

A friend from one of the kids' schools stopped by my table. I hesitated but then blurted out the Julian/credit card news to her because, years ago, she'd loved a story I'd written, and that recognition had informed every interaction since.

"Well, Julian has his issues for sure," she responded.

If this were a movie, the entire audience would jump in their seats because of the amplified sound of my insides screaming, juxtaposed with my absolute calm expression—a look I'd damn near-perfected. It was one thing for me to complain and worry about my kids, but no one else could.

"More importantly," she asked, "How's Noel?"

More importantly?!! What the hell did *that* mean? What kind of sick person was she? No way would I talk to her again. Screw that old story she liked. Luckily, Noel had been doing better that week, so I didn't have to lie. He'd gone from weighing 111 pounds and often not making it to the bathroom in time, to being twenty-five percent back to his old, adorable self. "Much better. Thanks."

I gaped at my watch as a way to get rid of her. "Shoot, I've got to go." I guess I did have to lie.

She left and I sat, not moving. *Turn it into a story*. Woman with one healthy kid as the villain. The blank screen stared accusingly back at me. How could I think after what she'd said? *Keep moving*: my less-than-inspiring-but-absolutely-essential-mantra. I packed up my things and left yet another piece of myself behind on the cruddy coffee shop floor.

"I'm growing wings," my daughter Vika said when she got into the car. "You don't believe me."

I handed Vika a candy bar. "Here's your sweet, sweety," I said in a cockney accent, no idea why. The best way to fend off an argument with Vika was with desserts or toys. She could be bought. When she first arrived from Russia at six, friends bearing gifts lined up to meet her, so, naturally, she associated treats with love.

"Thanks, Mom. Love you, Mom."

"You're welcome, honey."

"LOVE YOU, MOM!" I had to say the word *love*, or else. If edgy words were daggers, I would have died a long time ago.

"Love you, too."

A typical conversation with Vika was utter nonsense, an argument or something dirty. She has a filthy mind, hates anything academic, and has very few friends. I'm resting all my anxiety for her future on the fact she cares what George and I think. That has to mean *something*, I tell myself.

"Mom, no one calls it a sweet, but you. It's called dessert."

Vika loves—lives!—to correct, which makes me crazy because I imagine it is one of the things that drives a wedge between her and potential friends.

"Right, mom? It's called dessert."

"Whatever. Words are just words," said the writer who thought precisely the opposite. The argument continued until we got home.

In the house, I shouted like a maniac, "I gotta go!" "Once Upon a Time I Had Patience" is the beginning of an essay. I'm old and need to pee. I could write an essay about the spectrum of bathrooms I'd peed in around L.A., but why would I want to?

I knew by Noel's expression when he walked in the door, his school bus driving off behind him, that he'd had a bad day. I'd made the mistake of telling that awful, villainous coffee shop 'friend' that he was "so much better!" so, naturally, the next time I saw him he was worse; one of those laws of the universe, like the whack-a-mole thing. Noel's mouth scrunched to one side. Not a hint of a smile from his eyes. He's a beautiful boy with perfect features. Noses are hard, but his was exactly the right size and shape. He has full lips, and his eyes are coffee brown. But the most distinctive thing about Noel is the fireworks of freckles spread across his face. He should be a model, I thought. He'd never had an awkward period. He could be the first autistic male model; a PR sensation! He could care less what he wore, but he looked great in everything. I'd be his keeper, drive him to appointments. A Hollywood mom. Now that was a job for me.

"What time am I taking my pill?" Noel asked about twenty times in ten minutes.

"Asked and answered," I said, then referred him to the schedule we had written for every hour of his day. He asked again. Then he went to the bathroom and peed all over the toilet. But I made him wipe it up, which I congratulated myself for because, often, if he was having a hard day, I did things for him.

"What will you do if I say I'm not going to the pool tonight?" he baited me.

"Let's take a walk," I told him and Vika. Yay me. That's what good mothering looked like around here: ignorance.

On the walk, Vika kept asking me if I could see her wings growing, and Noel continued to talk about misbehaving at the pool. I spent a lot of my time with the two of them and always felt stuck in a time warp where these two kids would never, ever grow-up.

I counted three posters for missing cats on the walk. Was a missing cat ever recovered? Perhaps it was best we had a dog. Then I saw a missing dog poster.

After the walk, I drove Noel to the pool while Vika stayed home alone. Vika always stayed home. I would have gone to the city dump with my mother, just to be with her, but Vika preferred staying home, which I supposed was a great thing since she didn't have her own home until she was six. She also didn't have a mother for a while, but by being home she could feel like she had both.

"Who's picking me up? Are you picking me up?" Noel asks when I drop him at the pool. If I didn't do it, he'd be upset. No one would ever love or need me as much as this boy.

"What smells?" George asked when he walked in the door.

George had this juvenile obsession with smell that I refused to respond to. This ignoring my husband thing was getting out of hand.

Still, he continued to sniff his way around the rooms in search of a culprit, as if some sort of reward awaited him if he could accurately nail the source.

Finally, he moved on. "How was your day?"

I went mute. Hours of unintelligible talk had rubbed off on me. I often went mute when he asked this because I was tired, and anyway, what did I have worth talking about? I'd never mention what that woman had said about Julian—partly because I didn't want it to hurt George like it had hurt me, but also because I didn't want to relive it. What about all these ideas for essays that would never see the light of day because I didn't have the time or the connections to get them into print? "How was yours?" I asked instead.

"My class got approved," he said. "It'll be every Tuesday night from January on." George was an entertainment lawyer, and he'd been asked to teach a class at Julian's college. I spent my days desperately thinking of jobs I could do, and my husband, who had a full-time, well-paid job, had been handed another. That was the difference between his world and mine.

"That's nice," I said, serving him some homemade pesto orecchiette with olive bread and feta and oil on the side. I'd become a fairly good cook, enjoyed hosting dinner parties, and several neighbors had said they loved my cooking. If I owned a restaurant, I'd come up with a fabulous—

"This pesto is a little too salty, hon. I'll make myself a peanut butter sandwich, and watch the game," George said.

Mistakes Happen: A humorous cookbook I could edit of famous chefs' worst meals? I huffed and puffed my way around the kitchen, furious that I'd wasted an hour cooking something that he'd thrown out. Of course, he was right. I'd tasted the pesto and it was too salty. George was sickeningly right. "Perfectionism: Overrated?" Might be a *Modern Love* story for me to write.

George yelled across the house that I needed to come see the final play of a championship baseball game, even though I could care less about organized sports.

"I have to get Noel," I shouted.

Vika walked into the living room and told George she was growing wings, which was just the sort of distraction I needed to escape. As I walked out the door, I heard George laugh. "I see them sticking out!" Would I ever be that carefree again like that? I left the two of them discussing fairies and the validity of the Easter Bunny to head back for Noel.

"Can we go out to dinner?" Noel asked when I met him by the entrance.

I knew what this was about. He'd become afraid of the night: the time when that evil monster that lived in the closet in his head, did his finest work.

I extended my arm around Noel, as if that helped anything. "Not tonight, honey."

Noel threw his swim backpack on the ground and said, "I have attitude."

Narcissism was never this adorable. "If you don't come now, you're not earning a bus ride."

"I hate myself," he said. "This is bullshit."

He kicked the wall several times. Kids and their parents stared at him. I actually laughed to make it seem like he was joking. Ha. If I had to write a scene with the worst possible person to run into in this moment, with the whole day huddled on my shoulders, and a dull pain pulsing betwixt my brows, it would be that woman from the coffee shop, the one who'd commented about Julian having issues. Yes, there she was, twice in one day like some sort of walking, stalking reminder of a life that had somehow out-maneuvered me. Her son, with a recent haircut and excellent posture, stared at Noel until his mother wrapped her arm around him and drew him towards her, whispering something in his ear. And what was I doing? Laughing. "Fake Laughing, but Laughing Nonetheless," is an excellent title.

She said nothing, the woman who had said too much earlier. As she walked away with her son, nonsense essay titles raced through my mind. "Do You Have Any Fucking Idea What I'm Going Through?" "Who the Hell are You to Judge?" "Walk a Mile in My Shoes? Blues? News?"

It had been a long day, and it showed.

Don't Climb a Tree to Catch a Fish

by Brian Luke

Skye was sitting at Starbucks—you know, that big one across from Tompkins Square—sucking on her ice and trying to finish Act I of *King Lear*. Her roommate Roma had tickets to see Michael Pennington, whoever that was, play the mad king at the Polonsky Center on Saturday night, and Skye had agreed to go along. She had been to enough Shakespeare with Roma to know she was more likely to stay awake if she read the play ahead of time. The language was rough going though, even with the annotations, and her mind was easily distracted.

The macrophoto covering the far wall of the store, for instance. A supremely beautiful African woman wearing a tall, multi-colored headwrap held out her arms, beaming from ear to ear like it was her life's ambition to offer a basket of red coffee berries to the good folks of the Western Hemisphere. Though Skye enjoyed her own work, at times, she couldn't remember ever smiling like that while on the job.

Her phone buzzed. Usually, Skye let calls from Angelina go to voicemail, but today she welcomed the interruption.

"Talk to me, boss," she said.

"I've asked you not to call me that, Skye. Remember?"

"Sorry, ma'am."

"That's even—oh, never mind. Listen, I've got a hot prospect. Can you be in by four?"

"I'm off today, Angie. I had three clients last night. Can't you get one of the other girls to take him?"

"Ooh, three in one night," said Angelina sarcastically. "Back in my day we'd do six or seven in a row and call it a light shift."

"Well, your day sucked."

"He asked for you personally, Skye. His name is Slater. He's got a Riverside Drive mansion worth over 45 million, according to Zillow. Our year-over-year bookings are way down, so we could really use him. Fucking internet."

This was 2014, a few years before the OnlyFans revolution. But already every amateur with a webcam and a dildo was busy uploading her own get-rich-quick scheme. Skye couldn't see remote sex supplanting the live action roleplays they offered at the Spa, but she knew Angelina was stressing. And she could use a break from *Lear*.

"Fine, I'll reel in the new fish. But you owe me."

"This one's a whale, Skye, not a fish. Make him a regular and I'll buy you a steak."

"I'd hold you to that, Angie, except I'm vegetarian. Remember?"

"Oh. I'm so sorry, Skye, I meant I'll—"

"Don't sweat it, boss," Skye said, and clicked off.

Angelina texted her the basics—Dominic Slater, born 1942 in Paterson, New Jersey, semi-retired financial mucker. Back in the apartment, Skye scraped up some public information on Slater herself before taking a shower and hopping the R train to Chinatown.

Skye had the staff put Slater in room 302, the Spa's classroom setup. On her way to work, she grabbed a shiny red apple from a sidewalk grocer and sent Angelina a picture of it, captioned: "Customer service is an attitude, not a department," a slogan Angelina had stenciled on her office wall, among several other equally drippy sentiments. That text earned Skye an immediate "Yes" with an exclamation mark, which made Skye think her sarcasm was becoming too subtle for texting. Or too subtle for Angelina.

Skye grabbed a size four schoolgirl outfit from wardrobe, killed some time playing on her phone, and made her grand entrance precisely ten minutes after the scheduled appointment time.

The slight, yellow-haired fellow tucked into the tiny school desk in the corner was *not* private investor Dominic Slater. Dominic was in his early seventies. This fellow hadn't reached forty. But he reeked of equity. Clothes, hair, the way he crossed his ankles, the cast of his eyes. All smelled of money owned, not earned.

Skye guessed this was Slater's son, Paul—not quite the fish Angelina had hoped Skye would land. But, given that he was the mogul's heir apparent, Skye figured she could work with it. She closed the door behind her, tugged at the back of her skirt, and meekly apologized for chewing gum in class that morning.

"But you see sir," she said, taking a bite of apple and chewing it slowly, "I'm at the age where I need something in my mouth. Like, all the time."

He was hesitant at first, but she got him on board soon enough. After they'd finished a brisk round of: *Please, sir, I really need to pass this class*, he got self-conscious like some guys do, pasting his eyes to the floor as he turned away to button his shirt. Without looking up, he asked, "So, what is a girl like you doing in a place like this." A tired, stupid question that she, as usual, declined to answer. But he startled her with his follow-up.

"I mean, a girl with your special skills."

"Special skills?"

He turned to face her.

"You don't think I came down here for—" he flicked his eyes at the plaid mini-skirt hanging off the chalkboard easel by the door. "I mean, I enjoyed it, very much, but ..."

It suddenly occurred to Skye that he somehow knew about her other line of work. For a terrible instant she imagined he would blurt out something incriminating, right there with God knows who checking in by the hidden ceiling camera. No one at the Spa knew about her side hustle; she meant to keep it that way, for their good as well as hers. She covered the space between them in two strides and, for the sake of the camera, planted a kiss on his mouth, then whispered sternly in his ear that it was time for him to shut up and get out. He looked startled. Submissively, he began to get to his feet, but she pressed him back into the chair and whispered in his ear a time and place, then looped her arm through his and perp-walked him out to the hallway, pressed to his side so she could elbow him into silence if he started flapping his gums again.

***

Wednesday at noon, Central Park, the Shakespeare Garden, a haven of quietude tucked between Delacorte Theatre and the 79th Street Transverse, free of cameras, lightly trafficked, with benches that allow early views of anyone approaching—perfect for sensitive work-related meetings like this follow-up with Slater's kid.

Skye got there early. No skaters or dog-walkers or couples posing for wedding photos, just one or two olds poking their way along the flower beds. She waited until everyone was out of sight, then stepped over the low border fence and picked her way through lilies and daffodils until she could crouch behind a row of thick, low-cut bushes set several feet back from the path.

Skye pulled a couple branches slightly apart so she could see through to the walkway. She felt silly, sitting there cross-legged with her ass in the dirt, peeping through bushes like some clownish pervert in a bad sit-com. But this Paul Slater character had come at her out of nowhere and she needed to be sure she wasn't being set up before she could talk business with him. She resisted the urge to light a Marlboro and passed the time chewing chocolate-covered espresso beans, flicking ants off her ankles, and thinking about why she did what she did.

It wasn't the money. The Spa brought in more than enough for her. She did enjoy the intellectual challenge of it. Each job was its own peculiar kind of nut, and she got a special satisfaction figuring out how to crack another one open. But mate-in-two chess problems could be just as challenging, and you wouldn't see her squatting over a pile of ants to solve one of those.

Emotional satisfaction was the biggest part. She had yet to take a contract where she didn't feel, rationally or not, that her efforts were making the world a better place. She liked the feeling. If it ever went away—the sense that she was cleaning up God's messes, one little prick at a time—she'd probably give it up and call it a day. Or not. Maybe she was just a depraved psychopath. There was always that possibility.

A couple minutes before noon, Paul came up the path, alone and not on his phone. He looked worried, but no more than would be expected in the situation. No suspicious characters trailed behind him and Skye concluded provisionally that the meet was legit. She watched him for a few minutes to be sure. He stopped at the sundial, checked his watch, looked around for her, then walked along the flowerbeds, idly considering the descriptive plaques. One got his attention. He stared at it for a while, and she could see a pained expression on his face as if something Shakespeare wrote about crocuses upset his stomach.

She crossed the flower bed and stood out on the path, looking in his direction until he swung back around and saw her. She sat down on the nearest bench. He took a seat a couple feet away. She scooted over next to him and sat there quietly, trying not to look like a hooker.

"So," he said finally, "how does this work?"

"Is it your father?" she asked.

He hesitated, then nodded.

I had a feeling it might be, Skye thought.

She pulled out the two black flip-phones she'd bought that morning, wiped his down and cradled it in her scarf until he took it from her. "There are two contacts on that phone," she said in a low voice. "Fred—that's me—and Bman. Passcode is 'F-R-E-D.' Change it early and often."

"Bman?"

"Bagman—handles the money. In the notes folder I put instructions on how to make the drop. I figured this might be new to you, so I added a crib-sheet on the do's and don'ts of pulling together a cash pile of this size. Do not deviate from those instructions. Often as not, it's fuck-ups with money that get people jammed."

He stared at the burner in his hand, his expression growing more somber as if it just now occurred to him that he was embarking on a course of action disapproved of across human societies.

"All communication goes through these," Skye continued. "When the job is done, we get rid of them, according to the instructions on your sheet. Once this meeting is over, I never see you again—got it?"

He nodded slowly.

"Got it?" she insisted.

He shook his head briskly, snapping himself out of a daze, then nodded more convincingly.

"Good," she said. "Now, the fees."

"There's something I need to show you."

Paul took out an iPhone. Shading the screen with one hand, he thumbed through a series of photos: animals, of all different sizes and shapes.

"Okay," Skye drawled. "And my roommate has an entire Pinterest board of cats wearing sunglasses. Super cute. But—"

"I don't think you saw the captions," he said.

Skye exhaled as Paul scrolled through again, pausing at each photo for her to take in the description:

Mexican grizzly bear, last one killed 1969
Zanzibar leopard, Tanzania. Went extinct 1990s
Javan rhino. Last one in the wild poached 2010
Saola, or "Asian Unicorn." Extremely rare and nearly extinct
Cat Ba (white-headed) Langur. About sixty-five survive
Vaquita Dolphin, "ocean panda." 10 left in the wild

"Thanks for sharing," Skye said. "Now—"

"These pictures are from my father's trophy room," he said. "Every one."

"Oh," Skye said, looking again at the last image, a light gray dolphin mounted on a metal spindle, mouth permanently open, lifeless eyes staring blankly into space. She'd seen that look before. Half the girls in jail had it. Her mother used to get it whenever the sperm donor got ready to start in on her again with his sharp tongue or his bony fists. Skye had caught that look on her own face at times, back when she was still using—dead eyes fronting her from a cracked mirror over some reeking toilet in the land of God knows where.

"I want you to understand why I'm doing this," Paul said earnestly. "I need you to know I'm not some sort of—"

"No," Skye snapped. "You do not need. I do not need. The less we know about each other the better."

"My father is a monster, and he's got to be stopped. He's not just a trophy hunter. He specializes in finding and killing the last of dying species."

Skye heard a sound and raised her hand for silence. An old woman wearing a rain poncho and knit cap, and clutching a frayed carpet bag to her bosom, was shuffling up the path, swinging her head from side to side as if her failing vision was barely sufficient to keep her from straying into the shrubbery. Skye commenced an ad lib run-on of how her best friend Haley said she wouldn't be her best friend anymore, "because I wouldn't talk to her Tuesday when she really needed to talk even though I was *on Tuesday night* talking to Caroline about how *Haley* ..."

Skye blathered on until the woman had moved past; Paul played his part by keeping his mouth shut and looking confused.

"I don't need the psycho-history," Skye said, once the bag lady was out of view. "If you've got intel that helps me do the job, fine, just send it to me on this." She held up her burner phone. Once he'd nodded, she typed a dollar amount into the text screen and showed it to him. He didn't blink or clear his throat or bite his lip. No discernible reaction to a number that represented months of toil at the Spa for her. The asset class, Angelina called them.

"I'll text a contract to you and Bman."

"A contract?" Paul asked. "You're going to put this in writing?"

"It's no more risky than anything else sent between us on these," Skye said, indicating the flip phones. "And I've been burned by misunderstandings before, so it's better to spell it out."

"It just seems ... unwise."

"That's why you guard this phone like it's—I don't know, pick your analogy. It's never out of your sight, and no one else ever sees it."

Paul pursed his lips, then nodded mutely.

"Once Bman has the deposit," Skye continued, "I go to work. He doesn't pay me until I've finished."

"How does he know you finished?"

"I make sure of that," she said, standing up.

"Before you go," he said, looking up shyly. "I've got a private office, over on West 74th? I thought maybe we could ..."

Skye froze him with a look. "I'm heading this way," she said, tipping her head toward the cottage on their left. "Which means—" she pointed to the right "—you're going out over there."

Once past the cottage she stopped and counted sixty, then poked her head around the corner to confirm he'd left the garden. She walked over to the plaque Paul had found so distressing earlier. A passage from Henry IV:

> *For though the chamomile,*
> *The more it is trodden on, the faster it grows*
> *Yet youth, the more it is wasted,*
> *The sooner it wears*

She snapped a picture with her job phone. She'd lied about the psycho-history. Having just hired her to commit homicide, Paul Slater was suddenly the most dangerous man in her life. The more she knew the better.

***

Skye sat in the back corner booth at Whiskey's Tavern. Her new job tablet, picked up for $250 cash at Target, was carefully angled so that no one could see its screen when walking past. Located around the block from the Spa and under the shadow of the hulking Manhattan Detention Complex across the street, you would think the tavern's décor would give its patrons some hint they were passing this time of their lives in a New York City Chinatown establishment, but the blinking orange "It's Miller Time" sign, motley of rusty state license plates tacked onto the wall, and quartet of bowling trophies sadly gathering dust behind the bar made Skye wonder, not for the first time, if they hadn't all been magically transported to the airport hotel lounge in, say, Dubuque, Iowa. Which was funny, if you think about it, since she'd never been to Dubuque. Or Iowa.

Skye's big Bose over-the-ear headphones and implacable scowl successfully put off the bar's drunks and hopefuls, and her afternoon so far had been interruption free—other than Big Jim, of course, who periodically lumbered out from behind the bar to freshen her extra-large sweet tea and ask in an unnecessarily loud voice if she'd like him to "punch it up" for her, gratis—an offer she steadfastly refused lest this be the day of all days some bored beat cop decided to bust her for underage drinking, thereby creating a record of her presence at Whiskey's at just the time she was using the bar's free wi-fi to log into Slater's security.

A recording made earlier in the day showed Dominic Slater sitting alone at the long, polished conference table in his trophy room, his back to the camera and a laptop open in front of him. He appeared to be playing an online video game. Whenever Slater shifted in a way that revealed his laptop screen, Skye grabbed a quick screenshot. She wanted to know what Slater was playing and why. He didn't seem like the videogame type. Too many flesh and blood targets still out there in the real world, demanding his attention.

Paul had been texting her details of his dad's activities and habits since they left the Shakespeare Garden three weeks ago. He also provided her with access to the mansion's network of security cameras. Nothing she'd seen so far made her think the old man was any kind of soft target. He rarely went out. He spent mornings in his cavernous home gym watching Fox News and placing loud, sweaty calls about leveraged buyouts and undivided interest. Afternoons he ran the show from his perversely clean home office desk: loud calls, micro-consultations with his live-in chef, scattershot marching orders barked to various household minions, including his son Paul, who when summoned stood just inside the office door, head down, hands pressed to his sides, waiting to be dismissed. After dinner, Slater generally had a drink in the trophy room before retiring to his bedroom, alone. Over the entire time Skye had been observing him, Slater's master bedroom suite had not entertained a single social caller, professional or otherwise.

When Slater did go out, he was accompanied by one or both of his bodyguards, a pair of healthy young fellows Skye dubbed "Big" and "Tall." Cheerful and clean-cut in their crisp purple and green sweat-free sweatsuits, Big and Tall looked like they entered private security not by way of law enforcement or the street but via bachelor's degrees in personal fitness management. It was not their size, strength, or evident flexibility that made Skye reluctant to tangle with them, but a quality exuded by their calm, alert demeanor, one less often seen and rather more difficult to overcome—competence.

Skye had no plan of entry yet, but she hoped an opening might appear through Slater's current project, a twisted job of trophy-hunting Paul explained to her by text.

Slater had somehow decided he wanted to replace the conference table in his trophy room with a custom-made piece carved from the wood of the world's oldest living tree. A few years back, a UC Davis botany professor named Richard Tencher announced he'd counted over 5,000 rings in a core sample he pulled from a California bristlecone, thereby establishing it as the oldest known tree on the planet. The professor passed away last year without having shared his data, so no one knew exactly where to find Tencher's tree. But Slater found a source who claims to have Tencher's notes and core sample and is willing to share them with Slater for the right price. Once he's closed the deal, Slater plans to harvest the Tencher tree and ship slabs of it back east to be carved, polished, and given a central place of honor in his private petting zoo of "things I made sure didn't outlive me."

Not much sport, Skye thought, hunting a target that can't fight back or run away. But the old man's desperate desire to get wood—pun very much intended—did offer an opening, since Paul told her his father intended to confirm the age of the core himself. Apparently, counting rings doesn't require a doctorate in botany, just patience and a good magnifying glass. That little hands-on task should get Slater out in the open.

Skye had written the project into the contract, describing the deal between Slater and his source and pledging to take him out before the tree info was exchanged. She included this clause not because Paul asked for it—her research convinced her that Paul didn't care about protecting nature nearly so much as he wanted her to believe he did—but because she knew her own tendency toward sloth and thought an artificial deadline might keep her working the job at hand rather than wearing out the couch binging past seasons of *What Not to Wear* with Roma. For instance.

Paul told Skye he was never included in his father's safaris and didn't know the identity of the source. Skye advised him to keep his ears open but not to pump his father or his father's team for information; investigators would later consider that suspicious behavior. She began her own probe into who might be trafficking Tencher's materials. Nothing she found on Tencher's colleagues showed anything other than boringly stable super-nerds who really, really like trees—no drain-circling drug addiction, bankrupting divorce, or acrimonious grudge against Tencher that might lead a comfortably tenured professor to do business with

Slater rather than just analyze the core sample and publish the results himself.

She then focused on Tencher's family. His wife had died of ovarian cancer years ago, but his two children were alive and kicking: Samantha, an environmental science major at UC Boulder, and her older brother Anthony, a computer programmer who was proving harder to locate. Samantha was all over the socials, so Skye built a dummy profile for one "Renata," a high school senior who'd gotten a lot of college offers but was leaning toward Boulder—if its environmental program was really all that.

Renata reached out to Samantha. And Samantha bit. She bit hard. Within a week they were messaging and even had a couple voice calls about Renata's upcoming campus visit. Samantha was cute and healthy and full of life—the sort of wholesome college girl Angelina encouraged them to recruit, the kind who always rejected the offer with an overly loud laugh and a quick, "but I'm not judging what *you* girls choose to do." Of course not. Sam was wrapped up in her budding career as an "environmental professional" and Skye couldn't picture her violating the tree-hugger code by snitching to Slater. So she steered their chats onto the subject of Sam's brother, Tony. Which proved interesting.

Sam called Tony her "beautiful, hot mess-terpiece." A computer science and game design double major, Tony had dropped out of USC after just one semester, the in-class quizzes getting in the way of his habit of sleeping until five in the afternoon. He took short-term programming gigs to make ends meet but mostly focused on his own design projects, which always started out with grand proclamations and super-human bursts of creative energy and invariably crashed once conception encountered reality.

Tony had been kicking it in Berlin during the previous year but came back to the states when their father died. Sam wasn't sure where he was now or what he was doing. He'd been working on some big new game design but was uncharacteristically tight-lipped about it; all she knew was that it seemed to be putting him under serious pressure of some sort.

Execution of Tencher's estate had fallen to his kids, so Skye tentatively identified Tony as the one selling oldest-tree-in-the-world data to Slater. Which didn't advance the job much since she had no idea how to find him. Yet.

Skye slid a grease-slicked jalapeno popper into her mouth, took a swig of tea, and clicked on her last screengrab. Her image enhancement plug-in gave the pic just enough clarity to recover the URL of the site Slater was visiting. She opened a new window and typed in the address.

The game was called *Die Welt von Harry Potter.* The homepage explained the game through parallel text blocks in German and English. It was an animated role-playing game involving Harry Potter characters drawn as they appeared in the movies. Opening play happened not at level 1, but at 7, a scenario mimicking the seventh and last movie, *Deathly Hallows, Part 2.* The goal was to solve various magic-related puzzles and descend one level at a time all the way down to level 1, which was modeled on the first movie, *Harry Potter and the Philosopher's Stone.* Each level culminated with the unlocking of a hidden room in which, according to the site, "players complete various sexual challenges suggested by Headmistress, after which they may complete additional sexual challenges of their own choosing before descending to the next level."

Skye was no Harry Potter fan, but she thought that the first movie was about middle school kids. A quick search confirmed that the lead actors had been eleven and twelve years old for that film, very much in line with how they were drawn in the game's final level.

So, the better you did in the game, the younger the characters you got to play with in the virtual sex rooms. All the way down to pre-teen.

Skye's temperature climbed a couple notches and wanted to keep moving in that direction. But she was in the planning phase of the job and needed to keep her chill. After shuttering her screen, she crossed to the bar and gestured for a refill of her sweet tea, then drank the whole thing down while standing by the stool, ignoring Big Jim's attempts to chat her up as she let the cool liquid coat the fire in her belly. By the time she slid back into her booth, she felt sloshy and ensugarated but on top of her emotions. Mostly.

Skye opposed sexually explicit animation on the principle that it was taking market share from the hands-on side of the industry. But she had to admit that Tony had created an incentive structure that would keep guys coming back—guys like those she knew from the Spa, anyway. And she could see why he was in hiding. Animated representations of underage sex were legal in Germany, but not in the U.S. Authorities here were unlikely to feel that throwing in a few German phrases—*"du willst mehr, meine schätze?"*—exempted developers from prosecution under the PROTECT Act.

Skye went back to the recording of Slater playing *Die Welt*. Except he wasn't really *playing* it. He wasn't moving the cursor or prompting characters. He'd made it to one of the sex rooms, but his hands never strayed to his lap; they remained at table height, resting on the polished surface, periodically picking up his highball and swirling the amber liquid around before taking a slow swallow. He wasn't playing the game. He was watching the screen, waiting. She figured she knew what he was waiting for. She fast-forwarded through the recording until she saw Slater sit up and lean into the laptop, cocking his head like he was listening closely with the better of his two aging ears. Skye turned up her headphone volume, but whatever Slater was listening to was too quiet for the crummy audio pickup in the trophy room.

She could hear Slater's response, though.

"Yes, that will be fine," he said in that curt, commanding tone he used with underlings, meaning, everyone he addressed. "We'll talk about the rest when I'm down there."

Slater snapped his laptop shut and got up to leave the room. So did Skye.

On the way out, she left Big Jim a Big Tip. Threw him some happy face. Because why not? Her great white whale was about to breach.

***

Skye got through Jacksonville and pulled into the first rest area she saw. She'd made it to Florida, and it was time to take stock and figure out next moves. On Monday, Paul had texted that his father was flying to Orlando at the end of the week. The advance notice gave her time to drive down—a break for Skye because flying creates a record of one's location. She'd borrowed Angelina's car, a wine-red Lexus stored at a garage up on 117th, telling her she'd booked a five-day team-building event with some Wall Street bros in the Adirondacks—a cover story that should hold as long as Angelina didn't check the odometer when Skye got back. The sixteen-hour drive had been a grind. She had only passed her Ohio driving test on the third try and had had no opportunity to improve her skills since then. She jerked and prodded the vehicle out of the city, gradually gaining confidence on the highway, but as the terror of imminent crash subsided, it was succeeded by a new torture, the minute-by-minute struggle to stay awake.

By day two, desperation prompted her to try an audiobook dug out from the bottom of Angelina's console, Vladimir Nabokov's *Lolita*—a multi-CD set covered with New York Public Library stickers, five years overdue. Nabokov wrote in a way that made her eager to see what crazy shit he'd lay on her next, so that helped her stay awake. The only break in Skye's narrative trance came when Lolita's mother got hit by a neighbor's car *exactly when Humbert needed her out of the way,* an "accident" so artificial that Skye pumped her horn, lowered the window and yelled out to a grizzled trucker as she passed, "He killed her, he fucking killed her!"

That was Georgia. She was rather punchy by then.

Slater has two properties in Florida: an estate on Jupiter Island and a beach villa on Keewaydin. Neither is anywhere close to Orlando, so Skye assumed Slater was going to Tony rather than bringing Tony to him. She still didn't know how to get at Slater, especially if he brought his bodyguards down. But she knew Slater was flying into Orlando, so that's where she was heading, to be in position when—if—opportunity knocked.

The rest stop outside Jacksonville was built like a hacienda from an old western movie, except these walls were unpitted and none of the paint was peeling. After rinsing her face and neck in cold water and raiding the vending machines for Red Bull and Funyuns, Skye headed toward the shaded picnic table furthest from the building. It backed up to a chain link fence enclosing an area of standing water. On the fence was a bright yellow warning sign: BEWARE OF VENOMOUS

SNAKES. Skye checked the concrete slab underneath the picnic table, making sure it was clear of venomous—well, *any*—snakes, and started to sit down, then changed her mind and climbed up onto the table, resting her feet on the bench. Skye took the BEWARE sign as another example of the gracious southern hospitality she'd experienced at every Taco Bell and Starbucks along I-95. Back in the boroughs, no one ever warned you of venomous snakes.

Skye lit a cigarette and pulled out her tablet. At her last pitstop, she'd come across something chewable on Samantha's Facebook history, a video of a grinning Sam in chest-high waders, netting fish from an electrified river, weighing them, and throwing them back into the water after they'd recovered their wits in the holding tank. Sam captioned the video, "THIS IS WORK?!" To which a user named "Antonio Tentoes" commented, "nah, sis, THIS is work," attaching a pic of two white, hairy calves propped on a patio table, foo-foo drink at hand, blue sea sparkling beyond a wrought iron balcony rail.

In the snap's background, a blurry but recoverable street sign: "Turtlemound Road." Just two Florida roads have that name, one in Melbourne, the other in Daytona Beach. Judging from Google Maps, no sea would be visible if the shot were taken in Melbourne.

She knew where Tony was hanging.

Progress, but not yet an endgame, due to two problems; one Big, the other Tall.

Skye sat on the table, picturing one line of attack after another while periodically checking the grass for signs of anything nasty slithering her way. She lit another cigarette and smoked it down to a butt, then one more, but nothing came to mind likely to satisfy her personal code of professional conduct: all contracts must be completed without getting her killed or collared.

She pitched her trash and walked around the hacienda, deliberately removing the job from her mind. It was warm and muggy, but it felt good being away from the city in a distant land where tall, thin trees had no branches and birds made sounds she'd never heard or imagined. The people looked much like the tourists constantly streaming through

Chinatown, just sweatier and with automobiles attached. The dogs were the same as everywhere.

A flat, grassy area to the right of the main building was designated for dog business. A DOG WALK sign had an arrow that was supposed to point to the right, except someone had bent it around the pole until the arrow pointed at the hacienda to the left, a mildly amusing trick since there was a big NO PETS ALLOWED warning posted on that building. Skye was wondering if the effort it took to bend the metal was worth the joke when she abruptly realized she knew how to complete the contract. She'd been working the entire job wrong-headed, *climbing a tree to catch a fish*, as one of the Chinese proverbs she liked put it.

She got in the car, started the engine and set her nav to Turtlemound Road in Daytona Beach but didn't back out. She sat in the parking lot, air conditioner on high, eyes flicking from one windshield bug splat to another as she turned the job up, down and around until she had the whole thing mapped, including how to get paid. Especially, how to get paid.

Back on the interstate, she played *Lolita* again. Earlier, whenever hometown memories of *her* live-in Humbert Humbert got sparked, she'd been quick to push those images away and pull her focus back onto Nabokov's story. This time was different. She gave her mind permission to go where it would. When Humbert's perverted machinations provoked a sense memory of panic or pain, she encouraged the dark haze of emotion to swirl and spin until it congealed and sank into her belly where, blind and deaf and without memory and beyond reason, it gestated as a single bare feeling, the hunger for prey. When that pelting hunger could not be contained, when it migrated out along the pathways of her nervous system making her knees shake and her fingers tremble, Skye knew she was ready to go to work.

***

Skye was supposed to meet Angelina at Robert's Chinese, the restaurant downstairs from the Spa, to return her car keys. She stood on the sidewalk out front, in no rush to go in. The sun was out, she'd gotten her money stashed—job fee from Bman plus the "bonus" from Slater—

and to make the morning even better, she'd dropped into Dragon Land Bakery on the way over and discovered that today was two-for-one day.

Skye took a bite of coconut cream and peered into the restaurant through the grime-streaked glass of the front door.

She didn't see Angelina. The place looked empty, other than a man sitting in a booth, staring down at his phone—another tourist under the misapprehension that Robert's was an actual restaurant serving actual food rather than a front for the Spa business upstairs. Something made her take a second look, though, and when she saw who it was, I wouldn't say she spit out her pastry, not exactly, but a chunk did dribble from her gaping mouth and fall to the sidewalk. Waste of good cream.

It was Babacar's day on security. She texted him she could use some help down at the restaurant when he had a minute. She leaned against the brick wall and chewed her lower lip until Babacar emerged from the unmarked Spa door, hands glistening like he'd been washing up in the restroom and hadn't taken the time to find a paper towel.

"We have an unwelcome visitor," Skye told him.

He started to enter the restaurant, but she stopped him with a hand on his forearm.

"Could you put him in the can, please, Bobby? I'll be right in. Thank you."

As he turned, Skye called out an afterthought:

"Don't break him."

She watched as Babacar pulled Paul from the booth and carried him through the dining room and into the kitchen, handling Paul the way Skye managed a plastic bag overstuffed with groceries—one arm to bear the weight, the other to keep everything settled and in place.

As she crossed the dining room, Skye picked Paul's dropped iPhone off the floor, powered it down, and slid it into her bag. In the back of the kitchen, Babacar stood with his massive arms crossed, watching the gray metal door shudder as Paul pounded on it from inside. The can had a toilet, a sink, a broken mirror, and, usually, a few supply boxes piled up along the wall. Maybe some toilet paper and hand soap, but probably not. The only thing distinguishing it from a million other backroom toilets in the city was this one had its lock on the outside.

Paul's muffled shouts, curses, and threats were audible but not especially interesting. Skye propped open the kitchen's back door, lit a cigarette, and asked Babacar how his teams were doing. By the time Paul exhausted himself she was caught up on Senegal Premier League standings and thoroughly briefed on how Ebola was wreaking havoc on preparations for this fall's Africa Cup.

"Is he carrying?" Skye asked, once the sound inside the room subsided.

Babacar shook his head and reached around her to turn the lock. When Paul started bellowing again, Babacar relocked the door and Skye said, loudly enough to be heard through the metal, "That's okay, I can come back tomorrow when you're feeling better."

The room got still again. Skye nodded to Babacar and he opened the door. Paul took a step toward the opening but pulled back when he saw who was standing behind her. Skye stepped into the room and waited to hear the lock behind her, then leaned against the door and considered Paul.

He looked like hell. His complexion was a spongy, mottled red, his face streaked with tears or sweat or both. His hair looked like he'd run a marathon yesterday afternoon and neglected to shower before going to bed. His clothes were twisted out of place, and he stood hunched over, rubbing his shoulder, and looking at Skye like he couldn't decide whether to kick her in the stomach or fall to his knees thanking her for coming to his rescue.

"Hurt yourself on the door?" Skye asked.

Paul looked at his shoulder and scowled. "No. You can thank your gorilla for this."

Skye's eyes narrowed. "You're not on your home turf here, Paul," she warned. "I'd suggest you watch your language."

Paul started to retort but saw Skye's expression and thought better of it.

Skye noticed that in his free hand, the one not massaging his shoulder, Paul clutched a small black flip-phone.

"Can I see that a minute," she said, holding out her hand.

"What? No. No, you can't."

She kept her hand where it was, waiting him out.

"Fine," he said, sighing dramatically as he handed over the phone. "Are you going to let me out now or what."

The phone was locked. Skye typed in 'F-R-E-D,' the original passcode she'd told him to change right away. The phone unlocked. She glanced up at Paul and shook her head, then checked the activity log and saw he'd made no calls since being thrown in the can. The perils of not committing any numbers to memory.

"Sit down," she said, pointing to the toilet seat.

"I asked when you were going to let me out."

"And I told you to sit down."

Paul stared at her for a moment, then trudged the one step to the toilet and fussily lowered himself onto the seat. He sat there, legs crossed, plucking at the pleat of his slacks like he was on the guest couch at Leno waiting for a commercial break to end.

"You really are a fuck-up, aren't you Paul?"

"Excuse me?"

"A royal fuck-up. I told you to get rid of this phone. I told you we were not to see each other again. Yet here you are."

"I tried to reach you all day and you didn't answer! What was I supposed to do?"

"Not this."

"I'm going to get rid of the phone after the job's done, like you said. Obviously, it's not done."

"Bagman dropped me the money this morning."

"He did what?" Paul asked, his voice rising. "Why would he do that? My father flew back yesterday. I saw him this morning. He's already planning his trip to that bristlecone forest, for Christ's sake!"

"Did you read my text?" Skye scrolled through his flip-phone to a message with *Daytona Beach News-Journal* screenshots, then held it out for his view.

Paul read the headline: "Game Designer Found Strangled in Apartment: Suicide or Autoerotic Accident?" He looked up at Skye. "Yeah, I saw—still don't know what it means."

"I guess you didn't read to the end." Skye tapped on the image. "Anthony Tencher," she intoned, "was son of the late Richard Tencher, acclaimed conservationist and professor of forestry at the University of California, Davis."

"Tencher's son," said Paul, slowly. "So he was …"

Skye nodded. "Your father's source."

"And you," he said, pointing uncertainly at the phone. "You did that?"

Skye shrugged. "Some sex games should never be played without a buddy." She hooked a thumb into the waistband of her black jeans. "I mean, a buddy who can be trusted."

Paul gazed at the dirty floor tiles at his feet. When he looked up, Skye saw something in his eyes she hadn't seen there before—fear. Fear of her.

He cleared his throat, then spoke carefully. "Tell Bman to refund my money. Or hand it back yourself. Cause that wasn't the job, was it?"

"Wasn't it?" Skye scrolled to the beginning of their message stream. "Check the contract."

Skye watched Paul's lips as he read silently. She didn't need to look at the text. She had it memorized:

> *Dominic Slater has a source willing to sell the location of the world's oldest tree. Contractor pledges to take him out before the information is exchanged.*

"Contractor," Skye said, "that's me. And the 'him' to be taken out …"

"Is Dominic, my father!" Paul blurted. "Not the source—obviously!"

"Pronouns generally point to the person mentioned most recently," Skye said calmly. "In this case, that would be the source, as I explained to Bman when I told him the job was finished. So, I would say—" she paused, picturing the twisted metal sign at the Florida rest stop— "yours is the bent reading."

Paul pressed the heels of his hands into his temples like he was trying to contain a great pressure in his head.

"This is life and death," he said, his voice shaking. "And you're playing fucking word games with me. Goddamn lying little whore."

Skye sighed at the utter predictability of men under stress. She checked Paul's bearings to make sure he wasn't about to lunge at her, then pursed her lips as if recalling a conversation.

"*My father is a monster, and he needs to be stopped,*" she quoted. "Well, he's been stopped—your beloved tree is safe."

"I told you—he's back at home, *with* the coordinates, making plans to go get that tree!"

"He's making plans to get *a* tree. Not *the* tree, I guarantee you that."

"How can you guarantee …?"

She arched her eyebrows, a teacher waiting for her struggling student to answer his own question. When his changing expression told her he was starting to get it, she continued: "This tree job will not be his last. Knowing your father, as I unfortunately do, he'll keep going after furry things until they cart him into the woods on a gurney, with a hospice nurse to squeeze his trigger finger. If somebody wanted to stop him for good—your father, not the hospice nurse—knowing exactly where he's headed in that huge bristlecone forest could be especially useful. And worth paying for."

"And you're in possession of this valuable info," said Paul haltingly, still coming up to speed, "because you're the one who sold him the made-up coordinates?"

"Turns out, Tencher has a sister who hates trees, really loves money, and—" Skye held out her hands in mock surprise "—happens to look just like me. Who knew? I wouldn't say the coordinates were 'made up,' though. I'd say: 'carefully selected to place him precisely in the middle of nowhere.'"

Paul shifted on the seat, picturing it.

"Where no one can hear him scream," he said finally.

"Or smell his putrefaction," she added.

"So," he said sourly, "this is about squeezing me for more money."

"I'm a professional, Paul. I do my due diligence. You're no more a protector of wildlife than your father. This I know. I also know you stand to inherit a mountain of money when he passes—in, what, fifteen years or so if left to natural causes? Meanwhile, you're forced to make do with floor scraps."

Paul stared at his loafers.

"I've seen the way he treats you, Paul, and it's not pretty. *Yet youth, the more it is wasted, the sooner it wears.* Are you wearing out, Paul? Had enough of your youth being wasted?"

Paul looked up at her, sullen but resigned. "What are you proposing?"

Skye closed the flip-phone with a *snick* and stuck it in the back pocket of her jeans.

"I'm going out for a bit, Paul, but I'll be back—in an hour, a day, not sure exactly."

He started to object but she stopped him with a raised finger.

"If you get thirsty, there's the tap. It usually works. If you feel like yelling some more, knock yourself out. On the other side of the wall is the karaoke machine we fire up Saturday nights. If you scream loud enough, the neighbors will think someone came in early to practice."

Skye rapped on the metal door.

"I'll come back with two new burner phones—*if* I've decided to help with your 'wasted youth' situation. Then we'll talk numbers."

Skye reached behind her for the door handle.

"And how to make sure you follow the fucking rules."

Company Man

by Joe Graves

2287 CE

Hondo and his two friends stood in the Main Projection Chamber, waiting for their final checks to be approved before they could travel back in time to catalog the first human mission to Mars.

Hondo had one job. It was the same job anytime the three of them were together. It wasn't a real job; it was more like a self-prescribed promotion. His job was simple: to keep his friends out of trouble, and so far, it had been the hardest job he had ever taken on, for Aiden and Zeke were as equally fun to be around as they were likely to break the rules.

Hondo had grown up isolated and homeschooled, in a family of time travelers and secrets. Aiden and Zeke were his first friends outside the family and the first to ever speak critically of his family and their company. He enjoyed what they had to say, or more so, the conviction from which they said it. Speaking in casual, or even base, ways about something everyone had treated as sacred was intoxicating.

"You never answered my question," Zeke said to Aiden.

Hondo peered into the corner where their handler was half-asleep in her chair, then to the control room window where the technicians busied themselves with final checklists. No one was paying attention, but he was ready to hush his friends if needed at any moment. He had been doing this for the past four weeks of orientation, often keeping the instructor from finding the notes they passed, the jokes they made, or the critiques they offered about… well, everything. Zeke, especially, had some quick-witted, insightful critiques of every lesson they had learned so far in their history classes. He was not only his first friend outside the family, but also his first black friend, and his view of the world was unlike anything Hondo had experienced back home.

"What question?" asked Aiden.

"The question I asked you earlier today: If you were to go back and change something in history, but you could only change one thing—what would it be?"

"Just one thing?" asked Aiden.

"Yes, the *one thing* you would change if it were up to you," repeated Zeke. "Quieter, you guys. They are going to hear you," said Hondo.

Zeke looked around and shook his head. "They can't hear us." "They might if you keep talking so loudly," said Hondo.

"Okay—okay, we'll be quiet: Hondo the Company Man ... always worried they will hear us."

It was a line he had said as a joke for the last four weeks of intensives—son of a board member, member of the family that owned the technology, the second nephew to the current CEO. It was a nickname he would have to accept, and he would be happy to, if it meant he could use his influence to keep his friends from getting marks on their record. But that would only be possible if they listened to him. The company studied history; they didn't change it, and any conversation about change would be a mark he couldn't get removed. With too many, they could kiss any shiny promotions goodbye.

Aiden ignored Zeke's comment and answered the question anyway. "I'd kill Hitler—as a baby," whispered Aiden. "That'd be the easiest way to do it, as a baby."

"Ha!?" said Hondo, much louder than he planned, and their old handler shifted in her seat and looked up at them. He did the very thing he had warned them about. They all stood still, smiling, pretending to be up to nothing, when they were in fact breaking the one cardinal rule: Don't change the past—don't even discuss it. She turned to the control room, and seeing they were still busy with the final details, bowed her head again.

"Hitler," whispered Aiden. "Absolutely."

It was an unoriginal answer, but it made sense given Aiden's half-German ancestry. He always seemed bothered by this part of German history: the rise of fascism and the pain it caused. People did this often; they'd hold on to the worst parts of their ancestors' history and claim that if only this or that were different, the world wouldn't be in such a mess. But killing Hitler would cause too many ripples. The same would be true if Zeke, because of his African ancestry, tried to do something about the Atlantic Slave Trade. It simply wasn't possible without risking their lives. History is not a sequence of isolated events; it is an ecosystem. Remove a foundational structure—however cruel—and the entire terrain reshapes itself. Languages shift. Borders dissolve before they are drawn. Economies never form. Migrations never happen. Families never meet. Children are never born. And somewhere along that chain, the line that leads to the observer breaks.

"You do realize how ridiculous that would be?" asked Hondo, saying it as sternly as he could without raising his voice to a level that would be heard by their handler. "You do that, and we'd all go missing."

"Damn the consequences! It'd be worth it." He laughed, then turned to Zeke. "What would yours be?"

Zeke looked at him and then stopped smiling. He opened his mouth to answer but didn't form any words.

"Come out with it," said Aiden. "I'd—"

"All's set. Let's get into our positions," said one of the technicians, his voice crackling through the speakers from the other side of the control room's glass.

Their handler shot up and walked over to them, adjusting her suit. "Yes, dears. The time has come. Hondo, you're first. Then Aiden. Zeke, hop in after them, just as we showed you."

They squeezed into the small projection chamber and held hands, typical among young cadets. Holding hands didn't assist the technology in any measurable way—not technically, but it did make Hondo feel better about it, and that was worth something. Then, with nothing but a blink, they were gone. Traveling through time was always quicker than one would expect and exciting … so they had been told. Hondo had hoped to enjoy his first projection. Yet, he found himself distracted. He couldn't help but consider what his answer would be. What would he change if he could?

He'd be lying if he said he hadn't considered it.

It was in the midst of these thoughts—trying to remind himself of why these rules existed in the first place—that he and his friends were standing in a small, wooded area, his ears attuned to the timeline, with leaves blowing overhead and then the sound of kids talking. That's when Aiden pointed to the yellow bus they were told to look for.

"Hurry, let's catch it."

He would have to set these questions aside.

They ran towards it and joined the kids in line as they exited the bus. Standing in line, they fumbled with their "phones," an ancient technology reflective of the time they were visiting, but by the time they figured out how to turn them on, a counselor was walking down the line of students to confiscate them.

Hondo was disappointed that he wouldn't have the opportunity to use one of those devices, but it didn't matter, he told himself. He didn't need it. (And he didn't have to worry about such difficult issues as the ramifications of changing the past, either.) For a whole week, he, Aiden, and Zeke worried about nothing but having fun and being kids. It was the best week of Hondo's life.

They were fourteen, but they were expected to pass as twelve-year-olds—the oldest age allowed for the young astronauts' camp, located a short hike from the launch site of the Mars mission scheduled for later that year. Undercover as campers and standing half a foot above most of the others, speaking with voices that had already dropped, they did their best to blend in. They had to make it the whole week without raising any red flags, and only on the last day of camp would they be given a tour of the launch facilities. Attending the entire week was the way to gain in-and-out access to scan the rudimentary launch equipment without unintentionally causing ripples on the timeline. This is how everyone traveled back in time: showing up early, staying till the end, and not making any waves in the process. It was the only way to keep everyone they cared about safe in the present.

On the final day of camp, they stood behind a waist-high railing, their camp badges bright against their assigned T-shirts, while a guide explained fuel ratios and countdown redundancies. The pad rose in the distance, and it was hard to get a clear view of it, even if they leaned over the railing, which they were promptly told not to do.

"We will move to a new viewing area in a second, and you'll be able to see it better."

Zeke didn't stop leaning over the rail and he wasn't looking at the launch area to their right. He was looking down and to the left towards a stack of canisters and computers with technicians working. Hondo tapped his shoulder, hoping to get his attention without getting them in trouble. That's when Hondo noticed what he was looking at. Off to the side, near a cluster of storage containers, a kid about their age moved quickly between shadows. He kept his head down, timing his steps between passing technicians. It was clear that he wasn't supposed to be there.

"Do you see him?" Zeke whispered.

Before Hondo could answer, a security guard changed direction. The kid bolted behind a barrel. "That kid? Why?" he asked. It was the late 21st century, a century known for the unusual number of homeless families due to the rise of a rather brutal authoritarian government. They were told to expect it, especially outside the safety of their camp. *Like rats scrounging for something to eat*, his camp counselor had said.

"If he's not careful, he'll get caught," said Zeke.

The kid was hiding, but the guard was walking right towards the boy. He'd be caught for sure. "Not our problem."

Zeke lifted his hands to his mouth, as if he was about to yell down towards him—maybe to warn him, or distract the guard, or both—but before he could, Hondo grabbed his arm and pulled him away from the railing. Zeke shoved him off and looked down into the launch area. It was too late. The guards had seen the kid and grabbed him. Before they knew it, he was zip-tied and dragged off, yelling. Everyone in their group paused and turned as they listened to the guards calling him a *rat, camp trash, illegal*, and every other slur common for that time period.

Zeke was not happy, but Hondo grabbed his arm again anyway. "Look. It wasn't our problem. If you're not careful, you're going to cause a ripple."

Zeke stared at Hondo in a way he hadn't seen before, his eyes deep. He looked angry. "Company man, right?" This time it didn't seem funny. It didn't feel like a nickname. It felt much worse, and he couldn't understand why. He was only doing his job. He was only trying to keep Zeke out of trouble.

Around the corner, they held their gaze carefully to capture the rudimentary launch equipment just like they had been trained. When camp was over, they headed to the bus stop, where they disappeared into the woods. From there, the agency brought them back home without anyone noticing. In all, their mission was a success. A minor ripple at the railing—quickly contained before it reached review status. Hondo even received commendation for it, which, for reasons Hondo couldn't understand, wasn't celebrated by Zeke in the least. He never once said thank you for keeping him from making such an obvious mistake. Zeke didn't understand the company like Hondo, and maybe he didn't fully appreciate just how important obeying the rules was to the company's leaders. Zeke would never make it far if he didn't start listening to him more.

When they returned, their families celebrated at a restaurant overlooking the river, the kind of place that pretended it had always been there even though it wasn't much older than Hondo. The tall ceilings and larger, stone-framed, curved windows felt more like historical appropriation than an honest homage, as if the whole building was trying to feel more important than it was.

While their families sat together waiting for their dinner to arrive, Hondo and Zeke stood outside on the balcony. They had left Aiden to the torment of his mother who told story after story of how difficult he was as a baby.

The night was cool, and the river looked like black glass against the streetlamps. The restaurant door quieted the laughter inside.

Zeke leaned against the railing, staring out at the water. "Do you know the problem with all of this?" Hondo looked down at the river. It wasn't an authentic river, of course. A fabricated one, next to a fabricated building, all made to look like an Earth that no longer existed. "It's quite the waste of water, isn't it?"

Zeke turned and looked at Hondo, his brow squished. "What?" He turned back and looked at the water. "No, not the fake-ass river. I mean our mission—*the* mission."

Hondo would much rather discuss the injustice of a fake river and its role in the water crisis in underserved areas than to hear about how Zeke disagreed with his family. Not to mention, he was still a little annoyed that Zeke hadn't even once thanked him for saving him from a life as a lower-rank historian.

He turned and leaned against the rail and looked up into the stars. "I can't stop thinking about that kid."

"What kid?"

"The kid who got arrested while we were scanning the shuttle. He had the exact same view of the rocket as we did; in fact, I bet that, from his angle and access, he had an even better view of the equipment. A true behind-the-scenes. So, why send us back as campers? Why not as someone like him?"

"Don't be ridiculous. And get arrested like him? Who would even accept that kind of mission?"

"Why not?"

"You'd be ok spending the week running for your life, getting caught, sent to prison, or worse?"

"Sure, it has its risks. But don't you think that seeing the world through his eyes might give us more data on how to improve our future than spending a week on ziplines and swimming in a lake with a bunch of rich kids? Even if we got arrested—maybe *especially* if we got arrested."

"I... I don't know?" and Hondo truly meant it. He wasn't sure what point Zeke was trying to make.

"I think it will tell us exactly what we'd need to know to make a difference, and that's why they'd never let us."

"That's not fair. My family has invested all of our resources into improving the future." "For who?"

"For everyone!"

"If that's true, then... then... well, they wouldn't mind letting me be the first to catalogue the African slave trade from the perspective of a person of color, right?"

"As a slave!?"

"Or something similar. Send me back to experience history the way my people had. If you want to improve the future, we should study the past from *my people's* perspective."

Hondo's face turned red, and he was hot, and he found himself angry for reasons he couldn't understand. Why would Zeke suggest such a thing? There are far more comfortable ways to study that part of history. Whether it's from the perspective of a slave or a slave owner, the facts were the same. And none of this race stuff mattered; if the world didn't change its trajectory, it would only get worse for everyone.

He had always found Zeke's perspectives intoxicating, so why was this bothering him so much now?

Zeke asked, "Do you want to know the real reason they'd never send us back as homeless kids?"

"Sure." Hondo really wanted to say "no" and move on from the whole conversation before he said something he'd regret.

"It's because it'd be too hard to make you look like one. Aiden and I would blend right in.

But you … well … history has been kind to your people."

"That's not true! You know as well as I that white kids were homeless in the late 21st century."

"Did you see any when we were there?"

Hondo wasn't going to answer that. Of course, he hadn't seen any, but that didn't mean they didn't exist.

That's when he realized why this was bothering him so. He was fine with Zeke complaining about the privilege of white people as long as it wasn't directed at him. Why was Zeke treating him like an enemy? He was only trying to help. He had only ever tried to help. He had heard enough and knew he had to walk away from this. He pushed off the railing when Zeke grabbed his arm.

"Look, thank you for helping me on the railing. You were right, if I want to make a difference, I need to keep my job."

Hondo took a breath. "You're welcome. All I was trying to do was help."

"I understand. It's just… well, history is a lot harder for people like me than for people like you, you know."

"Yeah. I know."

That was something Hondo could understand. While some talked about the past as if it were the golden era, it was anything but. Hondo could acknowledge that there were some simple pleasures in the past that aren't available anymore. He loved seeing unpolluted rivers, waterfalls, and trees—so many trees—but he also knew that in some parts of history, people who looked like him were not kind to people who looked like Zeke. He understood that, and that's why he did his best to help him get through the orientation without any marks. That's why he wanted him to be a historian. He knew the agency could learn a lot from Zeke.

"We good?" Hondo asked.

"Of course, Company Man." Zeke smiled, slapping his back. "We're good."

2297 CE

The folder was thinner than Hondo expected. It had been ten years since his first mission, and he had been receiving threats from his family to be moved off the timeline. He worried this was the next step in their insistence. The folder lay on the table between them, matte black and unmarked. That alone told him what it wasn't. It wasn't a mission. Missions came in thick packets, layered with contingencies and redundancies, all the ways things could go wrong cataloged in advance.

This was something else.

His new handler sat across from him, his hands folded, posture neutral, eyes unreadable, like any good manager: A skill they wanted Hondo to have—and if his fears turned out to be true, a skill he'd soon learn.

"You're late," he said.

"Traffic."

"This won't take long." The handler slid the folder toward Hondo with two fingers.

Hondo didn't open it right away. "Is this another extension?" he asked. "I just finished a clean run in Australia. No ripples. Zero."

"I know. That's why you're here."

Hondo waited for an explanation. When it didn't come, he opened the folder: One page. Just one. His name was at the top, his clearance code was beneath it, and a location was stamped in bold: Buenos Aires – *Department of Timeline Preservation.*

"This is a mistake! I asked to stay on the timeline—just a few more cycles. I'm not—" He stopped himself. *Not ready* sounded childish. "I'm more useful out there."

"You've been useful," he said. "That's the problem." "Argentina," he said. "Why Argentina?" "Perspective, I guess."

"From what?"

The handler was about to answer when the door behind him opened. Hondo didn't have to turn around to know who it was. His mother's footsteps were measured, the sound of someone who never hurried. She didn't need to. She stopped beside him, close enough that he could smell her perfume. It smelled old, like the way linens smell when they've been in storage too long, mixed with a bit of artificial flower.

She looked at the folder.

"So," she said. "They finally stopped indulging you."

Hondo closed it. "I wasn't done traveling."

She took the seat beside him without asking. "You were done years ago. You just didn't want to admit it."

"This is management. You said …"

"*I said* I would let you earn it," she interrupted. "This isn't an executive role. Don't flatter yourself."

The handler stood. That was his cue to disappear. "You'll receive your relocation details by morning," he added, already halfway to the door.

"You could've stopped this," Hondo said quietly to his mother.

She folded her hands in her lap. "I could've delayed it. That's not the same thing."

He stared at the folder again. "I didn't want to end up like my cousins stuck in stuffy offices, unaware of what's really going on in the world."

"Good. Then don't. Go see the world, as you say, but this time, in the present."

His wrist buzzed. A message notification pulsed faintly against his skin. He glanced down before he could stop himself. It was a message from Aiden.

He didn't open it, but his mother noticed anyway. "Still hearing from him?"

"Sometimes."

"He's a part-time historian, I hear. In and out of rehab. Tragic, really."

It *was* tragic, and Hondo wished he had done more to help him over the years. Then he got another ping. This time it was Zeke. He looked at his mother and asked, "Did you tell all of my friends about this?"

"I thought you'd need some encouragement. Go ahead, take the call. I'll leave you." "I didn't ask for this."

His mother stood, "None of us do." She paused at the door. "Make me proud," she added. "Or at least don't embarrass us."

When she was gone, Hondo picked up the folder again and answered the call.

Zeke's voice came through thin and wind-worn, layered with distant surf and the low murmur of people nearby.

"I finally made it." "Made it where?"

"The coast," Zeke said. "West Africa. Later today, I'll be walking the ports. Cataloging the markets, the ships."

Hondo pictured him squinting into the sun, skin dark against darker bodies, trying not to stand out in a place where standing out could get you killed.

"They actually cleared you for it?"

Zeke laughed. "*Cleared* is a strong word. More like they stopped finding excuses." "You always said you'd get there."

"And you always said I shouldn't." There was a pause. The surf grew louder. "Are you sitting behind a desk yet?"

"She told you about my promotion?"

"Yeah, and should I say *congratulations* or *my condolences*?"

"I didn't ask for it." "I know."

"I tried to stay out there," Hondo said. "On the timeline. I begged. But they're sending me to the Office of Timeline Preservation in Argentina. So much for traveling the timeline."

"Still—it makes me feel better." "Why?"

"Because if something goes wrong, at least it'll end up on your desk." "You shouldn't be joking about that."

"I'm not joking," Zeke replied. "I'm relieved. I wouldn't be here without your help, and we all know keeping me out of trouble is really the most important job you've had. Now it's official. You'll get paid to do what you've tried to do anyway." He laughed, and Hondo found himself wanting to laugh along with him but couldn't. "Let's make this a tradition—every year on the anniversary of our promotions, let's chat."

Nothing about either role felt like a promotion, but Hondo agreed anyway, "Sure."

"I've got to go. I'll be heading back to the 1600s soon. If you're curious, check my feed. You'll be able to do that in your new office, I'm sure."

"I will. And be careful."

"Always."

2302 CE

Hondo sat in his office the way he did most afternoons: leaned into his monitor just enough to make it look like he was working, his fingers resting on a keyboard to further sell the lie, while he watched the latest episode of a show that was far too boring to watch at home, but more interesting than anything left on his to-do list. His lunch sat heavy in his gut, the kind of meal chosen because the restaurant was nearby, reliable, and came with a receipt he could add to his expense sheet. If his family was going to make him work in middle management, he'd take advantage of every benefit.

He had just lifted his mug of this morning's coffee, now cold, when one of his analysts knocked on his door.

"Yes?"

Hondo took a sip out of habit, then spat it back into the mug.

"A ripple," the man said.

Just what he needed. At least ripples were interesting and far better than the mindless, brain-numbing tasks of reviewing employee timecards and doing performance reviews.

"Where?" he asked.

The analyst handed Hondo a set of coordinates. Hondo closed the video he was watching and opened the Global Timeline Interface. The analysts had recorded the ripple in 1619 along the West Coast of Africa.

"Zeke?" he asked—out loud—not meaning to.

"Who?" asked his analyst.

"I want a full report on every historian in the field for this time and location. Now."

He didn't need the report; what he needed was for the analyst to leave his office so he could gather himself. He already knew who it was. There was only one active historian in that part of the timeline. Zeke had been researching a particular slave ship, spending multiple trips scanning and tracking it, going back even to its construction, when it was retrofitted to hold human bodies in the cargo hold. It had helped the agency gain unprecedented details on the nature of the African slave trade. He had been doing this for years—multiple missions, each with minor ripples that Hondo cleaned up without anyone noticing. He stared at his computer screen, sipping the cold coffee this time as if it were no longer disgusting. The bitter taste of cold, old coffee matched the moment.

His analyst returned. "You were right, sir."

"What?"

"It's someone named *Zeke*?" He laid the ripple report on his desk: *Historian ZF-419*. Zeke's internal designation was typed across the top. He had caused a *4.98rp* ripple before dropping down and hovering around *4.1rps*. It was the worst possible ripple one could get and still be handled by middle management. Anything more, and it would have alerted the entire department.

Immediately, Hondo had control of Zeke's feed, but he had to wait for it to connect. The image came in blurry as the feed switched, giving him access to Zeke's line of vision. The first thing he saw was the ocean lapping against a wooden dock and the waves drifting towards the horizon. As the sun sat low in the sky, seagulls filled the air. Then Zeke turned, and the digital image stabilization kicked in, slowing the image down so Hondo could see everything more clearly. At the end of a long dock sat the same large ship Zeke had been studying for the past few years, its flag at the top of its mast fluttering in the wind. And running the length of the dock were people with dark skin like Zeke's, all bare-backed, standing in a line, chains connecting them.

Zeke slowly lowered his gaze to his hands. They were chained with thick, rough iron shackles, pitted and reddish with old rust, biting into his wrists each time the line pulled him forward. Then, with his chained wrist, Zeke reached up and wiped his face, and when he brought his hand back down, there was blood.

Hondo slammed his desk. This was precisely what he said would happen. "We need to pull him out of there, first chance we get," Hondo yelled to his analyst.

"Can't right now, boss—too many ripples."

"I know we can't do it now, but as soon as possible," he said, knowing he'd stay up all night if he had to. He wasn't going home until Zeke was safely back in the 23rd Century.

***

The light in the break room flickered, and Hondo had already submitted three support tickets about it. "The ballast needs replacing." When Hondo asked what a ballast was, the building manager explained it and added, "It's not like those old ballasts from the 20th century—not related to them at all, just a familiar term from an outdated technology."

He looked back up at the ceiling. He wasn't going to complain about the light again. The building manager had enough to worry about. It was people like the manager who cared about things in the present, allowing Hondo and others to invest so much time in the past, and, by extension, the future. Trying to rationalize this—how his investment in the past protected the future, but only possible because of the building manager's ability to fix flickering lights in the present—made his head hurt, especially given the hour of the night. So, in the light of a flickering bulb, Hondo made a fresh pot of coffee.

It was 1 AM, Zeke had been loaded onto the ship, packed into the lower level, bodies lined up like a drawer of neatly folded socks. They couldn't pull Zeke out with so many people watching. Pulling a historian out in broad daylight with so many people around him went against everything historians believed in. The last time that happened—

when a guy just vanished into thin air—an entire religion was born. It took half a year of adjustments to get that religion worked out, but it could never really be wiped from the timeline altogether. A small group still gathers for worship in the hills of Switzerland—more of a cult now than anything.

In the meantime, all he could do was watch and wait. With a hot cup of coffee and some stale snacks he found in the cupboard, he woke his monitor back up. Zeke was staring at the wooden frame in front of him. The space they held him had to be less than 3 feet tall. He had to crawl to get into his spot, and the bodies were crammed into the space so tight that it was hard to tell whose arms were Zeke's and whose were his neighbor's.

For the next hour, Hondo sat and stared, slowly sipping his coffee. He sat so still, and sipped so carefully, that his office lights kept turning off. He'd have to throw off the small blanket he had wrapped around him and wave his hands like some flamboyant dancer just to get them to turn back on.

Hondo kept a pulse on Zeke's vitals, and while his blood pressure was raised, it wasn't even close to registering shock, which was shocking. *Why wasn't Zeke freaking out?* Around 3 AM, Zeke finally closed his eyes, and Hondo leaned back, relieved. He must have fallen asleep. It seemed many others had fallen asleep as well, but not enough to drop the ripple meter to a level where they could pull him. By this time tomorrow, the ship would be out to sea, and in the madness of the waves crashing, they could pull him without anyone noticing.

With Zeke asleep, Hondo finally gave himself permission to turn away from the monitor.

Stacked on the corner of his desk were every available report, thick manila envelopes filled with paperwork. He had already been told the summary and important details from his analyst before he sent him home for the night, but with some respite from Zeke's feed, he figured he'd do his own digging.

First, the mission reports: Zeke had been cataloging the slave market near the Kwanza River.

He was supposed to be a well-respected indentured servant of a prominent trader, similar to his previous missions, which would have given him the freedom to roam the port without disrupting the timeline. It was while he was working as an indentured servant that he encountered his first ripple.

Second, the ripple report: It was filled with every available detail outlining the infraction. Zeke had found himself among the mob boarding the slave ship. Because of his dark skin, they must have mistaken him for an enslaved person, and he was shackled and put into the line. He put up a bit of a fight and cursed the guards in a language they didn't understand, but a tone they could easily translate—which is how he got the bloody nose.

Finally, the third report: It included a full report on Zeke's ancestry. This would ensure there weren't any historical prejudices that could undermine the mission. With his previous ripples, this wasn't needed, for they had never registered above a *3.8rp*. This time was different, and an ancestry report would be required in his final reports on the incident. The agency would never send someone like Zeke within walking distance of his ancestors, given their low social status. It was too risky. Had they been comfortable or wealthy, it would have been fine. But whenever a people group experiences oppression, the agency is careful not to place their descendants too close to the action. Even the best historians can be temperamental when pushed to their limits.

He flipped through Zeke's ancestors. Before being sold as slaves, they served as a kind of primitive judges, settling disputes and carrying out justice when crime took place. They were sold out by a rival village and eventually shipped to Jamaica. As far as Hondo could tell, his reports had no ties to his ancestry line. He was about to close the folder when he noticed an image on one of the reports about his family. He pulled it close. It was the ship used to transport them across the Atlantic, and on top was a flag he recognized. He pulled up the archive of Zeke's feed and rewound it until he was back on the dock, looking at the ship. He paused and zoomed in.

It was the same flag. It was the same ship. Zeke knew. He was on the same ship as his ancestors would have been.

Hondo logged in and looked up the details in the timeline—details that wouldn't be included in the ripple report, for no one had flagged it yet. It was a bit ironic, Hondo thought, having it flagged for something as obvious as a literal flag. The ship that carried Zeke would sail to the Americas, then back to Africa, circle the Cape, dock on the eastern coast, and transport one of his direct ancestors to the island of Jamaica, where, if you traced his line, it led to Zeke.

Hondo pushed his chair back.

***

"Boss, did you get any sleep?" his analyst asked.

It startled him, and he turned. "No, and we need to pull him. Go ahead and get the paperwork filed for an early release."

"Are you sure, boss?"

"Yes. Do it. Now."

No sooner had the analyst left and the door closed when Zeke's ripple meter went off. Hondo turned to his feed. Zeke was awake, the sun now skirting through the planks of wood, lighting his face. He lifted his finger to the dark wood above him. The wood was damp and soft beneath his nail, leaving pale grooves that stood out against the blackened grain. In the ceiling's grime, he dragged his fingernail into the moist lumber, leaving clear marks in their modern dialect—and with each letter, the ripple meter beeped.

"This is the one," it read.

The ripple meter hovered at 4.2 — well above the 3.0 extraction threshold. Anything above that required executive override. If he pulled him out before that, he'd end up with a mark in his permanent record. What was he thinking? None of that mattered! He had to stop thinking like a company man and think about what would be best for Zeke. Whatever Zeke was up to, he had to stop him; it didn't matter what demerits they got. He had to be brought back home.

Hondo grabbed the black box on his desk with one hand and keyed in Zeke's exit code with the other. He reached for the switch and flipped it, but nothing happened. He had put the code in wrong!

The ripple meter ticked to 4.5.

Zeke wiped the words from the ceiling with his palm. The meter dipped slightly. Then he carved again into the damp wood.

"Hondo, thanks for the help." The meter jumped.

Zeke erased it and wrote once more. "I'll miss you, friend."

"Damn it." Hondo re-entered the authorization string, hands suddenly unsteady. The meter climbed—4.7.

On the screen, Zeke moved with calm precision. He pried loose a thin shard of metal from the frame above him. Then another from beneath the floorboard. A third piece slid free from a narrow compartment hidden in the hull. Hondo watched as he entered his extraction code again, now feeling it was far too long to be useful in emergency situations like this: now 4.9. Zeke struck the metal once. A spark flared and vanished. He struck it again. Fire caught inside the compartment. 5.34.

Hondo finished the exit code, double-checked it was right, and slammed the extraction button as the screen turned white. It was too late.

He sat back in his seat. His monitor displayed the wreckage, a ship blown to pieces. Zeke had been pulled, his body sent to the nearest facility in West Africa. He was dead before he reached the table.

***

After surviving the shock of losing his friend, Hondo had new problems to deal with. "The board was on the line," which meant his mother was on the line and he'd never hear the end of it.

They had a dead historian, a ship explosion, including all of the lives of those who were supposed to live and go on to have children who would have children—a major disruption of the present.

Hondo's analyst had been lost in the shuffle—not a direct descendant of anyone on the ship but connected tangentially enough that he no longer existed.

Hondo leaned into the speaker on his desk to hear the board's secretary read the official report, which, even for the board, had been heavily redacted.

"According to the recently updated logs, the vessel experienced an internal explosion. No survivors were recorded. Extraction protocols were initiated within seconds. Historian ZF-419 was retrieved moments after the blast and transferred to the nearest facility. He was pronounced deceased prior to surgical intervention."

Zeke had carried elements of his rudimentary bomb onto this ship over the course of a couple of dozen missions. And Hondo was so focused on covering Zeke's little ripples along the way that he hadn't once thought they were connected. It was brilliant, just like Zeke.

"Never easy to lose an agent," said one board member.

"A horrible catastrophe indeed!" said another, "Agents taking history into their own hands, deciding what to change."

"We're lucky none of us disappeared!"

"We must contain this, or we risk him being an example to others."

"We will have to make *him* an example."

"Now, now, everyone. Let's not get carried away," inserted Hondo's mother, "Hondo, can you please explain what happened in your own words?" she asked.

Hondo swallowed. "I—Zeke—he… I…"

"Yes, *Zeke*. Of course." Her tone was softer now. "In cases like this—when it's personal, I mean—we can receive your official statement at a later date, but having the chance to address the board now is a privilege you shouldn't take lightly."

Hondo closed his eyes.

"Right, that's enough for now," inserted his mother. "We can wait for your official report."

"In the meantime, we should also tell him. Right?" a board member asked. "About his reassignment? Wouldn't want him to wait to hear about it."

Hondo looked up.

"Yes. Hondo, you'll be reassigned to an executive role," his mother added. "Outside Time Preservation. You'll take mandatory leave while we conduct a full review. When you return, you will be assigned to a different role."

As if things couldn't get any worse … another promotion.

***

The ground was warm beneath Hondo's shoes. Fine red dust worked its way into the seams and clung to the hem of his trousers no matter how often he brushed at it. The air smelled of sunbaked earth and salt carried inland from the coast. Somewhere beyond the trees, the ocean's waves crash against the eroded shores.

It was a beautiful country, even after all that had been lost. It felt wrong that it took a funeral to bring him here.

Zeke's family didn't exist anymore, at least not in the way they had. They were still living in their homeland, and it was unlikely that Zeke would ever be born in that line. The ripple was too significant for that. The ship he blew up never made it back to the other side of Africa, and this disrupted the packaging of enslaved people enough for his family to be overlooked in their village.

Hondo wasn't the only person at the funeral. The man who had come and sat beside him cleared his throat and Hondo turned. He almost didn't recognize Aiden. His hair fell down his back now, streaked with gray. A beard hid most of his light olive face, but his eyes were steady in a way they hadn't been when Hondo had last seen him.

"Didn't think I'd see you here." Hondo whispered.

Aiden smiled and whispered, "Didn't think I'd survive long enough for it."

"How are you?"

"Been sober three years now."

"That's good … Sorry, I wasn't there for you. I feel like I should have done more."

"It's fine. It was something I needed to figure out."

They hugged, and Aiden pulled out his phone. "I've got a kid," he said, swiping. He was about to go on about his new family when the first speaker interrupted them.

One by one, official personnel stepped forward to share remarks. They all had the unique ability to use a lot of fine words without saying anything of substance. Hondo wasn't scheduled to say anything. He wanted to but was afraid of what he'd say. He was afraid he'd say too much. There were conversations appropriate in front of high-ranking officials and conversations just for friends. He didn't need to risk his future with the company.

Near the end, when it was almost over, Aiden leaned in. "What was that all about?"

"You noticed, huh?"

"Felt more like a mission debrief than a funeral. What really happened?"

"It was… well, it's complicated. Classified, you know."

"Classified? Really? Fine, keep your secrets, Company Man."

Aiden laughed, but Hondo didn't find it funny. Aiden was right—Zeke too—all those years. He was, in all measurable ways, nothing but a company man. The thought sat in his stomach with such weight, he wondered if he might throw up. That's when someone from behind him leaned forward and tapped his shoulder.

"Hondo, congrats on your recent promotion," he said. "I'd love to share my CV with you if you'd ever be interested in looking at it. I think I'd make a great manager if given the chance. Let me know if I can…" and the man went on, whispering during the funeral, as the last speaker finished his mission debrief-style remarks and Hondo felt that the one person who kept him from being nothing but a company man was no longer here, nothing but ashes in an urn.

Hondo brushed the hand of the stranger off his shoulder and stood up. He adjusted his suit as everyone turned to look at him. If he didn't say something, he'd regret it forever.

At the podium, he took a breath, adjusted the mic, and began. "I'm Hondo, and I've known Zeke since our first orientation. We went on our first mission together. Me, Zeke, and Aiden, too," he said, gesturing to Aiden. "I still remember that first mission. I remember standing in the projection chamber, so nervous. I didn't want anything to go wrong. But I was traveling with Zeke, and nothing went right when he was around." A few in the audience laughed nervously. "And on that platform, before ever even stepping onto the timeline, Zeke asked us a question—one we were told never to ask." He looked at Aiden, who nodded. "*If you could change one thing in the past, what would it be?* I loved those kinds of conversations, but only if they were secret. I'd never bring it up in any official capacity. I'd bet a day's wages you all do the same—in back rooms and behind closed doors, but never where anyone of importance can hear it. And that's what bothers me the most. Because maybe someone important should hear it." He wiped his eyes, which were starting to fill with tears. "Zeke never had the chance to tell us what he'd change, but in the end, he showed us." Hondo laughed. The kind of laugh when nervousness and grief work their way out in all the wrong ways. "I tried to stop him. I was going to stop him from making the world a better place. Generations of his family no longer know the horrors of slavery. Sure, we lost some people, but it's not like they died. They just never existed, and those aren't the same thing. Other people exist now in their place, and they live in a world that is just a little bit better than it was a week ago. It was all he ever wanted, and I tried to stop him, just like I was trained. And I would have, but I got his extraction code wrong. Switched the numbers—an accident, or maybe somewhere in my subconscious, it was on purpose. I'm not sure." He laughed again, shaking his head, and then straightened up and looked out at everyone. "Whatever the reason, I'm glad I did. And if I had the chance, I'd do it again, only this time it would be on purpose."

He left the podium and went back to his seat as the audience sat in stunned silence.

Aiden leaned in toward Hondo and whispered. "Not much of a company man after all, huh?"

I Walk Away Considerably More Unhappy and Disappointed in the Human Species

by Roy Bentley

Like right after the first time that I had sex. I
was 19. In the air force. She was twice my age,

Colombian. Approximated my name as *Bethlehem*.
I was enthusiastic to step away from being green

to intimacy, Sex, and so wound up at a single-wide
by the train tracks that ran through Rantoul, Illinois—

she cranked open a few louvered windows. You get
the picture: I'm That Guy Who Will Do. Just some

airman with a '71 Firebird and nowhere else to be.
But this was my first time, and she gave me the Clap.

Maybe if I had spoken a little Spanish and had, later,
known to say, cheerfully, coldly, *We have gonorrhea*

and she hadn't shouted what she shouted. Something
negative about the women of the Midwest who would,

according to her, fuck anyone and without protection.
As if she wasn't my first. Which she was … or had been.

So, how did I feel walking away from her house trailer
by the train tracks? How do you guess? Not too good.

Like someone had robbed me and I might never hear
the word *gonorrhea* and fail to recall Rosita Flores.

Like there's having sex and there's getting fucked
and needing a boatload of antibiotics to move on—

like it feels to have Donald Trump as president and
a clown-car full of Christian nationalists in charge.

Labyrinth and Minotaur

by R. Luce

At thirty, Dave Nichols had done his duty as primary caregiver to his brother, Luke, who was about to graduate with a degree in engineering from MIT. In addition to the pride that came with helping Luke survive the loss of their parents and giving him a future, Dave had been proud of his own accomplishments: BA and MA degrees paid for with hard work, what little he got from his parents' "estates" (he found the word *estates* ridiculous in his parents' cases) and student loans; a job working for one of New York's oldest advertising firms; a great income; a plush apartment in Bay Ridge; and what looked like opportunities for advancement in the near future. Though he didn't necessarily love advertising, he felt like he had made good on his childhood determination to "make it" despite his early experiences and the struggles that came with trying to negotiate the world without parental support for the past fifteen years.

He enjoyed having money, buying high-quality products and services, and being able to afford to splurge on himself and his brother occasionally. And now that his brother was graduating and would soon be working and taking care of himself financially, he was anticipating new ways of enjoying the money he was making … at least, he had been enjoying it right up to the day when he was told that his services at the VML agency were no longer needed.

When Dave asked for the reason, his supervisor stumbled across phrases such as, "We hold our employees to the highest standards of conduct particularly in their interactions with clients" and "sometimes we have to make decisions that we don't like, but which become necessary …." When the imperious, pinch-faced little man finished stumbling through the many words that amounted to "You're fired," Dave said, "Cochran complained, didn't he?"

"You called him a moron."

"No. Actually, I called him a *fucking* moron." As Dave said it, the supervisor's face started turning red. "I've told you a number of times about him and the way he treats me, making demands of me that aren't in the contract, coming up with constant changes he wants made that contradict what he had agreed to in previous meetings … all while belittling me, swearing at me, treating me like a child; you did nothing. And now you are going to fire me for doing what you wouldn't do yourself?"

"We will not have a client treated that way … calling him a moron," the man said.

"'Fucking moron,' that's what I called him." Dave's temper getting the better of him, he continued, "As far as I'm concerned, you are the one who should be fired; you aren't as smart or as capable as that fucking moron Cochran. I smell a lawsuit in the air. Can you smell it, you idiot?" Smells like satisfaction to me. With that, he walked out of the door strutting with a young man's cock-sure belief that he could go down the street, walk into another agency and be given a great job at a much higher salary. Reality would take a while to set in.

Over the next couple of weeks, he worked full time searching for a job amongst New York agencies, but when potential employers called VLM for references, they didn't like what they heard. It was readily apparent that his former supervisor put the word out on the street that Dave Nichols had committed the unpardonable sin of infuriating a top client, and the client had threatened to move his lucrative account to another agency. Word spread like a confession in a what's-said-here-stays-here AA meeting out into the local community faster than the confessor could get through the hand-holding end of the meeting, out of the building, and into the parking lot.

After numerous polite rejections and non-responses to his applications, calls and queries, it became obvious that there wouldn't be any interviews, and no offers, from top paying advertising firms. The blackballs had been thrown in all directions, and Dave would keep falling on his backside as they rolled under his feet. Meanwhile, the bills came in and tore at the flesh of his savings. The apartment took a huge bite out of what he had; utilities chomped away steadily, demanding their usual portions as did laundry service and food costs; then there was the insurance company and the storage facility that held his car. All these gluttonous beasts adding their mysterious service fees that fed unnamed entities deep within their systems that even the employees who worked there couldn't explain.

From the day of his firing, Nichols estimated he would go broke within two months if he didn't find employment, and that was based on the belief he would probably have to live on Ramen noodles and bologna for some of that time. He gave up everything that wasn't necessary, packed his nightlife at the clubs into a mental box to be stored amongst his hopes "to be opened soon" and gave all his energy to looking for something he could do that would pay.

Like a PT boat in a war zone, Nichols dashed around the lumbering behemoths of New York, applying to publishing companies, agents, corporations of all kinds looking for writers and who offered salaries that would allow him to keep his apartment and pay expenses. He was meeting with people he knew who might know the people he wanted to know and brazenly making pitches to people he could find unguarded by their overzealous office staff, and he was "working" his phone and computer for many hours each day trying to make connections without much luck.

Early in the second month of what he called "the job search shuffle" (search, apply, make follow up calls, hear nothing or be told the "position has been filled"), he allowed himself to think of moving, going someplace where he could afford to live even if the pay was less, even doing something else for a while. Jobs he never dreamed he would consider suddenly started sounding more appealing to him. That's when he began toying with the idea of government work.

It made sense to Dave that selling political ideas was not all that different from what he'd been doing with promoting products and services. The challenge was to find a position that would pay him well and stretch his talents. The research skills he had acquired in college, his excellent writing abilities, and his experiences working with high-profile individuals (other than Cochran) led him to believe he might qualify for the position of communications assistant he found posted on the U.S. Senate Employment website. "What the hell," he told himself. "It's just another application. Worst they can do is say 'No.'"

A week later when his phone screen showed he had a call from Washington, D.C., he took a moment to contain his surprise and quell the nervousness that scattered like the beads of a shotgun shell throughout his body. He waited through four rings while he calmed himself. "I can sell ice to Eskimos," he told himself as his self-confident, carefully practiced, "Hello. Dave Nichols," fell out of his mouth and onto the phone's receiver, and the process of schmoozing the caller began.

***

It had taken some time and effort for Dave Nichols to justify his decision to hit the send button at the end of the online forms the caller had sent him. He had to first convince himself that he didn't care that the senator was a Republican. He would have preferred to work with a senator from the "other side of the aisle"—as politicians refer to the supposed "colleagues" they also called "sons o' bitches" behind closed doors—none, other than Senator John Bedsloe, needed a communications assistant at the time.

Dave's personal belief about politics was a cynical one: the party of the moment drinks from the shot glasses of power and self-importance until its adherents become so drunk that they start tearing the house down around themselves just for fun. In some cases they get so wasted that a drunken lout among them leads a chant to find somebody to lynch. With that, they run off into the night with pitchforks and torches and burning anger, ready to destroy everyone who isn't them. When they wake up the next day, they try to cover up their obvious crimes, get indicted by the press, lose public support, and create an opportunity for the "other side" to step up and repeat the process.

But he was running out of options and beginning to believe he could adapt. Other positions he had applied for weren't coming through. He had moved out of his apartment the previous week, stashed his belongings in a storage building, and was now staying at the YMCA in Washington, and had just enough money to eat for a few more days. Given his circumstances, it wasn't difficult for him to decide that politicians were simply faces of a political party line. They were not all that different from non-politicians whose faces get printed on cereal boxes or toy packaging or on wanted posters. He told himself that politicians and political parties were no different from the producers of Superior Brand dishwashing liquid trying to displace another company's Ultimate Brand dishwashing liquid. Both, just soap. Both made from the same basic ingredients. Both poured from similar bottles. Both created about the same amount of suds that would last for about the same amount of time. But each wore its uniquely designed label, and each claimed to be much better than the other.

Outside of Texas, Senator Bedsloe was not much liked even by the people of his own party. His wealthy campaign donors thought him boorish, a wannabe sophisticate bereft of the essential skills and delicacy required, a battered bull thinking of itself as an elegant steed. But that slight majority of Texans who bothered to vote him into office liked his tough guy image, what they called his "tell-it-like-it-is" style (whatever that was supposed to mean) and his pride in declaring himself white, conservative, anti-immigrant, damned-sure proud to stand up for the "forgotten middle class" and a "real" American. He had a long-standing reputation for spoon feeding his constituency what they wanted to hear, and they ate up whatever he dished out and then, licked the bowl he had served it in. He got his donors what they wanted, voted the way they wanted, and promoted their agendas for as long as the money and the "atta-boys" rolled in the way the senator wanted.

"It doesn't matter one way or the other," Dave mumbled to himself as he stated that he was a loyal member of the senator's party and hoped no one would take the time to check his voting record. As he pressed the submit button, a phantom pain shot deep into his belly.

***

A couple of days later when he told his brother over the phone that he was in the final round of interviews for the position with Bedsloe, Luke begged him not to take the job, called the senator all the filthiest words he could pull into his consciousness, laid out a litany of reasons to hate the man and his politics as he pleaded with Dave to wait until a better opportunity came along. Apparently, Luke believed any opportunity was better. Dave faked a laugh at his brother's intensity and his commitment to political beliefs that would be appalling to the senator and his ilk.

"When did my hotshot, little brother, smart ass, college graduate become so passionate about politics?" The question was asked and followed with another fake laugh. "Anyway, I'm not taking a political stance, I'm taking a job and I'm going to take it if it is offered. At least it will be interesting.

Politics: It's not all that different from what I did in advertising. I was a slut for them, wrote what they needed written because it paid. I'll be doing the same thing for him. Being a whore pays well!"

After a string of reordered expletives and a few comments about Dave selling his soul, Luke gave up, stopped talking, sighed, and said, "I love you in spite of yourself, bro," and ended the conversation with an excuse for cutting the call off. As the phone clicked to silence, Dave realized that he "felt green" … green like when as a boy he had tried smoking three unfiltered cigarettes one immediately after the other and felt the nausea and regret as his stomach and chest rebelled and his skin turned gray—a feeling only understood by those who have felt it and never want to feel it again. He hadn't liked what he had heard himself say, and he hadn't liked the way the conversation ended … "in spite of yourself."

He sat down on the hard red park bench outside the deli where he'd brought his pastrami on rye wrapped in white paper, and the hot, paper-cupped coffee he needed for surviving the day. As he ate, he watched the street filled with traffic and the sidewalk teeming with bodies moving like racing ants among patio stones performing tasks that humans don't understand. He found himself thinking about the concept of a soul and wondered if he'd ever had one.

***

"It isn't political," he had said, trying to convince his brother in their previous conversation. "It's just writing what he wants said and getting paid for it. It's not like they're my thoughts. They're his. I just dress them up."

"And your writing helps Bedsloe bring more people over to his way of thinking even when they're fucking themselves in the process. You'll be as guilty as he is, and you know it." Luke had spoken with a layer of heat in his voice.

"It's just a job, and after I get on my feet again, I can look for something else without losing what little I have left of my things!"

"I'd rather have nothing ...." Luke's words from their last conversation had bitten his brother. Dave found himself being somewhat defensive about them. Though he pretended to slough them off, they roiled in Dave's mind during his interview with Bedsloe's Chief of Staff. However, he had managed to focus enough to impress the interviewer who set up a face-to-face between Dave and the Senator at the Senator's fourth-floor office in the Russell Senate Building the next afternoon at 2 p.m. "The Senator likes to have the final word in hiring staff that he might have to work with directly."

When he left the office, Dave was still hearing his brother's arguments, arguments that stayed with him throughout the remainder of that day and into the next.

***

He arrived for the interview wearing his New York tailor-made charcoal gray suit; his red, white, and blue checked tie; his large turquoise ring; a matching masculine-looking bracelet; and brilliantly shined shoes. He made a striking figure with his handsome face, strong chin, blue eyes, and dark brown, carefully trimmed hair, his broad shoulders, slim waist, and powerful muscular and toned body. He walked confidently into an office where he was met by a woman who introduced herself to him as Mrs. Kepper, the senator's secretary.

Mrs. Kepper was an early-middle-aged blonde, dressed in a tight-fitting business suit, short skirt, white blouse, and a jacket. Hers was a straight-lipped face carefully made up to reduce the appearance of wrinkles at the corners of her eyes and to lighten the dark sacs under the lower lids. She spoke as if she were a tape recording of the type that can be found at a museum: eliminates the docents and can do their jobs until the machines that hold their voices die. Dave Nichols noticed her doing a quick head-to-toe scan of him. He sensed that she had made her decision as to his value and wasn't impressed. He'd been around enough to know that secretary's run organizations; they just let their bosses think that they (the bosses) are the powers behind their operations. He could feel his confidence fading when his attempts to make small talk with this woman wasn't going to be reciprocated, so he walked along behind her as she proceeded officiously and silently across the room to the senator's massive red oak door and its inches-thick ornately carved moldings. She knocked and within a few seconds, a booming voice came from the other side of the door saying, "I'm ready. Send him in, Ruth." Mrs. Kepper, Ruth, pushed down on the latch, walked the door open on its hinges, then stood like a butler motioning for the applicant to step inside the room. As he took several steps toward Senator Bledsoe to shake his hand, Nichols heard the door close behind him. The senator had risen from his chair and was walking toward him with that politician smile on his face that said, "You are the most important person I know at this minute in time, and you and I both know that's not true but let's pretend, shall we?" The senator stuck his paw out like a trained dog waiting for the treat that was sure to come after such a well-practiced gesture. The men exchanged their strong handshakes like gentlemen before a wrestling meet, trying to out-squeeze and intimidate the other.

"Come in, young man. Have a seat here in this big old leather chair and lets parley," the senator said. Nichols sunk into the chair, felt it envelop him, the Texas-twanged "parruhlaay" still ringing in his ear; he wondered if he was perceived as being an opponent or the senator didn't know the meaning of the word. The senator walked away briefly, returning to his desk to pull out a bottle of whiskey from a drawer. He studied Dave like prey, removed the cap from the bottle, took two engraved whiskey glasses from the side table and held them in one large hand as he poured whiskey into both. Then he brought the glasses toward Dave, handed him one, said "Cheers," clinked his glass against Dave's. Both men took a swallow, and then the senator sat down, dropping his weight into the chair opposite Nichols, causing the sofa to groan at the attack by his backside. The men sat looking into one another's eyes as if checking to see who would blink first.

Nichols was impressed by the size of the man. Bedsloe was large, not fat, just large, maybe six feet two or three, broad shouldered and big boned. His face was perhaps a little rounder than a man of his stature would like, not strong-chinned, but it was hard like a stereotypical Texas cowhand, a Marlboro Man, an oil rigger, or banker's face when he denies a loan; he had the look of exhaustion around his brown and sunken eyes, the skin darkened almost to the color of burnt umber under his heavy protruding brow. He had one of those thickening, slightly bulbous noses typical of heavy drinkers. His expensive suit looked somehow badly fitted for a body in a sitting position. His big bones pushed at the fabric and pulled the jacket up behind his large neck and the sleeves high above his wrists; his pant-legs showed the bare skin of his legs above the socks.

After thanking the senator for the excellent whiskey, Nichols expressed his appreciation for the interview. Then he waited while the senator looked over the top of his whiskey glass. Bedsloe had swallowed the remainder of the liquid in one large gulp, but he held the glass in place barely beyond his lips as he looked at Dave as if studying something in his face that he hadn't quite figured out but intended to. Then, he lowered the glass to his lap and said, "Nice suit. New York?" As Nichols began to respond, the senator talked over top of him, "You'll need to tell me who your tailor is. Might want to get myself a couple of new suits."

In the pause at the end of the interruption, Nichols said he would be glad to provide the information. And then he waited again. After the forever that a long silence can be among strangers, the senator spoke: "Is it true that you called Sam Cochran a fucking moron and got fired for it?" The senator rattled off the question almost as nonchalantly as asking, "Where are you from?" Nichols could feel his pulse speed up. His brain tried to process the surprise of the question, allowed the thought to enter his mind that the job was slipping away. In an attempt to match the senator's style, Dave swallowed the remainder of his whiskey, set the glass down on a coaster on a side table, took his time, looked into Bedsloe's eyes and said confidently while controlling any shame that might escape to his face, "Yes, sir. I did." And then he waited for the senator to ponder his response.

"Is it true you said the same thing to your boss?"

"Yes, sir. It is true."

"So, are you likely to say that to me?"

"Senator, I have no intentions of saying it, especially if it's not true. If either of those guys had just had a bad day, I could have accepted that and kept my mouth shut. Problems had been going on for a long time, at least a couple of years, and my boss wasn't doing anything to help. What Cochran wanted was to be his own advertising agency and use me as his personal whipping boy, and my boss let him do it."

"Your boss told you to bend over and take it for the good of the company?"

"I probably wouldn't have said it quite that way, but yes."

"Sam Cochran is a fucking moron, and I've told him so myself. You've got balls. As to your former boss, I can't say, but from what you just said, my guess is you aren't wrong." Bedsloe got up, picked up both glasses, and refilled them as he continued talking. "I like my employees to have balls. Even the women. I've seen the work you gave to my staff, liked the way you rewrote a couple of press releases and made me sound pretty goddamned good. You've got a flair for words, son." He had brought the glasses back, handed Nichols his hand-warmed glass, and smiled as he sat down. "You think you can make me look good, spin me when it's needed?"

"Yes, I could."

"Good." The senator paused. Then he repeated himself before moving on, "Good. That's good! Now tell me about your politics. Tell me where you stand."

"Stand on what, sir?"

"Oh, how about you telling me about your coming over to the Republican Party? You voted Democratic in New York for the past four years, what is it you decided you like about us Republicans.

"Well, sir, I ah, ah," struggling for words, "I … well … to be honest, I figured marking that on the application form was the only way I would get a chance for an interview, and I hoped I could impress you enough once I got here that my voting record wouldn't matter. It was wrong for me to do that … but in reality, I couldn't see what difference it made. Truth is, I am a good writer, and I can create what you want words to say whether or not I personally agree with them. Isn't that what you would be hiring me to do?

"I've got to know that my staff people are with me a hundred and ten percent. The job is about loyalty to me and to my vision. Total commitment, son. I can't be worrying you'll stab me in the back. You're either all in, or I can't use you."

Something about the way the senator said, "use you," hit Nichols like a flash fire—the hot breath of the Minotaur as it prepared to eat its prey. He remembered his brother's assessment of the senator, what he himself had known but tried to dismiss as unimportant. In those few seconds, the thought occurred to him that he had become a walking sales pitch, a man ready to sell himself to another man who had succumbed to his own delusions of power and control. Bedsloe's phrase about bending over and taking one for the company came to mind.

As he looked at the senator, he could almost hear his brother's voice crying out like the voice of a gull above the ocean crying out to nearby gulls. He had no words prepped and ready for saying. Yet, they fell out of his mouth as if placed there by someone else, surprising him as he said them as easily as he might have said he had enjoyed the whiskey: "Senator, I have wasted your time, and for that I apologize. But I can't give you what you want. I'm not willing to give you my soul. Come to think of it, I'm not sure I want to work as a whore for anyone anymore. Think maybe I need to go in a different direction."

The senator's face first turned brilliant red and then drained to a ghastly gray, the slits between his eyelids narrowed, and his forehead acquired wrinkles that had not been there even a moment previously. He set his drink down and said, "Yes. You have wasted my time. Now get the hell out of my office." He walked to his desk, pressed a button on his phone. Mrs. Kepper opened the door and once again stood like a butler waiting for a command. "Mrs. Kepper, we are finished here. Show him out."

As Dave walked across the threshold, he heard the senator utter, "Fucking moron," before the door hit the doorjamb. Mrs. Kepper maintained an unreadable face as they walked. Dave Nichols smirked as he walked toward the door that would release him to the hall … a self-satisfied look of joyful, unrehearsed self-satisfaction that continued as he took the elevator down to street level and stepped out into the light of day. And there in front of him, a phantom image of himself sitting on a low bough of a manicured tree, the grinning boy he had once been, dropping to the grass as only a gawky teenager can, to walk alongside him toward home, wherever that might turn out to be.

Ohio

by Kelly Fordon

Off Lake Erie   a cold wind   And a colder one, passing through me.
An old oak dangles   off this bluff
—still   the roots hold—
a person in a better state of mind   might call that tenacity.

*

Hunger   on the third season of *Alone*.
An Ohioan stranded
in Patagonia   keeps bitching
cursing the bramble   the weather   his holey tent
The Great Hunger—   it's not.
He asked for it.

*

I was young once   and swum in Lake Erie.   More often than not,
I'd emerge with a rash.   In those days   you had to traverse
the beach with care—   needles   tampons   plastic filters,
more garbage than sand.   Now it's mostly cleaned up.
so that's one good thing,
as they say…

*

Often   I amble.   Just yesterday   I happened on
   a SWAT team   surrounding a house,
fifteen men with guns drawn   marching in formation
   up the driveway
drugs I heard first   then kiddie porn.   The conspiracy theorists
descended.   This is Ohio.   I'm not sure what's happening here.
Most days   I land on despair.

Wheels on the Bus

by Christina Singerie

"The wheels on the bus go round and round, round and round…" The tiny, little handcuffs did not stop the child from touching the button that made the yellow plastic toy sing. The baby pushed the button that made it honk a horn. Then, again, "The wheels on the bus go round and round…"

As we stood in line for the bus, the mamma and baby were behind me. I turned to look at them and the other people one after the other, all with cuffs on their legs and chains on their wrists—except the little girl dressed in a pink jumper, diaper looking a bit swollen. I could see that the mom's cuffs were cutting her hands as she held her baby on her hip. That's when the guard came towards us, shaking the mini cuffs and shackles as he talked to the baby, saying, "Look at these! Aren't they cute?" All three of the other guards assigned to our group laughed as he put them on the baby. I turned. I couldn't watch.

The guard tried to take the baby's toy but relented when mom pleaded, "it's her favorite," and "she'll cry without it." Every time the child hit the buttons on the toy, her chains rattled. "The wheels on the bus go round and round…"

The cheerful yellow of the toy was so different from the inside of the bus we were riding. The hard plastic bucket seats were in rows, dark blue, two by two, and the inside of the bus was dull gray. The petroleum smell of heavy plastic in closed space filled my nose, covering up the human smell of sweat like a tarp. The black lined windows were up high so we couldn't see out.

And that stupid toy kept on and on, "the wheels on the bus go round and round…"

Early in the trip, the bus stopped often and made a lot of turns. There were sounds of loose stones crunching, glass smashing. Then, the road became smooth, the bus maintained a constant hum, seeming to hold the same speed for what felt like an endless time. We hadn't been told where we were going or when we would get there. There was nothing to do but wait.

"The wheels on the bus go round and round..."

When the guards put us on the bus, I was first, so I ended up in the last row right in front of the toilet. The smell of antiseptic mixed with the scent of the bus's diesel fuel overwhelmed me and made me feel like I would vomit. The guards attached our leg shackles to chain rings welded to the floor. "It's like a seat belt," the guard said. I guess it was good we didn't have the stomach chains, but the ones that hooked our handcuffs to our feet gave us little room for movement.

In front of me sat the child and her mother, and when she turned her head, I saw she was crying. I felt the bitter betrayal in each tear that ran down her smooth cheek. I tried to imagine being in her place, being worried about whether she could keep her baby safe. She was looking away, trying to hide her tears. Then she wiped her eyes and hummed along with the song, smiling at the baby and pretending she wasn't upset. For her or the baby? I didn't know.

"The wheels on the bus go round and round...."

Across the aisle from me were two teenage girls. They looked like Disney Princesses, long curling hair, perfect little noses. They were beautiful. They were probably on their way to school when they were caught, judging by the navy blazers, khaki skirts, knee socks, loafers, and full make up—only teenagers have time to do full makeup. And sometimes when they turned to each other, a small bit of expensive perfume wafted my way. They spoke in low whispers. My heart broke to think what was in store for them or what they already might have had to deal with. When they had first been directed to their seats, the guard had taken his time chaining them to the floor, bending over, his head at their knees, saying something I couldn't hear—something that made them look afraid—then he laughed at them. Bile burned the back of my throat. I had to look away. I wondered if they were conjuring a Prince Charming who would come and save them. I wanted someone to save me, too.

Across the aisle from the mother and the child, a man, with a sculpted jaw, sat alone. He had a black eye. He took no notice of the menacing toy. His jaw maintained the same amount of clench whether the toy was squawking or not. He reminded me of Clint Eastwood, hard lines on his face, only darker. He and Clint would have been on opposite sides in that western.

Beyond him, two men sat on the right side of the front row. I thought they must be father and son, they looked so much alike, same big, brown eyes, same hair, dark black, thick and combed to the side like Dean Martin. The old man was hunched over and had an oxygen tube in his nose. They were focused on each other, their eyes in constant contact. The middle-aged son was breathing slowly, his lips saying, "in" and "out," and urging his father to do the same. He touched his hand on his dad's shoulder as best he could, chain rattling, gently patting him. I guessed the older man's tank might be running low or maybe they were just conserving what they had. There was love, care, and kindness between them ... I wanted that for myself, would have given anything to be less alone. I wondered what the old man had lived through, if he'd seen this before, if he knew something we didn't. If he did, why was he on this damned bus?

"The wheels on the bus go round and round...."

The woman across the aisle from the two men, a little older than me, was hard looking. Weathered. Like Clint Eastwood, behind her, she looked like someone from a western, too. But not the hero, not even the sidekick. She was the Native American woman, maybe a beggar, that the hero passed on the hard trail, a foreshadowing of the battle to come—another of those westerns showing brown-skinned people in the dimmest light. When she turned towards me, I avoided her knowing eyes.

Toward the front of the bus were the cages. They were separated by bars like you'd expect in that western movie jail. The cage walls, though, were made of gray, wire mesh, tightly woven so you couldn't really see through them. I only saw shadows, the impression of bodies inside them. I guessed they wanted to make sure those in the cages had no interactions with the people around them. I wondered if it was a blessing. They spanned the space between our barred off compartment behind the driver. They had been empty when we got on the bus. When they brought on the people who they put in the cages, I couldn't see their faces. Opposite the cages, a guard sat hunched on a seat bench like the ones we were sitting on, but with three seats instead of two, that faced the cage doors. I could see the flickering light on his face. He had his phone in his hands, and he was scrolling. Sometimes his shoulders moved like he was laughing, making the bundle of keys attached to his belt clack on the plastic seat. The caged prisoners must have been resigned because they didn't make a sound or try to cause any trouble. I wondered if they were dangerous.

"The wheels on the bus go round and round...."

I didn't know why I was on here. I was an American, for the love of God. I didn't even know how to speak Spanish. Except we sang Feliz Cumpleanos when the family was together for birthdays.

Not that we had been together much for the past few years. My family changed once we realized we didn't vote the same. I voted for this! I thought my sister was exaggerating when she said they would come for us. She was so mad that I didn't agree. Instead of arguing, we just stopped talking, except to check in. My mother, Mami, always said my sister ought to be in movies. I thought it was my sister being her dramatic self. God bless, Mami. I'm glad she couldn't see this.

"The wheels on the bus go round and round...."

I didn't know where my sister was now. She and her family might be in the camps already. God, I hope not. From what I heard, the camps were terrible. Some said they packed people in like sardines. Some said they made people work in fields. Everyone said there was no fresh food. And people, especially young and strong, disappeared. The young were stolen and trafficked, the strong were killed for the fear they inspired. No one knew if it were all true, but everyone knew you didn't want to find out.

I lost touch with my sister a few weeks ago. She said that she and her husband and their baby (just nine months old!), were going to Colorado, but they hadn't called before my phone was taken away when I was nabbed. My sister had told me that some of the states were safe, Colorado, California, Illinois, New Mexico and Nevada. She begged me to leave Ohio. Why didn't I leave Ohio? Why didn't

I listen? Why did I chance this? I thought it would be okay. I thought if I just played by the rules, I'd be fine. I didn't know the rules would change.

"The wheels on the bus go round and round...."

I hated that toy.

I tugged at my wrists, pulling them this way and that. I squeezed my hands smaller so they might fit through the cuffs. I remembered the movie about the mountain climber who fell into the rocks and his hand was caught. He cut his own arm off because he was going to die otherwise. 127 Hours, based on a true story. Did I have a hundred and twenty-seven hours?

"The wheels on the bus go round and round...."

The government's agents had been taking people for a while. To the camps? Deported? I never thought it would be me. I wanted criminals to be deported. I wanted people to come into America only if they'd been vetted. I wanted people to be legal. I wanted to be safe. Who wouldn't want that? The government told people to leave if they didn't belong. I was American. Not exactly like a White American. But usually I passed, unlike my sister.

"The wheels on the bus go round and round...."

When, at first, the government came for the illegal people in the bad neighborhoods—gangsters—it didn't seem to matter that there were mistakes such as taking citizens or people with visas. These were honest mistakes, I thought. "A few broken eggs," they said. Anyone who got taken was gone ... we should be grateful. When someone filed a missing person's report or checked with immigration, there was no response. At least that's what my sister said when she was looking for her in-laws who had committed no crimes, they just lived in a mixed neighborhood. Then there was outrage, but it changed nothing. This was the omelet.

"The wheels on the bus go round and round...."

I was taken from the front of the Whole Foods store on the west side of Cleveland while I was waiting for the bus I took to work. Wheels, bus, wheels bus. They came out of nowhere. Masked men in black riot gear. Helmets, batons and guns, they surrounded the glass shelter, detained me and the others who happened to be there. The agents treated us roughly as if we were guilty of the crime of living.

They didn't tell us where they were taking us when they were putting the handcuffs and shackles on us. They just told us to "shut up." They loaded us into a small police van and locked our shackles to the floor. Jingle, rattle, clang. We arrived at a large warehouse used to track the flow of humans rather than any type of goods. The warehouse was newer, like a Costco, where the skylights dimmed when the clouds covered the sun. The walls were modular, a flag blue fabric, like in an office with cubicles. And so many people in lines. When they arrested us, (Is that what they did? Arrest us?) they took our purses, wallets and backpacks so that we had no form of identification on us, then accused us of having no ID. Boom! We were in line for the bus to take us somewhere. People were whispering, "Are we going to the camps? Oh, God, the camps!"

Wheels, bus, wheels, bus. My head was spinning. My wrists were cramping.

The man in front of me in line, a man I recognized from the neighborhood, protested to one of the guards. "Look man, my name is Alfred Wilson. I had my ID in my wallet, but the guys who brought me here took it. They took all our stuff. They put it into a white bag labeled 'evidence.' If you can ask them, I can get you an ID. I'm American."

Two officers (Is that what they were? They had blue uniforms, like police, with white arm bands, some said MP, others said MG. What did that mean?) came up behind Alfred and one touched the tip of his stun baton to Alfred's neck. Alfred fell to the ground, face first, unconscious. I could smell the burning skin. The officers grabbed him by his arms, flipped him over and started to drag him off. The last thing I saw of Alfred were his white Nikes as they disappeared behind a blue fabric wall.

The message was clear. Better not talk or get out of line. Keep your head down.

The whole time, I was thinking, this isn't really happening. My thoughts went over all the times I could have asked questions, all the times I didn't. I accepted. Timid, even though I wanted answers. Why didn't I make myself question before? Why did I believe the people I had voted for? Why didn't I dig deeper? Why did I embrace the lies? Why did I think it wouldn't be me? I pinched myself to wake up. And when I did, I was still in the line that led to the bus.

"The wheels on the bus go round and round…"

***

The bus slowed down a little. Were we here? The camps? I was shaking. The chain that went from my cuff to my feet jangled. I tried to breathe, to slow my mind, but nothing worked. I was recalling the rumors about what the camps were. The women were raped or sterilized. The men were starved and used for medical experiments. People went missing. I could remember the black and white photographs, the click-click of the war footage. The shoes. We'd learned this lesson, hadn't we? This couldn't be that? Could it? News reporters had stopped talking about the camps long ago. Attention had moved on. Here I was, and no one would know. No report on TV. No report on the internet. I felt my heart race and my arms prickle. It was a prison that could erase me … erase us.

"The wheels on the bus go round and round…"

The young mother was sobbing. The teenage girls were crying, too, mascara darkening their eyes. The Clint Eastwood guy clenched his jaw tighter, and I could hear the crunching of his teeth, louder than the stupid toy. The old man with the oxygen tank had tears streaming down his cheeks and was touching his son's face as if trying to memorize it. Only the old woman was still, her head not moving, her body sitting straight up. The bus was electric with our trembling and the echoes of our chains. The girls crossed themselves, as did the father and son. I, too, hoped God would intervene.

"The wheels on the bus go round and round…"

I wrestled harder with the handcuffs. I could feel the sting as the metal cut my skin. Was I going to die if they put me in the camp? I wasn't as young as the girls beside me, but I wasn't that old. Maybe I would be just as invisible as any other middle-aged woman and survive it.

The bus ground gravel to a stop and we heard the door pistons hiss. The guard who had sat opposite the cages got up and unlocked the door between us and the driver. Suddenly, there was yelling, then a crash and a bang as a gun fired, the sound followed by smothered bumping sounds coming from the front of the bus. I heard the rattle of keys and a shadow appeared at the front of the bus. I could see it wasn't the guard who had been with us before, the clothes weren't blue.

The person unlocking the cages was in camouflage, brown, beige and green. I tore at my wrists, I swore to myself, swore to God, if he would save me, I would never be so timid again. I would fight. Not just for me, but for those innocent girls who might lose their sparkle, my sister who was smarter than me, her family, and the people who have hardened over years of trying to fit in or refusing to. I swore I would speak up. I would not turn away.

The person, dressed in earth colors, opened the door that separated the cages from the back of the bus where we were shackled.

I stopped pulling at the handcuffs. Blood trickled into my hand. I could see it was a woman. The military had released all women from service months ago, saying women lowered the standards. Was she one of them?

The keys shook in her hands as she bent over to unlock the old woman in the front. The clang of the chains hit the metal of the bus floor.

"We gotta go," she said as she moved over to the man and his father. Jingle, rattle, clang.

"You can come with us to Illinois, or you can stay until the next bus to the camps comes this way," she moved back to the man with the hard jawline. Jingle, rattle, clang. And then to the girls.

"I promise, you wanna come with us. But if you're coming, we gotta go now. It's still three hours to the border. To the safe houses. It's nothing fancy, but better than the camps."

She moved next to the woman and her child. The little one began to cry.

"We have your purses, wallets and ID's. We can't take your phones. They can be tracked."

Jingle, rattle, clang.

The young mother stood and put the baby on her hip. The baby wailed. Like everyone else, she rushed to exit.

I was the last one … the back of the bus. She unlocked my feet and my bloody wrists. Jingle, rattle, clang. She looked at me, brown eyes to brown eyes, her crow's feet deepening with her smile of understanding. My warrior queen in shining armor. An American fairy tale.

We stood up, and I saw the sunshine-yellow plastic toy on the seat in front of me. I scooped it up as we escaped.

anti-fascist love poem blues #3

by Jim Dwyer

I get out of the house I leave my phone I start walking I head
anywhere & maybe on my way to anywhere I'll see a redbird or
two or three
& maybe (right time right place) they'll be perched amidst
the wild entangled green of a maple tree that's behind a
Kwik-Stop Market or a Taco Bell & if right then I start
laughing because beauty because surprise because
everything really is connected to everything else then right
then I am alive…

I get out of the house I leave my phone I start walking I head anywhere
& lucky man that I am I get to hear it one more time—the dirty
graceful rhythm & blues of the city noise—the funk that
gets me dirty
that keeps me graceful the ecstatic racket I never tire of the
clamorous bangarang of Dayton Ohio this astounding awful
place the only place I could ever call home…

I get out of the house I leave my phone I start walking I head
anywhere & sweet Jesus of the celebrated herbaceous habits
of Snoop Dog & Willie Nelson it's there on a random
breeze the now ubiquitous neighborhood smell of
marijuana—
& it's a frantic furious hard driving high tech world
full of high-tech folks getting baked on various
varieties of high-tech reefer but around here things
are different
around here I'm geezer happy to report that most of the
aroma I'm running into of late has the exact same
bouquet
as the rank old skunk weed we used to

smoke back when it was a felony to smoke
it—
it's a glorious jump for joy kind of
thing to be so out of it so behind the
times you can just live your life…

& speaking of being a geezer & just living your
life two weeks ago I turned 75 & I'm here to
tell you that I don't have to work at it anymore
because at this point I am drop dead
irresistible w/o even trying…

75 years old & I'm here to tell you
that despite how sane & logical it seems
these latter days to give up on hope &
embrace cynicism & despair like a pair of
erstwhile friends despite knowing that as bad
as things are it's guaranteed that they're even
worse than that despite all the nightmares of
history currently repeating themselves
because that's what both nightmares &
history always do
despite it all & everything else

I am still helpless--
I keep on falling in love--

in love with Aretha Franklin's version of YOU SEND ME
in love with the way light creates shadow
in love with the silent rest between lightning crack & thunder roll
in love with the forgiveness feel of rain on my face
in love with honey & peanut butter sandwiches
in love with slow dancing & French kisses
in love with never getting anything exactly right
in love with the way beauty breaks my heart & makes it more human
in love with every single sucker punch blind alley
no exit kind of morning when I know

that I just can't go on but then I do what most
everyone almost always does anyway
I get my ass in gear & I go on with my life (my one & only life)
where anything—anything within the laws of physics—
can & usually does happen—
every single reason for cynicism & despair
every single reason to never give up hope—
day after day after day
there's no escape from who we are
day after day after day
suffering absurd brilliant deluded
day after day after day
standing together in the dark at the crossroads
standing together with no choice but to choose
day after day after day
there's no God no savior no superhero
riding racing flying to our rescue
day after day after day
what we need most
we can only get from ourselves and one another
say that again
what we need most
we can only get from ourselves and one another ...

Der Weiße Schild[1]
(The White Shield)
by George Pallas

A light rain fell as two figures, one male and one female, made their way through the darkened streets of blacked-out Berlin. While the young woman's gait was measured and precise, her companion moved stiffly and limped. As they approached one of the university buildings, the man spoke. "Make sure no one sees you. Absolutely *no one*."

"I know, Karl." She shuddered against the December chill and pulled her thin coat tighter, a vain attempt to keep out the cold.

"Very well. Meet me over there after you finish." He pointed to an enormous linden tree in the yard near the street corner. "But if I am not alone, do not come near. Go back home and do not let anyone see you."

"I will," she said.

"The moon is full tonight, Hanna, and these clouds should clear later. We can expect the bombers overhead then."

"Yes," Hanna said. "I understand." Then the two parted, taking separate entrances into the building.

Nineteen-forty-three had been filled with bad news for Germany. In February, what remained of the Sixth Army had surrendered at Stalingrad. German armies, which had seemed unstoppable two years earlier, were now in retreat in the east and had surrendered in North Africa, while Allied bombers pounded the Reich day and night. Earlier that summer, in July, British incendiary bombs unleashed a hellish firestorm on Hamburg, killing tens of thousands and reducing much of the city to charred rubble.

Karl Jäger, once a proud soldier of the Reich, no longer believed. His disillusionment began with a severe leg wound on the Eastern Front, an injury that prevented his continued military service. A

---

1 Pronounced "dare VY-suh shilt."

university student now, he walked with difficulty and lived with near-constant pain. But more than his crippled leg weighed on Karl. The government, that is to say, the Party, was lying to the people. Germany was not winning the war and could not win it. In fact, it faced almost certain defeat. From their vast lands in the east, the Soviets pushed ever westward. Meanwhile, the American invasions of Sicily and the Italian mainland had forced the collapse of Mussolini's regime and taken the Reich's erstwhile ally out of the war. Everyone knew that an invasion of Western Europe was only a matter of time, although no one spoke of it. Promises of wonder weapons and ultimate victory rang hollow as German troops moved ever closer to Hitler's shrinking Thousand-Year Reich.

Even more unsettling were the disturbing rumors about the goings-on in the camps in the former Poland. It was common knowledge that the concentration camps were dreadful places to be avoided, but there were hints that the big camps in the east were far, far worse. Rumors surfaced now and again that people went into those camps and never came out. They went, as one escapee was purported to have said, "up the chimney." Some of Karl's acquaintances discussed these things, furtively, of course, but most Germans seemed to instinctively understand that they didn't want to know too much about the camps.

These factors combined to convince Karl that the government and the Party were leading the fatherland into a dark and dangerous corner. It was then that he decided to form Der Weiße Schild. Der Weiße Schild was not much of an organization, consisting only of Karl and his fiancée, Hanna Richter, with occasional help from a few friends. Nor was its reach extensive. It was limited to just a few universities in Berlin. Karl and his co-conspirators had little hope of effecting dramatic changes. They wanted mainly to make a statement and clear their consciences. On this evening, Karl and Hanna carried small packets of leaflets they planned to leave in prominent places around the main university building. Karl had crafted the text himself:

> *Germans!*
> *The government and the Party is lying to you! The Party assures you that victory is certain. This is a lie! Our armies have suffered crushing defeats in the Soviet Union and in Africa. The Russians are at our very*

door, and the Americans and British are sure to follow soon!
German cities lie in ruins, devastated by enemy bombers. Göring's
Luftwaffe is powerless to stop them. The miracle weapons we're promised are
fantasies!
Don't believe the lies in the Party press! Look around! Believe the
evidence of your own senses!
--Der Weiße Schild

To be caught with such a leaflet meant certain death in the Third Reich of 1943. The Party, and therefore the government, viewed any dissent as treason and defeatism, and *Völkischer Beobachter*, the Party newspaper, frequently reported executions for actions such as Karl's. But he was determined to resist the regime in his small way. As fully committed as she was to Karl as her soulmate, Hanna insisted on being part of his mission.

Karl swiftly scattered his packet of leaflets around the building, then slinked across the open yard to the tree where he and Hanna were to rendezvous. Hanna was already there.

"No troubles?" he asked.

"No troubles," she said. "I am sure no one saw me."

"Or me. Come, let us get away from here."

A visitor two days later shook Hanna's confidence. The man at her door identified himself as a Gestapo agent, and he had questions for her.

"I am Herr Zimmer, Fräulein Richter. An unfortunate incident has occurred at the university you attend. Defeatist individuals recently littered one of the buildings with treasonous leaflets." Hanna felt her chest constrict but tried to control her breathing and remain calm as the agent continued to speak. "Someone observed you, Fräulein Richter, entering that same building two evenings ago, the very night the leaflets appeared. Now, what would you know about that, Fräulein?"

Hanna steeled herself. "Nothing. Nothing at all."

"Then perhaps you could explain why you were in the building after hours." The agent's lips twisted into a sinister smile.

She was sure Zimmer could hear her heart pounding but pasted on a smile. "Of course, Herr Zimmer. It's really quite simple. I had an unfinished assignment. I left it in the office of my professor." At least she'd actually had the foresight to leave an essay on her instructor's desk.

Zimmer eyed her, his expression inscrutable. "Ach, I see. Yes, you did leave some papers for Herr Doktor Weber. Is that *all* you left?"

"But of course!"

A moment of uncomfortable silence followed before the baleful smile returned, and Zimmer said, "Very well. I shall go now. Please be sure you confine yourself to your academic papers. It would be a pity for something to happen to a pretty fräulein like yourself."

The man turned away, and Hanna closed the door behind him. Then she collapsed into the nearest chair, emotionally drained. She sat for nearly an hour, trying to regain her equipoise. At first, she felt certain she'd deceived the Gestapo agent. After contemplating for a while, though, she decided she hadn't and that Zimmer was toying with her. It was a chilling thought. Maybe she wasn't really cut out for this clandestine work after all. But Hanna persevered. For the next two months, she and Karl repeated their secret leaflet distribution about once a week.

There were no more scares until late November, when the Gestapo, in the person of Agent Zimmer, appeared once again at Hanna's door. "Fräulein Richter," he said, "you must come with me." His grim expression frightened Hanna, but she did her best to maintain her composure.

"What is it, Herr Zimmer?"

"Come with me," he repeated, saying nothing further. Resigned, Hanna put on her coat, locked her apartment door, and followed the Gestapo agent.

Hanna's heart sank when Zimmer took her into the imposing Gestapo headquarters at 8 Prinz-Albrecht-Straße.[2] Herded into a small room, she faced Zimmer and two other men in street clothes, presumably more Gestapo. Zimmer did not introduce them, nor did they identify themselves.

---

2 Prince Albrecht Street, named for Prince Frederick Henry Albert of Prussia (1809-1872). The East German government renamed it Niederkirchnerstraße (Niederkirchner Street) in 1951 to honor a resistance fighter

"Now, Fräulein Richter," Zimmer said, "you will tell us about the leaflets."

"I know nothing about any leaflets."

"Ach, but Fräulein Richter, you were seen placing them in the university administration building. We have witnesses."

Hanna's heart sank. Did someone actually see her, or was Zimmer bluffing? Regardless, she was in real trouble now. All she could think to do was repeat, "I know nothing about any leaflets."

"Come now, Fräulein Richter, your boyfriend has already confessed! Tell us what you know. Omit nothing."

Hanna was stunned. "You're lying! Karl wouldn't have…." In her shock, the words had tumbled out before she could hold them back. Zimmer's lips curled into a smile that was, if possible, even more menacing than before.

"So you *do* know about the leaflets. You are correct about one thing, Fräulein Richter. Your young man has said nothing, despite using some of our extreme interrogation techniques. Nonetheless, he is guilty. He carried a stack of that vile propaganda when we arrested him."

Hanna's mind reeled, and she felt physically sick. Had the Gestapo caught Karl distributing the leaflets? That seemed unlikely, as he took precautions to avoid detection. Perhaps someone informed on him. Maybe it was Gerhardt. He was so eager to help in the beginning, but lately he had all but disappeared. Would she ever know?

"Zimmer's face darkened, and he pounded the table as he said, "Tell me about the leaflets! Everything!" Hanna sank into a chair and said nothing. "Stand up!" Zimmer shouted, and Hanna reluctantly obeyed. For hours, agents hurled questions at her. Periodically, her questioners would depart only to be replaced by fresh agents. Hanna herself, however, was exhausted, and she lost all sense of time. Standing during endless questioning was bad enough, but distant screams and cries, and the occasional moan, told her that other prisoners undergoing "interrogation" were faring even worse than she. Finally, Zimmer reappeared and barked an order. "Take her away and lock her up!" Two other men in the room each took one of Hanna's arms and frog-marched her to a cell.

What passed for justice in the Third Reich moved swiftly. Within the week, the Gestapo hauled Karl and Hanna before the dreaded People's Court, a kangaroo court whose function was to conduct show trials for propaganda purposes in political cases. It was no surprise that Roland Freisler, the Judge President[3] himself, ascended the bench to hear their case. Freisler, infamous for browbeating hapless defendants, wasted no time. "This is a most disturbing case of high treason!" He shouted. He glared directly at the defendants. "The evidence of your guilt in this file is overwhelming! You insult the Führer and sow defeatism among the people!" Whatever was in the file, both Karl and Hanna knew that in the People's Court, "evidence" was whatever the prosecution and judge wanted it to be.

Knowing he would not escape alive, Karl chose defiance. He glared at Freisler and said calmly but firmly, "The Führer is lying to the people. Our sacred fatherland—"

He got no further. An apoplectic Freisler banged his gavel so violently that Karl thought it would break. "Silence! You have no right to speak of the Führer that way!" He turned to Hanna. "And you, Fraulein, why did you choose to degrade yourself by engaging in this treasonous behavior?"

Hanna followed Karl's lead. "The only degrading thing is this so-called 'trial.' Der Weiße Schild spoke the truth."

"TRUTH? The *Führer* is Germany's truth!"

The proceedings continued in this vein for less than an hour. In a foregone conclusion, Freisler found both Karl Jäger and Hanna Richter guilty of high treason and sentenced them to death. He did not permit the defendants to present evidence or call witnesses, and there were no appeals from the verdicts of the People's Court. Shortly after, a squad of soldiers led the pair to a courtyard where they tied them to posts set against a wall. In her terror, Hanna found the courage to strike back at the regime one more time by refusing a blindfold. "I am not afraid to see you murder me," she said. Karl also refused the blindfold. Moments later, a sergeant gave the order, and the soldiers fired.

---

3 Judge President was the highest position in the *Volksgerichtshof*, the People's Court. The People's Court had jurisdiction over political offenses.

***

In his small room, Ulrich von Hardenberg studied the brief article in *Völkischer Beobachter*, the party newspaper, which trumpeted the previous day's trial and executions. Fate had been unkind to Ulrich; he lost an arm in fighting on the Eastern Front. At least the war had taken the left-handed soldier's right arm, but he still struggled to adjust to both civilian life and to the loss of a limb.

More than the horrors of the battlefield haunted him. Despite clumsy efforts to hide it, von Hardenberg had seen the atrocities with his own eyes. He observed special action squads rounding up civilians and escorting them to the hastily dug pits where firing squads would murder and bury them. Combat soldiers were told that the roundups snared only a few "criminals," but Ulrich knew this was not so. Nighttime brought no relief; the horrors of combat and the murder squads—he could think of no more honest term for them—regularly tormented him in his dreams.

Now Ulrich contemplated what he read in the paper. He'd read some of Der Weiße Schild's leaflets, and they touched him deeply. Now, the government, the Party, had silenced the eloquent voices behind the pamphlets.

Ulrich thought some more. Then he drew the window shades and sat down with pen and paper. With his remaining hand, he began to write: "Der Weiße Schild lives…"

Left Brain Right Brain

by Jaclyn Youhana Garver

> *I live a life of wishing, but it doesn't always*
> *matter.*

In the 2024 American presidential
election, 73.6% of voting-age Americans
were registered to vote. That's 174 million
registered voters out of a possible 236.4
million eligible voters.

> *For example, I wish those numbers weren't*
> *so large, because I find it difficult to imagine*
> *millions: Have I read a million pages in my life?*
> *Kissed a million kisses? Will I by the time I die?*
> *God, I hope so.*

Of the Americans registered to vote, 65.3%
actually voted. That's 154 million people who
cast a vote.

> *Malcom Gladwell famously decided*
> *that 10,000 hours of practice made someone*
> *an expert in their field. Which also sounds*
> *impossibly large, but 10,000 is only 1% of a*
> *million. One would need to become an expert*
> *100 times over to hit a million.*

Of those who voted in the 2024 presidential
election, 49.8% voted for ███████████.
That's 77.3 million Americans.

> *I wonder how many blades of grass are in*
> *my little fenced-in backyard. Our fence is cute,*
> *but our yard would look much larger without*

it. Behind the fence is a small and protected swampland with large trees. Sometimes deer come out. Without the fence, they could enter my backyard. They might eat my peach tree, whose sire had a sire had a sire (I wish I knew how many) from peach trees my grandfather grew in his backyard in Channahon, Illinois. My grandfather was born in Iran. He moved to Illinois a few weeks before my father married my mother. My papa didn't speak English very well then. He didn't speak English very well during the thirty years I got to spend with him, either, and I loved to listen to him speak. The way he called me bratid Papa—*Papa's daughter, Papa's heart—is my favorite. Still, I think I'd prefer to ditch the fence.*

Or at least paint the insides of it pink.

Sometimes I remind myself of that number who voted for ███████████ and of the way the United States of America's representative democracy works: Those 77.3 million Americans elected ███████████ to represent all 340.8 million Americans.

Which means ███████████ was elected by 22.7% of the population of the United States.

And many of those 340.8 million were ineligible to vote. Back in November 2024, the 236.4 million eligible voters comprised 69.4% of the population. Those ineligible to vote were underage or not citizens. Maybe they had other residency issues, a move near the election date that led to improper

or missing paperwork. Some states don't let
felons vote.

> *Some poets may believe that numbers*
> *are not poetic. But poetry—its creation*
> *and consumption—can heal like a kiss or*
> *combination of muscle relaxers and steroids.*
> *And both can—and, I'd argue, should—make*
> *you dizzy.*

I sometimes remind myself of that
number—22.7% of Americans, compared
to the other 77.3% who were underage or
ineligible, or they missed voting day, or (bless
them) they knew better—to make myself feel
better. Especially when I make the ghastly
mistake of reading a comments section
anywhere online.

> *Maybe the angry ones are loudest, or maybe*
> *some algorithms simply prefer the angry ones*
> *and shove their dipshittery to the foreground, as*
> *though they think I prefer anger to, I don't know,*
> *that cozy West Coast barber who gives gender-*
> *affirming haircuts, or the hot musician with the*
> *silly moustache and amazing black hair who*
> *takes mashup requests like "Do Flo Rida's 'Low'*
> *in the style of Slipknot."*

Or maybe the algorithm is purposely
misleading, overamplifying those who fear
anyone unlike them (people whose skin is a
different shade … who love a person some
others deem objectionable … whose assigned-
at-birth gender is wrong … whose life at home
was so terrible that the horrors of American
immigration are preferrable … whose religious,
or non, beliefs don't fit precisely into the

rhombicosidodecahedroned-shaped hole of
their own belief puzzle).

But not people with disabilities, mostly.
Folks with learning or physical disabilities
seem to be one of the few minority groups
who don't strike fear into the hearts of the
fearful. Maybe because they often have no
power; their brains work differently or they're
nonverbal or their bodies aren't strong—
what's to fear?

> *Except autism, of course. So many would*
> *seem to prefer their children die of measles,*
> *mumps or rubella—but autism-free—than*
> *live a healthy life autistically. A hypothetical, of*
> *course, since the two don't have a thing to do*
> *with one another, of course.*

Sometimes, though, when I'm feeling
particularly like I live alone with strangers
(it isn't hard to do), I remind myself of the
fact that only 22.7% of Americans voted
for the racist misogynist who puts children
in cages and mocks people with disabilities
and changes the Department of Defense to
the Department of War and then wonders at
the violence aimed at politicians and media
personalities and schools and …

Well. He doesn't seem too concerned with the
violence at schools, now, does he?

> *Every time I look at that number, that*
> *22.7% of people who both live in the United*
> *States of America and voted for* ███
> ███*, I experience a tiny pebble of relief, a*

few ounces off my shoulders, less than the weight of a Fannie May milk-chocolate vanilla buttercream. Those candies are worth much more than their weight, anyway, and can be relied upon to leave me in a good mood for all sorts of reasons: the way the middle melts on my tongue. Transports me to Louis Joilet Mall in 1988 right by Bergner's and Claire's and, that one time in a dream, when the door opened to a Tyrannosaurus rex who chased me down the mall hallway and ate me. Transports me to my grandmother's voice and, at the end, when the Alzheimer's was really, really bad, how you could give her a box of Fannie May, and she'd keep forgetting that she'd already had three, so she ate three more. And then three more. Someone—my mother, an aunt, one of Nani's live-in aides— would inevitably take the box away. But, hell— when I'm ninety-something and senile, you better let me eat the entire box of candy.

If I love you, I might even share.

Das Vierte Reich[4]
by R. Luce

Auschwitz,
Buchenwald
Treblinka, and Sobibor …
their names come easily to mind
even now in twenty twenty-five.

Majdanek, Kulmhof and Belzec[5]
take more time.

Now, there is Tecoluca, Matsapha,
and somewhere-Rwanda,
and prisons yet unnamed
and God-knows-where
chosen by men in suits of black and blue,
white shirts instead of brown,
and Windsor-knotted, Trump-red ties.

Those same men looking down
into the streets today, pissants
shouting and waving above their heads
vulgar declarations—now clichés—
"Fuck Trump!" "No King! No Tyranny!"
and "Save Our Democracy!"
doubtlessly demanding once again
return of freedoms filched
and fenced for pennies on the dollar.
Annoyed by yet another of these daily dins,
a reichman gazing upon this madding crowd
declares the obvious … perhaps,
to reassure himself, or
perhaps, others in the room:

4 The Fourth Reich. Pronunciation: Das Veer·teh Rī·shh [long "i" as in "rise"].
5 Pronunciation: Mai·daa·nuhk, Kulm·hof, and Bel-ghick.

"Bald werden solche Leute stumm gemacht.[6]
They must ... they will ... be silenced ... soon."

But, his words fall unremarked
like dust in listless air the open window breathes
into this room of preening men
busily scrubbing their hands of humanity, scraping
barnacles of decency from their shells, brushing
blood from their fangs at well-maintained
and glistening
white,
men's
room
sinks.

6 Soon, such people will be silenced." Pronunciation: Baallt ver·den zol·cha Loy·ta schtoom
ge·makt.

American Eros

by Candice M. Kelsey

Whether to honor or betray, the blood current
rising in my face for every promise expired,
rotting behind Capitol glass and gilded Senate

chambers. For each human detained, deported.
A feral ghost-dog, its bark unchained and jaw
coiled in a tin ledger tallying racist narratives,

their hate will stalk them. Neighbors, journalists,
protestors, empathy flung over rickety fences
of a fragile, perpetually gaslit union. Most days

I am the Mississippi River. Slow, burdened, bent
under centuries; mother of cities, bastard daughter
of floods; long-suffering, carrier of debris, still

moving. Today I am both the Atlantic and Pacific,
roiling over oil spills and industry lies. How I am
the lover they mocked, placated, ignored. Lady

Liberty reads my Tarot cards; warrior Audre Lorde
is in my DMs; Harriet Tubman orders my steps.
I am the banshee singing dark anthems in subway

stations and city halls. All that I am. Confidante
to organizers, stylist to radical women in waiting;
mystic, woman, girl, nightmare, and whore. I am
swarming beneath a star-spangled smile, tracking

each crack in this nation. They, nominal inamoratas,
are poisoned water, have eyes like lantern flies, old
lust of Apollo. Billionaires riding roughshod over
climate's bride—floods, fires, hurricanes unyielding.

Tried dooming me into surrender or strange apathy

and hope deferred. I reject them all through burning
towns, flooded plains, and histories unlearned. Let us
trade places: me in their office, fucking everyone

over; them in my classroom, teaching empathy. I'll
become them, shedding ideals like parasites from
a serpent nation; they'll become me, living check
to check, side hustling for more. I'll pull a slick con,
cancel SNAP benefits; they'll learn the grammar

of hunger in another tongue. I drape a tapestry over
my face, an ocean mask: Caribbean crossings, migrants
and waves that answer no flags. Perhaps they will hear

my tiger's heart—velvet paw, sharpened fang hot.
Somehow remember love can save. Their America
was never my lover: gaslighter, dangerous and cruel;

they unleashed courts like knives to carve my uterus
into obedience. I left them an epidemic of loneliness,
my pity and outrage wholly rabid for democracy.

Refusing compliance. Outside their embrace now,
I am insurgent, erotic. Behold! a bloodthirsty huntress,
witch, elusive thing they can't contain. And won't.

Oración for the Midterm Elections

by Mary Moody Hunt

Juanita cries for her teenagers every morning.
Maria, Emilia, and Miguel disappeared in the raid,
sponsors chickened out at the eleventh hour.
Grown sons, Mateo and Edwardo, with Bob and Linda
in another basement, another hiding place ready
for the sounds of slammed doors, boots upon the stairs.

Luis comforts her with muffled words, untranslated.
Though we are learning their language and they ours
in eight months' time I know so little – greetings, days
of the week, *arroz con pollo, habla más despacio.*
We pantomime and sometimes even laugh about it,
a respite for the knot of fear present in our bellies.

One of us upstairs at all times, Larry or me, watching
from the kitchen and living room windows when we hear
rumors of house-to-house searches. The other one
in the basement, ready to shuffle them behind the hidden
door by the linen closet, bolt themselves in, a basket
of laundry, two totes, boxed Christmas tree as cover.

Sunday mornings Juanita sets up her altar by the
dryer—framed image of the Virgin Mary, candles,
incense, artificial flowers, photographs of the missing,
the dead, his parents and hers. She prays for them all,
for us, for one more clandestine visit from their sons,
and always, always the phrase *elecciones intermedias.*

Civilization (I See a Train)

by Jeffrey Hanson

My imagining places me there.
Pines loom through fog.
A chrome moon, says cocktails.

Here they are, cart, white linen
silver salver, neat drinks.
Ah, yes, Civilization.

But where are you?
Far below the cliffs

the sea keeps reaching.
How easy to keep reaching
when the heart is memory.
Yesterday reminds me

Don't go too far, Jeff.
Where must we end?

How do we face the cold lands
to depart for the gravel and
grizzly slush of home?

Meeting Donna Haraway
at the Sydney Opera House

by Noah Fischbach

We become at once victims
collectively slain by cruel empire
and witnesses to a murder most
foul; intimately acquainted by fire
amidst the roaring crowd.

For a moment, I think of me,
that cyborg self;
lost in awareness,
grappling with a fearful
world, neglecting the divine crimson
wrapping itself like a Christmas
garland around my bones.

I pause, condensation gripping
pores and glass alike.
A bright and joyous rendition of

Bach's Jesu, Joy of Man's Desiring
allows spirits to swell forth,
out of this accursed structure
toward our same divine muse
responsible for this chance meeting,
this affiliation of transgressors,
forcibly reclaiming words and worlds.

Over canapes, we reckon with our mor[t]ality,
our being,
our shared perversity,
in hopes that it may one day be deemed
holy.

Signs of Hope

by Lynne Zele

Scratchy voices squawked urgently as I played on the warm concrete. My father, a Cleveland police officer, sat nearby on a lawn chair in our driveway listening intently to the cacophony of sound coming from his small police radio.

I can't recall if it was 1966 or 1968, but I do remember thinking that the chaos blasting from dad's radio had to be happening too far away from my sunny street of modest duplexes and yards teeming with children, dogs, and backyard barbecues for me to be afraid. I was just a kid then and thought all things unpleasant were far away, but I was wrong. I would later learn that the deadly 1966 Hough and 1968 Glenville race riots in Cleveland had erupted a mere 15-minute drive from our Euclid home. When I grew old enough to understand how close we had been to the violence that took place, I finally understood the concerns and fear of the adults who had been around me at the time.

The reality of my first brief childhood exposure to masses of people fighting for their rights fully sank in when I started my first job as an adult and discovered some jarring reminders of that turbulent period of my childhood. I was a news editor at a Cleveland television station. In the corner of a storage room, I spotted a dusty collection of gas masks and other riot gear. I was told the protective equipment was used by the news crews who had covered the violence more than a decade earlier. Before that day, I had never contemplated the very real danger everyone in the vicinity of those riots had been exposed to.

In the years since then, I had fumed with righteous indignation at times over injustices and spent a lot of time advocating for my profoundly disabled daughter's rights where I engaged in a form of resistance through verbal and written persuasion. Beyond that, I had never felt compelled to exercise any real opposition to anything with my boots on the ground (actually my Skechers), until this past year. Nearly six decades after those race riots and non-violent civil rights marches penetrated cities nationwide, I found myself experiencing and outraged by the kind of oppression which those people sixty years earlier had to deal with, but this time, I was not a child who could let her parents do the worrying while she played in the front yard. I was faced with having to take a stand against our current federal government's aggressive, violent ICE raids, the administration's dismissal of judicial orders the president disagrees with, the regime's attacks on freedom of speech, and its weaponization of the Department of Justice to persecute perceived enemies. Our democracy was at stake, and I knew it would take effort from every American to stand up and demand that our country remained a democracy. Thinking about the situation wasn't enough; action had to be taken. Picking up my pen or my phone to urge action just didn't feel like enough. I couldn't sit on the sidelines any longer. So, at the age of sixty-eight, I hoisted my first sign at my first protest rally: the "No Kings" rally, October 2025.

Days before heading to our local event in Mentor I obsessed over what words to stencil onto my sign because I knew words mattered. But condensing a response to the deluge of democracy-busting atrocities spewing out of Washington every day into a concise slogan was an impossible task. I had to find something that—for me, at least—conveyed all of my disappointments with the regime in just a few words. I finally settled on the following personal sign of hope: *Got democracy? Only if We the People oppose Trump's Tyranny!*

Armed with our homemade placards on that unseasonably warm Saturday, my husband, Joe, and I arrived at the protest site and found it to be an uplifting scene. The protest hadn't even officially begun yet, but a sizable crowd was already lined up along busy Mentor Avenue. I hadn't known what to expect, so I was totally surprised and pleased by what was unfolding in front of me. My first surprise was the atmosphere. It was festive. People were smiling, cordial, peaceful and polite. There was a feeling of community. Of hope.

Then there were the actual signs, many similar to my own, and others filled with rage and sarcasm. Wit definitely ruled the day. Many protestors wore T-shirts that cleverly expressed their feelings about the government's policies and leaders. Other people wore inflatable costumes. Those adorable people-powered blow-up frogs and unicorns would become increasingly emblematic signs of peaceful dissent on the 2025 protest front. If I hadn't known what we were there for, I would have thought we had stumbled onto a huge, ever-expanding block party.

My next surprise was who was there. It was predominantly older protestors. My husband prefers the word "seasoned." Like us, those activists appeared to be predominantly children of the fifties, sixties and seventies. Maybe it shouldn't have come as a surprise that our seasoned ranks were the largest component of the rallies nationwide. Unlike our children and grandchildren, we spent our entire adult lives witnessing the struggles of the civil rights, women's rights, LGBT rights, and disability rights movements.

Once Joe and I joined the seemingly endless throng along the street, I was surprised by the reactions of the steady stream of drivers and passengers cruising by. The vast majority honked, waved, or gave a smiling thumbs up. I hadn't expected that. There were a few who lifted a middle finger instead of their thumb, but very few. And the response from the crowd remained respectful. There were no jeers or taunts from the protestors that I saw.

During this divided time when families and friendships have been fractured by our polarized political landscape, I didn't realize how much it would raise my spirits to be around so many other patriotic kindred spirits who feel the same angst and anger as I do. I didn't have to bite my tongue or edit my words for fear of offending anyone or triggering an argument. I also didn't expect to get so emotional. My heart swelled and my eyes welled with tears as I chanted, cheered, and raised my sign in the middle of the roughly 5000-member crowd. While I had felt awfully powerless and alone prior to the "No Kings" day, I experienced firsthand the energizing strength in numbers.

Before leaving, I spent a few moments completely absorbing the sights, sounds, and sensations of that joyous empowering scene and committed them to memory. It was like the end of a sublime vacation when you breathe in the ocean air and listen to the tranquil sounds of the surf one last time so you can hold onto that relaxing vibe a little bit longer as you return to your hectic daily life. I wanted to capture as much of that sense of communal mission and resistance as possible to tide me over for what I knew would be continued dark days ahead. That day, my husband and I were fueled by a sorely needed boost of optimism. Babysitting our young grandson after returning home that afternoon, the lessons of the protest reinforced just how crucial it is that we stand together to protect our precious democracy and ensure a bright future for all our children and grandchildren.

Later, after stashing our signs in the basement for our next rally, I was actually looking forward to watching the news for the first time since the previous fall. My television screen and social media were filled with breathtaking images of monstrous spirited rallies like the one we attended. There had been 2700 No Kings rallies held throughout the country and in cities around the world with well over seven million participants in all. For me, that day represented a heartening beacon of hope for our nation. Seven million signs of hope.

About the Authors

Steve Abbott has had poems published in numerous journals and anthologies. He has published five chapbooks and two full-length collections: *A Green Line Between Green Fields* (2019) and *A Language the Image Speaks* (2020), 46 ekphrastic poems accompanying the artworks that inspired them. He was a founder and a host of The Poetry Forum (Columbus) for nearly 40 years. He edits Ohio Poetry Association's annual journal *Common Threads*. www.steveabbott.us

Roy Bentley is the author of *Walking with Eve in the Loved City*, chosen by Billy Collins as a finalist for the Miller Williams poetry prize; *Starlight Taxi*, winner of the Blue Lynx Poetry Prize; *The Trouble with a Short Horse in Montana*, chosen by John Gallaher as winner of the White Pine Poetry Prize; as well as *My Mother's Red Ford:* New & Selected Poems 1986 – 2020 published by Lost Horse Press in 2020.

Linda Davis won the *Saturday Evening Post* Great American Fiction contest for her short story "The War at Home." Other story and essay publications include *The Iowa Review, The Literary Review, Literal Latte, Kallisto Gaia Press, Gemini Magazine* and *Mothering Children with Special Needs.* She was the editor of the online literary journal, *Lit Angels*, with Francesca Lia Block. She received her MFA from Antioch University.

Thomas Dukes was born in Gainesville, Florida, and grew up in Aiken, SC. He received his BA and MA from The University of Texas at El Paso, his PhD from Purdue University. He lives and writes in NE Ohio in the company of his husband, a cat, and a dog.

Jim Dwyer is a devout fallen away Catholic from Dayton, Ohio. He doesn't believe poetry can change the world, but he keeps on working and writing because he just might be wrong.

Alan S. Falkingham currently lives in Cincinnati, Ohio, but was born in Leeds, England. He attended Nottingham University and worked for 30+ years as an IT professional, but now writes short stories, flash and micro fiction, and has recently completed a full-length mystery novel manuscript. Alan's work has been awarded and published in the *Fish and Bath* Fiction Award Anthologies, *Vine Leaves Press, Writer's Playground, Adhoc Fiction,* and the *Flash Flood* and *Potato Soup* Journals.

Noah Fischbach is a poet and writer currently pursuing his master's degree in rhetoric and writing from the University of Findlay, where he also serves as the poetry editor for the Slippery Elm literary journal. Noah has been published in multiple print and online publications such as Slipstream Press, Ekstasis, and the *Sigma Tau Delta Rectangle.*

Kelly Fordon has published two award-winning short-story collections: *I Have the Answer* (2020) and *Garden for the Blind* (2015), and two poetry collections, *What Trammels the Heart* (2025) and *Goodbye Toothless House* (2019). Her work has appeared in *The Kenyon Review Online, The Boston Review, The Michigan Quarterly Review, Rattle,* and *The Saturday Evening Post.*

Jaclyn Youhana Garver is the author of the novel, *Then, Again* (Lake Union Publishing). Her story "The Butterfly Catcher" appeared in *This World Belongs to Us: An Anthology of Horror Stories About Bugs,* and she coedited *Requiem for a Siren: Women Poets of the Pulps* (both from Beyond Press. Her poetry chapbook is *The Men I Never.* She serves on the board of directors for the Midwest Writers Workshop. She lives in Fort Wayne, Indiana.

Joe Graves is an author of fiction and nonfiction exploring faith and the human experience. His fiction blends speculative elements with ethical questions, while his nonfiction focuses on leadership, justice, and community renewal. He serves as President of the Ohio Writers' Association and a member of the Science Fiction & Fantasy Writers Association. His science fiction novel *My Family and the End of Everything* is out now, and his work has appeared in *The Pearl, 365tomorrows, Abingdon Press,* and various anthologies.

Jeffrey Hanson received a PhD in English and Creative Writing from Ohio University. After teaching for 25 years, he retired and moved to Washington State. Much of his poetry is autobiographical. After working at construction and doing six years in the Navy, he began his college career at 31. He has recently published a book, *Doubtful Stamina*.

Stephen Haven published his fourth book of poems, *The Flight from Meaning* (Slant Books) in 2025. His earlier books include *The Last Sacred Place in North America*, selected by T.R. Hummer for the New American Prize; *Dust and Bread*, for which Haven was named Ohio Poet of the Year; and *The Long Silence of the Mohawk Carpet Smokestacks*, published in a 2nd expanded edition in January 2026 by The Ashland Poetry Press.

Jim Hodnett is a retired educator and psychologist who began writing in 2011. Though he was born and raised in Arkansas and has resided in both Texas and New York, he has called Columbus, Ohio, home since 1992. He has published five stories, all of them, he is proud to say, in OWA anthologies. He shares his home and life with Dr. Joe Heimlich, an environmental education researcher and consultant.

Mary Moody Hunt is a writer and poet whose work emphasizes social issues and the marginalized. Her poetry has been featured in *Mobius: The Journal of Social Change and Rat's Ass Review*. Her short story, "Ticket to Nowhere" was included in the 2024 anthology of the Ohio Writers Association: *Should This Book Be Banned*. Hunt lives in central Ohio with her husband Roger.

Blanche Kabengele describes poetry as *"A bathtub filled with bubbling philosophical hooch", holds a doctorate from the University of Cincinnati's College of Education* and is the author of *Conjugal Relationships of Africans and African Americans, and Quiet as it's Kept, Me too, and other Poetic Expressions of Life!* Blanche has poems published in *Poetry Against Racism & Hate USA, The Prose Poem, Willawa, The Woolf and the WAYE*. Find Blanche at blkabengele@gmail.com.

John Kachuba is the author of thirteen books of fiction and nonfiction. His most recent book is *The Bottle Conjuror*, an historical fantasy novel. *Haycorn Smith and the Castle Ghost* is a paranormal novel for middle-grade readers. Other novels are *Dark Entry* and *The Savage Apostle*. *Shapeshifters: A History,* was a 2020 Bram Stoker Award finalist. He is a speaker about the paranormal at conferences, libraries, and universities and on TV, podcasts, and radio.

Candice M. Kelsey (she/her) is a bi-coastal writer and educator. Her work has received Pushcart and Best-of-the-Net nominations, and she is the author of nine books. Her work appears in *Bust, The Rumpus, Painted Bride Quarterly, Poet Lore, SWWIM,* and other journals. A reader for *The Los Angeles Review and The Weight Journal,* she recently served as an AWP Poetry Mentor.

Stephen C. Kraynak, an Ohio native, received his MA from The Ohio State University and his MLS from Kent State University. This is his third piece of nonfiction published by the Ohio Writers' Association. Twice, he has been a finalist in the Tucson Festival of Books Literary Awards Competition. He writes and revises while walking in the morning Sonoran Desert sun.

R. Luce (Ron) is the author of *Once Upon a Waning Star and Walking on Nathan's Grave* (novels), *Pie in the Sky and Other Illusions We Live With* (short stories, poems, a novella, and a play), *The Millfield Mine Disaster* (nonfiction) and other works. He has been the recipient of awards for his novels and was a finalist for the Carlo Annoni International Playwriting Award. He has a PhD in English from Ohio University, Athens.

Brian Luke is the author of *Brutal: Manhood and the Exploitation of Animals*, and co-author with Barbara Luke of *The Complete Crimes of Donald Trump, Part 1: Crimes of Race and Sex*. Brian and Barbara co-host the book review podcast Bestseller and live in central Ohio with their menagerie of ten chickens, four cats, and a golden retriever named Finn.

p.j. melton is a Mansfield, Ohio, native who currently lives in Vermont. p.j.'s work has appeared in the *minnesota review, The Iowa Review, Café Review, Superpresent*, and other publications.

George Pallas was born in Chattanooga, Tennessee, and grew up in the Nashville area. He moved to Ohio after graduating from Vanderbilt University and began a career in information technology. As a writer, he has several short stories to his credit. His first book, *Stalking Horse*, is a mystery novel. George lives in Chicago with his wife, Sharon, and his dog, Sheldon Cooper

J. Martin Pfau first published poetry in the *Indiana University Southeast Review* where he won Best Short Poem and Best Long Poem at the 1993-1994 Indiana Collegiate Press Awards before he quit writing. He returns to the fold after a 20-year absence supported by his wife Anna Belle and elderly cat, Lily. He lives in Denver, Colorado.

Joseph Randolph is a multidisciplinary artist and professor from the Midwest. He is the author of *Vacua Vita* and his debut novel *Genius & Irrelevance* is currently under review. His writing has appeared in *Action, Spectacle, The Penn Review, F Magazine*, and elsewhere, and he received second place in the 2025 Bath Flash Fiction Award. Music is available on streaming platforms; paintings are on Instagram@jtrndph.

D. B. Ruderman is an associate professor at The Ohio State University, Newark, and runs a poetry-writing workshop for people convicted of non-violent drug offenses. A past winner of the Hopwood Award, his poems have appeared in *Anomaly, Word/for/Word, and The Nervous Breakdown*. He is the author of two monographs, most recently *A Poetics of Duration from Blake to Patti Smith* (University of Toronto, 2026), as well as numerous essays on poetry, poetics, and pedagogy.

Stephanie Schamess is a recent arrival in Columbus, having spent most of her life in Massachusetts where she taught child and adolescent development at Hampshire College. She has always loved to write and has relished the opportunity to devote more time to it since retiring in

2002. Her work has appeared in *Persimmon Tree, Tiferet, Chicken Soup for the Soul* and *Gallery of Readers Anthology.*

Christina Singerie has been making up stories since she was a child. Most of the time it got her in trouble, but she continues to be pathological in her pursuit. Whether working out something personal, or creating a world where dragons read tarot cards, her dearest tool has been a pen in her hand. She believes in the transformative power of storytelling and hopes her stories make a difference to you. Find her at chmsingerie.com

Mistinguette Smith writes from where her identities intersect and fissure: race, gender, sex, age, land, place. Her poems and short stories have appeared in *Abandon Journal, Beloit Poetry Journal, Pluck! A Journal of Affrilachian Literature,* and *Meat For Tea.* Find her at MistinguetteSmith.com

M.R. Vian is a writer and former experience designer living in the Midwest, with short fiction published in multiple anthologies and a second novel in the works.

Michelle Tackla Wallace is a writer from Cleveland, Ohio. A daughter of Lebanese immigrants, she often finds herself negotiating different cultures and values, a struggle that informs her poetry. She has an MA in English from John Carroll University and works as writer and editor in the healthcare field.

Lynne Zele spent over three decades working as a multiple regional Emmy award-winning television news producer, writer, and reporter at WEWS and WJW in Cleveland. She was also a longtime family caregiver for her late beloved daughter, Aubrey Jeanne. Now retired, Lynne has written an as yet unpublished memoir about her transformative caregiving journey.